Best Wishes
Billy Graham

Other titles by W.G Graham
Available   on Kindle and Paperback
At
Amazon

Scottish Historical Fiction

The Cateran
Glen Arnoch
Sgian Dhu

Historical Fiction

Evil and the Child
Walter
Incres Island

Adventure

Oor Bit
Stern Walk
Yesterday's Soldier

West Barns Mysteries

Charlie's Gold
The Deep
Double Deal
Persona non Grata

Crime Fiction

3rd Key
4th Key
Cannon
Dead Men Don't Talk
Any Street Any Town
Anguish

OOR BIT

Chapter 1

Summer 1947

There were three things eight-year-old Mal liked about school – going there, coming back, and meeting his pals. Today was their first week back at school after the summer holidays. He reached the gate oblivious to the screaming and shouting...and that was only the teachers.

Calum, his cousin, saw him and crossed the tarmac battlefield to meet him. "Goin' tae Oor Bit efter school, Mal?" he shouted in his ear.

"Maybe. Don't know. Might have tae go tae ma Granny's. Mammy will tell me at dinner time."

The bell rang. Scrums dissolved. Bullies let go of pigtails and arms bent up the back. Slowly, the mélange of aspirants to the greatness of Scotia's future shuffled towards their respective lines, where Mr Wilson, the janitor, descended upon them with all the grace and charisma of Attila the Hun, belting the unprotected heads of the slower ones with the wee strap attached to the end of his whistle.

Teachers retreated to the temporary safety of the school hall, leaving the rotund janitor to sort things out, which he did with an ear-splitting blast of his whistle. Mr Wilson blew again and, as usual, his cheeks looked as if they had been blown up by a bicycle pump. Mal thought that some day they'd burst and there would be specs and false teeth splattered all over the playground.

A hush fell, as ominous as when England had scored at Hampden. Mr Wilson blew again, this time a little less harshly, and only the birds as far away as Coatbridge defecated on their way to darkest Africa.

The first line moved, each child stamping their feet and marching in time to the piano from the school hall. 'Gutties' – rubber shoes – were no use for this job. Tackety boots were the order of the day; with these, you could stamp down as hard as you could on the stone corridor floor. A half thousand pairs of boots stamping in perfect unison, just like yon news pictures from the war of the Gerries at one of their rallies. Mal had hated Hitler. Even, with all the Luftwaffe at his disposal, the wee Gerry had not hit the school once. Now, there was no chance, unless one of the bombers was running late – two years to be precise.

It was now the turn of his class to move off. This they did to the piano belting out 'John Brown's Body', stamping their way to the stairway, leading to the first floor to glance with eight-year-old wonder at the lassies climbing the adjacent stairway.

The brass floor strip into their classroom was the demarcation line to self-discipline, now all hell was let loose. Old and new scores, and a few for good measure for the future, were settled. Suddenly, an instant hush descended upon the room. Mrs MacFadyen, a tall sharp-faced woman with a tongue to match, stood in the doorway, surveying her domain.

Mal reached his desk, his eyes drifting from his pals to 'Miss Sprinkle' - the nickname given to the unfortunate teacher who had a tendency to spit out her S's with all the velocity of a fireman's hose. And he thought how lucky he was not to be sitting in the front row of the class, and save the cost of an umbrella, while across the passage his cousin made a face at him. Proudly, he returned one of much greater facial contortion.

Mal looked towards the foot of the class where Miss Sprinkle stood over the hapless Drew Little. Poor Drew, he thought, not too bright. He had been 'left back', the expression used for those having to repeat a second term, and had been nicknamed 'Static' by his fellow classmates as he was never on the same wavelength as anyone else.

Static's non-acceptance by his adopted class was not only due to his not having started in their original class - which had also excluded him from playing in their much-beloved waste land called 'Oor Bit', but also because of his appearance. Whether Static had had chickenpox, or just some other infantile disease that had left his complexion the way it had, Mal did not know, but to all the boys this had been due to Static 'dookin' for chips. And, although the unfortunate boy had tried to explain that he had contracted German measles, Jimmy Smith, their class leader, had dismissed this by declaring that if this had been the case, he'd have had come out in

Swastikas.

Mal opened his schoolbag and took out his reading book from behind his 'playpiece', as his mind returned to Tuesday, the second day back.

Miss Sprinkle had given them arithmetic, when instead of writing down the sums on the blackboard, she had wandered around the class repeating the figures. Unfortunately, each time she had repeated the same figure, Static had written it down, until he had a sum all the way down one page, up the other, and halfway into the next classroom.

Teacher had not been amused. Pulling him out of his seat by the ear, she had introduced him to 'tinkle', which she affectionately called her strap. Unrolling the thick black strip of leather, she had brought it down with all the wrath of God on the outstretched hand. Unflinching, Static had stood there, his eyes fixed a little above the perspiring head of teacher, until finally looking her straight in the eye he had defied her to do her worst. Giving up, but unwilling to admit defeat in front of her minions, teacher motioned him to take his seat, with the final words, "let that be a lesson to you to pay attention." Some lesson, Mal had thought. If Static had only paid half attention, he might only have written down half the figures!

Mal raced out of the door before his mother changed her mind, delighted that he did not have to go to Granny's to do her messages at the Co-Op. They were going to play cowboys and Indians. He had his best pistol and holster strapped to his waist, the one he'd got for Christmas. Five minutes, and two imaginary horse changes later, he'd reached Oor Bit, just in time for them picking sides.

"You're an Indian the day, Mal," Jimmy Smith informed him with all the authority of gang leader, and what two or three inches in height advantage could do.

Mal looked in dismay at the old bath, now used as a cattle trough. Today, it was filled with two lassies and wee Ian Shaw, who was acting as driver of the 'stagecoach'. "But I've got my gun and holster, Jimmy! I'm a cowboy!"

"No you're no." Jimmy's voice held a veiled threat at this challenge to his authority.

"Here's Static!" wee Ian burst out, pointing his cane with its piece of string dangling from the end.

"Whit's he wantin?" Jimmy turned with the dozen or so others in the direction of the gatepost.

Static came towards them with all the timidity of a blind bullfighter approaching his quarry, hands deep in his pockets, asking, "gie's a game?"

"Naw!" said the self-appointed leader.

"How no?"

"Cause. That's how no."

"Och, give him a game," one of the female passengers piped up. "Efter aw, he's in oor class noo."

Jimmy Smith shook his head. "He didnae start in the same class as us, so he cannae play here in Oor Bit."

"We could make him a cowboy, caught by the Injuns...tie him to a tree!" Ian suggested hopefully.

"Aye, I'll do that!" Static agreed eagerly, taking his hands out of his pockets, happy to be accepted in the game, if not quite in a starring role.

Jimmy smiled wickedly. "Better still, how about wan o the horses pulling the stagecoach?"

Amid a chorus of agreement Static donned the ropes of the makeshift reins.

"Gus, you`re the Injun chief. You and your band come oot o the trees and attack the stagecoach. We're the cowboys...you can come too, Mal," Jimmy conceded. "We'll come oot later and chase efter you. Okay?"

Now that the script had been explained, all made their way to their appointed positions, the Indians to the trees by the burn, the cowboys following Roy Rogers to the opposite edge of the trees.

"Go!" Jimmy called out, waving at the Injuns to commence their attack.

"Faster!" wee Ian howled at Static, who was doing his best to resemble a horse running on a treadmill.

The Injuns were now right behind them, the lassies letting out shrieks of terror, with wee Ian urging Static on with his whip and flicking reins.

"Noo!" Jimmy cried, urging on his horse by slapping his thigh, with Mal close behind waving his gun in the air and galloping his mount in time to his own mouth music.

Now it was time, they were within range of the Injuns. Mal aimed his gun at the nearest Indian, pulled the trigger, and the percussion cap, better known to experts of such weaponry as 'keps', exploded with a bang. "You're deid!" Mal shouted.

"No I'm no, you missed," his Injun shouted back.

Mal looked up to where his leader was galloping his horse neck and neck with the stagecoach, and shouting at Static to go faster. Static, his face beetroot red, was still running on the spot as fast as his eight and a half year old legs would carry him, with Ian flogging him from behind.

"Faster! The Injuns are nearly there!" Jimmy hurled at Static, slapping him on the shoulder, and Static obliged by turning the grass beneath his feet to mud.

Suddenly, Static went down. Jimmy pulled up his horse, laughing at the top of his voice.

Mal holstered his gun, all at once realising what his leader had been up to. He bent down and helped Static to his feet. "That's enough Jimmy, that's no fair!"

"The game's no finished. Come on Static, you wanted to play! Are you some sort of big lassie or something that cannae keep up?" Jimmy asked, his face twisted in a smirk.

"You couldna keep up, Jimmy. If Static ran any faster, we could enter him in the Derby," Mal roared at his leader.

A silent ring formed itself around the two protagonists.

Jimmy pushed Mal in the chest. "Oh, so you`re on Static's side. Maybe ye would like tae go and play wi him? Eh?"

"I didnae say that, Jimmy. But he's had it. Okay!"

"No. It's no okay! I'm the leader here."

Mal did not see the blow until it was too late and he was tasting grass and docken leaves. Shaking his head to clear it, he rose, unsteadily, and instantly found himself on his second helping of vegetation. Above him, the ring widened. He shifted his gun to a different position, wishing it was real, and struggled to a kneeling position.

"That's enough!"

Mal looked up. Static put out a hand to help him to his feet.

"Says who?" Jimmy demanded.

"Me," Static answered, his voice a low rumble for a wee boy, and hit the erstwhile leader a blow on the nose that sent him sprawling on the ground, and looking up at the legs of a full tribe of savage Indians.

"Want some mair?" Static asked, his fist and teeth clenched, his eyes staring down at the cowboy leader.

Amid an astonished silence, Mal rose unsteadily to his feet. "Can he still play, Jimmy?" he asked, implying that there could be more from where that came from.

"Sure," Jimmy nodded, knowing he had met his match but not wishing to appear beaten in front of his followers. "You two can be cowboys, and I'm the Injun chief. Aw right?" His voice regained its usual authority

"Suits me. Suit you Static?" Mal winked at his rescuer.

"Aye," Static grinned.

"Well, whit are we waiting fur?" Jimmy turned to gallop his horse into the trees closely followed by his screeching band of warriors.

It was their third week back at school. Mal, Calum and Static were making their way home.

"How many bools have ye got, Static?" Calum asked, proudly swinging his bag of marbles.

"Nane," Static replied, with a shrug.

"How come?"

"Couldnae afford any."

"You mean tae say you dinnae play bools?" Calum asked incredulously.

"Wance or twice. I hiv tae save my money for other things."

Before they could inquire further, they had reached the end of the street.

"Oh well, see you!" Calum turned away with a wave.

Mal and Static waved back and turned their attention to crossing the road.

"Wid ye like tae come tae my place?" There was the merest hint of nervousness in Static's voice as he asked the question of his new friend.

Mal shrugged. "Aye...Okay. Mammy will no be expecting me just yet."

"Hey Static!" Calum ran and caught up with them as they were crossing the road. He held out his hand. "Here, hiv wan o mine."

Static stared at the two marbles Calum had pressed into his hand. He swallowed. Two pals! Both in one day! "We're just goin tae ma place. Wid you like tae come, Calum?"

Calum shook his head. "I cannae...I've... something else tae dae, but thanks aw the same."

A little dejected, Static watched him run off. Perhaps, he had been a bit over-zealous about having acquired two pals in one day.

Mal read the look. "He's feart tae tell ye he has Highland Dancing tae dae."

Static's eyebrows shot up. "You're kidding me!"

Mal shook his head. "Honest. That's why he cannae come wi us."

"Dis he hiv tae practice every day?" Static asked sympathetically.

"Only if his Mammy can catch him." They both laughed.

Static's house was on the second storey, where they found his mother busy sweeping the landing outside her open door.

"Hello Mammy. This is ma pal Mal." There was an unmistakable note of pride in Static's voice as he stood there awaiting his mother's reaction.

Mrs Little stopped briefly in her work to study this friend of her son. "Hello Mal. Where do you bide?"

"Anderson Street, Mrs Static...I mean Mrs Little." Mal felt the heat rush to his face. Whit an eejit.

Static came to the rescue. "Can Mal come in and play, Mammy?"

"Aye, as long as you take yer shoes aff at the door. I've just swept the lobby. I know what yer feet can bring in Drew Little. Ye ay come back frae school half a foot taller than when ye leave in the morning."

Static sat down in the doorway to untie his shoes. Reluctantly, Mal followed. Lorry Dickens! he thought, she'll see the hole in ma sock, unless I walk cross-legged.

Static rose. "Come on Mal, and I'll show ye ma collection."

Mal followed him through the kitchen to his bedroom. The house was spotless, though sparsely furnished. No better, no worse than his own, which immediately put him at ease.

Static sat down on the edge of the bed, legs dangling over the side. "Whit dae ye think Mal? Like them?"

Mal's eyes opened wide in admiration. Model aeroplanes hung from slender wires from the ceiling. Warships adorned the small chest of drawers.

"Where did ye get them, Static?" Mal gulped. "They're smashin!"

"Made them."

Static rose. Carefully holding one of the planes in his hand, he stroked it lovingly. "This is the first wan I made. It's a Spitfire. Ma daddy helped me."

"Wis yer Faither in the R.A.F., Static?" Mal asked in surprise.

Static shook his head. "Naw, he wis in the army. The Cameronians." Static pointed with his free hand to a small chest of drawers beneath the window. "That's him."

Mal followed the pointing finger to the photograph of a man in uniform. "Where's yer Faither noo, Static?" Somehow, he knew he shouldn't have asked the question, for Static had never mentioned his father before.

"Deid," he said simply, letting go of the model plane and taking hold of another and examining it. "Mammy said he was killed near the start o the war. I dinnae mind much o him, except noo and again when he came hame on leave, and he would bring a model plane for us tae build." Static twirled the propeller and crossed to the set of drawers. "Efter he wis killed, I started building battleships, and that's how I spend maist o ma pocket money...that's if ma Mammy has ony tae spare."

Mal lifted one of the model planes, and studied it admiringly. "It must have taken hoors tae make, Static. I wish I wis that clever."

"Get yer daddy tae help ye," Static suggested.

Mal wanted to laugh at the suggestion of his father having the patience, especially after a skinful on a Saturday night. He could just imagine where the gun turrets would be. His model would probably end up looking more like a cross between a battleship and something Flash Gordon flew in to Mars, not to mention Mammy going daft at aw the glue sticking to her tablecloth or linoleum. "Naw," Mal said with a shake of his head, "ma Faither's no that handy. He wis a bomber pilot during the war. Noo that the war's ower, the air force has him away testing planes and fixing them," he stated proudly. "But I cannae see him fixing model wans."

"Drew, yer tea's nearly ready! Does yer wee pal want tae bide fur some?"

Mal looked at Static and shook his head. "Mine will ready as it is. I'd better go."

Mal said his farewells as he ran down the stairs. Well, would you credit it! Half the folk in his class wouldnae talk to Static because he was thick. 'Thick?' he thought. Half the class couldnae do in a month of Sundays what Static had done. Well, just wait till he told them. Aye, just wait.

Chapter 2

Mal glanced at his mother then at the clock. It was almost nine. He heard his mother click her teeth and he knew instinctively that it was not from the dropped stitch of her knitting. Faither was already seven hours late, or for him on a Saturday night, still two hours early. He glanced at the clock again, marvelling at the bravery of the cuckoo exposing itself to his mother's deadly aim, on this occasion with a tea cosy. Would the daft bird never learn? Maybe that was why it was always cuckoos in a clock and not owls. Owls were too wise for that job.

He heard the unmistakable shuffle of footsteps on the landing. Zero hour! Faither had arrived.

Mal manoeuvred nearer to the chair by the bed, while Mammy torpedoed for the door, wrenching it open, and, with it, half of Faither's waistcoat, just as he was in the act of inserting his key in the lock, from his chain. Not a good start, Mal conceded, edging closer to the high bed.

"Look at ma waistcoat, you stupid woman!" his father roared, holding a strip of black material and two buttons in his hand.

Mal saw his mother's right foot twitch slightly. Then, as if having thought better of it, she swung on her heel, banged herself down at the table and picked up her knitting.

"Can a man no have any pleasure, even on a Saturday?" Faither burped.

"I work aw week. And me, wi trouble wi ma back," he moaned, sliding down in a chair opposite his cherished one.

"Trouble wi yer back is it?" Mammy retorted. "Trouble getting it aff the bed in the morning, but nae trouble getting it intae McWhinnies when ye like!"

Mal turned his attention to his father, who had trouble focusing on him, and was sure he was going to ask him who his twin brother was. Instead, spraying the air with fumes from another pint and a half of Tennents, he asked his spouse in a voice that was always certain to commence hostilities, "Where's ma dinner?"

"Same place as it was at two o'clock when you should have been hame."

Mother rose. Holding a cloth in both hands, she opened the oven door, and was aware of her husband grinning at her as she bent to extract the plate of mince and tatties. "Whit are ye grinning at, like some great gowk?" she asked, dumping the steaming hot plate down on the table before him.

Faither grinned and passed an unsteady hand across his mouth. "It wis jist seein you bending doon there that I remembered ma horse won the two thirty at Ascot, pet." He fumbled in his waistcoat pocket. "I've got something for ye."

"And me for you!" mother yelled, scooping up her dish of the day, her anger boiling over at her nether regions being compared to that of a horse, not to mention the added disappointment at once again missing another Saturday night at the pictures.

"Oh no! No again!" Mal moaned closing his eyes. Last week, the row had started over Faither declaring he was king of this castle, and Mammy had agreed by crowning him with his dinner. This week his Faither's hairstyle was about to receive another culinary change.

Knowing battle had commenced, Mal dived under the high 'hole in the wall' bed, his backside almost passing his knees in his haste to reach sanctuary, whilst the battle for domiciliary supremacy raged overhead. Five minutes later, the sound of the front door banging shut announced that hostilities had ceased.

Mal drew back the curtain that ran the length of the bed with all the stealth necessary to prevent the thunderous roar of silk being drawn along a curtain rod. Cautiously, he peeked out from beneath the bed like a mouse at its hole. Mammy was nowhere to be seen, hence the rattle of the front door.

He would dearly have liked something to eat. He could fairly go a 'piece', but to leave his sanctuary and enter no man's land was asking an awful lot from an eight-year-old.

Suddenly, Faither jerked up, awakened by his own snoring. For a moment, he sat there in a cold sweat at finding himself partially blind. Passing a shaking hand across his eyes, he discovered the remains of mince and tatties sticking to his eyelids.

Pushing back his chair, Faither levered himself to his feet and waited unsteadily for his brain to catch up before making for the kitchen cupboard which he did with all the grace of a tightrope walker with vertigo.

Apprehensively, Mal waited while the torrent of adult vocabulary wafted across to him from his unseen parent. Then, like a phoenix rising from the dishes, Faither appeared from between the kitchen sink and the table, a rasher of bacon in one hand and in the other, a piece of lard the size and shape of the thing that had sunk the Titanic. Again, Faither sank down until only his head showed above the table top.

Above him, a fly made a sudden appearance from the direction of the light bulb, where it hovered overhead while trying to decide whether to commit hara-kiri by joining his friends sticking to the fly paper, or go for the softer option and merely break his legs by attempting to skid to a halt on Faither's bald patch.

Clutching a frying pan in his hand, Faither arose. The fly, confused by this sudden shifting of his landing strip, tried vainly to adjust his flight path at the same time as Faither swung the frying pan, missing his target, but volleying a sauce bottle across the room in the best of Wimbledon traditions, while muttering niceties as he tottered to the cooker.

"Help!" Mal exclaimed to himself, "Fire Brigade time."

Faither's last attempt at Saturday night culinary activity, Mal remembered, had resulted in a scaled-down version of the Clydebank Blitz, with half the clothes on the pulley going up in smoke, his own vest taking the brunt – or was it burnt – of it?

Mal shook his head in sad recollection. Mammy had trimmed off the burnt bits, of which there had been plenty, and he had gone to school not knowing whether he had been wearing a shrunken simmit or a bra, as Mammy only let him wear his good vest for drill. Drill being the primary school version of gym.

Turning a knob at the front of the cooker, Faither struck a match and held it unsteadily over one of the gas rings. Nothing. Mystified, he stood there like first Neanderthal man discovering fire as the flame shot up the sliver of wood and up his fingers.

"Jesus!" Faither roared, shaking his hand and what was left of the curling match.

Picking up the frying pan, with its 'dod' of lard in the centre, nonetheless confident that he had this new-fangled contraption beaten, Faither struck another match, generating an explosion of oaths in conjunction with that of the cooker, as the match found the correct ring. The pan flying up into the air as he reeled back in shock, a foot slipping on the lard that had dropped to the floor at the same time as the pan swiftly descended on his head. With a grunt of incomprehension, Glasgow's leading gourmet slid to the floor.

Self-preservation now no longer a requisite, Mal broke cover and, in one swift movement, had turned off the gas, eyed his father lying moaning on the floor, and bolted for the door.

Mal ran down the stairs, his brain two steps to the fore of his racing feet. Mammy would be at Mrs MacWhirter's, which is where she usually went in time of crisis.

Mrs MacWhirter's house was in direct contrast to that of his own. Mrs MacWhirter was immaculate; no chance getting over her doorstep with dandruff.

The old lady lived alone, knew everything and everybody, and could be seen daily, partially hidden behind her bedroom curtain, watching the street below; known to everybody as 'peninsular'...a long thin thing sticking out to see.

Composing himself, Mal drew his sleeve over his hand, and pulled the brass doorbell, and took hasty step back, shifting his weight impatiently from one foot to the other.

At last, the door opened and, after a sideways glance at her still-polished doorbell, the tall thin lady smiled down at him. "Well, young Malcolm, what can I do for you? Is it your mother you are after?"

Mal nodded. He was only Malcolm on Sundays and at Mrs MacWhirter's. She stood aside to let him pass and, despite his urge to run into the house, took time to wipe his feet on the Welcome mat.

His mother sat at the table, a figure of complete composure, sipping tea from a Willow Pattern tea cup, her pinkie crooked at the correct angle. Seeing her son and heir, Mammy eyed him suspiciously. "Well, what are you after?" she inquired in a voice reserved for influencing people such as Mrs MacWhirter and the rent man.

Mal never could understand his mother's obsession with trying to influence the old lady into believing everything was so perfect in the Moffat household. How could she ever hope to fool the woman into believing Faither was a kirk elder, sober as a judge, etc, when every Saturday night he counted the steps of the stairs with his chin? A woman so alert to what was going on in the close, she could open her door and tell the neighbour's cat to stop stamping its feet.

"I was wondering Mammy, where my clean shirt is for Sunday School the morro?" Mal asked, imagining Mrs MacWhirter could already see the halo above his head.

Mother closed one eye suspiciously on him. The fly wee bugger's only doon here for a fairy cake and wan o they Gypsy Creams, she thought, taking a dainty sip of her tea.

"I will be up shortly." Each of her words carried a veiled threat.

Mal swallowed. He had to keep up the subterfuge in front of Mrs MacWhirter, or his mother would kill him. He changed tack. "Faither was just asking me if it was ham and eggs for breakfast?"

"Sweet Jesus...!" his mother exploded, starting up, all composure gone. Then, remembering where she was, started casually for the door. "Efter all, it is getting late and Mal...Malcolm does have Sunday School the morn's morning," she offered in explanation of her sudden departure, considering she still had half a cup of tea and the best part of a chocolate biscuit to get through.

"Well, I'll see you again Mrs Moffat." The old lady smiled sweetly, escorting them both down the lobby.

And, as the door closed behind them, mother and son bounded up the stairs to their home...while they still had one.

Mal turned right at the close mouth, heading for Granny's. Granny Findlay was his maternal grandmother, mother to his, Aunt Maisie and Calum's mother, his Aunt Jenny. Mal hoisted the shopping bag higher. He liked going to Granny's, except on Sundays. Mal moaned at the thought that one seventh of his life was spent on Sundays.

Sabbath was the longest day of the week, unlike Saturdays, which seemed to fly past.

On Sunday mornings, Granny would give him the wee envelope containing her contribution to the church, which he would first carry to the Sunday School, before attending morning church service.

He hated Sunday School, only because of the text he had to learn, which he never seemed able to remember. Sometimes, Calum would help him by miming the line of the text behind teacher's back. If, like last Sunday, his cousin was in a devil of a mood, he would mime the wrong line, which had come out last Sunday as 'sodum the morra', instead of Sodom and Gomorrah.

He'd got his own back on the way to church, thumping Calum on the ear and telling him to turn round like a good Christian and let him belt him on the other cheek. Calum had replied that he was not that good a Christian and belted him back instead. Granny was a good Christian. He remembered asking Granny while walking in the park one day, after she had bought him an ice cream cone (better known as a `pokie hat`), that "if Jesus was the Son of God, where was Mrs God?" Granny had said there wasn't one.

Not satisfied, he had countered by saying that Catholics believed the Virgin Mary was the Mother of God, so was the Virgin Mary Jesus's Granny? Granny had explained that only Catholics believed the Virgin Mary was the Mother of God.

'So God, Jesus and the Virgin Mary are all Catholics?' he had asked in all innocence, and had been told to eat his ice cream.

Once a month, he had to attend church parade. As a Life Boy, he, along with his pals, marched along behind the Boys' Brigade, or BB's, as they were generally known. Life Boys! That was a laugh for a start; they were lucky to see the sea once a year, either at Millport or Ayr. Even if they did, what chance had they of saving someone from the sea who just happened to be drowning on that particular day? As far as he was concerned, they would just have to be drowning no further out than the top o his wellies, seeing as he and most o his pals couldnae even swim! Aye, some Life Boys! They were about as useful at saving somebody as a cake o Lifebuoy soap.

On these particular Sunday occasions, all those on parade marched down the aisle to the front of the church, passing men wearing sombre suits and matching expressions. Women in their fancy hats, willing, as good Christians should, to forgive their neighbours as long as their neighbour's headgear was inferior to their own, once installed in the front pew there was no chance of falling asleep or misbehaving, not with the Rev Simpson beaming down at them and uttering "suffer the little children"; which is what in fact he did do to them for the next hour and a half, while knocking the stuffing out of the padding of the pulpit and reminding his congregation of the Ten Commandments. Then, in order to give his tonsils a rest, he would signal to the choir, which would in turn release those women in particular who had waited all week for the moment that they could compete vociferously with one another to see whose larynx could reach the rafters first.

Finally, when the hymn was over, and the stoor had settled once more on the rafters, or down the backs of their necks, the minister would stand up and glower down at them darkly, to remind them before they left to 'honour their fathers and their mothers, so that their days would be long upon the land' etc. And his cousin jabbed him in the ribs and asked 'how long have you tae go, Mal?'

He remembered one Sunday in particular, sitting on a bench in the park with his pals Calum, Static and Leaky Tap, staring at the swings all chained up until Monday, and thinking dismally that it was school again the next day, and that he'd better do his homework after tea time, when suddenly Calum sprang up. "You know," he began, facing them sitting there, "that it was lucky fur us Christians that Jesus was crucified. Oh, I know it wis no a nice way tae go," he defended, at their looks of astonishment. "But just think, a bishop or a priest stands afore the alter and says something in Latin...like Francis got the dominoes...or something that sounds like that, and makes the sign of the cross. Noo, just think if Jesus had been beheaded for example, whit would the bishop have done then? Francis got the dominoes...then wallop!" Calum hit the back of his head in a chopping motion.

The others laughed.

Leaky, his nose running as usual (hence his nickname), leapt to his feet to join in the game. "Or if he had been hanged? In the name of the Father, the Son and the Holy Ghost!" Leaky, turned his eyes skyward, his hand above his head - and jerked an imaginary rope.

"Or killed by a bow and arrow!" Mal tittered, clutching an arrow at his heart.

The fun over, they all stood about laughing, afraid to roll about on the grass in their Sunday best. Suddenly, a cloud obscured the weak April sun, followed by a flash of lightning and a peal of thunder. Fearfully, all glanced up, Mal remembering what Granny had said about thunder being the angry voice of God. Had God heard them making fun of His Son?

"I think ma tea will be aboot ready," Mal said, trying to keep the fear out of his voice.

"Same here," Calum rejoined.

Slowly, the pals began to drift towards the park gate, Mal wishing Calum had not thought of the game, for you never know. You never know.

He was almost at Granny's. The bag seemed to weigh a ton. Never mind, Granny always had something nice for him. Something nice that was, except if you made the mistake of saying you weren't well, then that was a different story, for Granny's solution for every ailment known to man and dog, was a dose of castor oil.

Just like the time Calum had made the mistake of telling Granny he had a bad cough. Her solution, castor oil. It had cured Calum's cough all right, for he had come across his unfortunate cousin clinging to a lamp post for dear life...feart to cough!

However, Granny's house was sanctuary. He could have burned his own house down, or sawn the legs off the table and still Granny would have set him down in front of one of her home-made pancakes and a glass of lemonade (better known as 'ginger'), while at the same time giving him a hug of sympathy. On occasions when he had complained about his own mother's short temper, Granny had merely shaken her old grey head and said sadly. "It's a failing she's got, laddie. It will leave her when she dees."

Then, how was it, according to his own Mammy and aunties, Granny had always been strict with them, yet the exact opposite with Calum and himself? The exact opposite that was, except for one occasion. Mal shuddered at the recollection. His bottom lip trembling, he had burst into Granny's.

"Whit's up this time?" Granny sighed, crossing to the fireplace to put the black iron kettle on to boil.

"Wee Ian gave me his moose tae keep while he is away on holiday, and it got oot."

"In the hoose?" Granny cried in dismay.

"Aye, in the hoose."

"Malcolm Moffat, ye mean tae stand there and tell me, there is a moose loose aboot yer hoose?"

He had not seen the wet dish cloth Granny had been holding until it hit him on the back of the neck. Letting out a yell, he had backed away in horror. Granny had clouted him with a damp cloot! Granny was on his Mammy's side! Oh, what betrayal!

He had tried to analyse Granny's logic. Burn the hoose doon...okay. Break a windie...okay. A wee moose loose...sternest aggression. Grown ups!

"Where's yer Mammy noo?" had been the old lady's next question.

"Standin on the table when a left."

His Mammy had been at her sewing machine when he'd broken

the news that Bertie, the moose, had got away. He had never known his Mammy to be of the athletic persuasion, but her triple jump... floor, chair, table … had been spectacular. A certain qualifier for the Olympic Games, and she had immediately showed her versatility from athlete to can-can dancer by standing there on the table, with her skirt above her knees.

He had dived for the floor, peering under the sideboard, hearing his mother's screams from above. "Stop screaming Mammy, ye'll frighten the wee thing!" he had shouted up at her.

"Frighten the wee thing! I'll gie ye frighten!" she had hurled back at him.

There was the sound of a shoe being thrown. "I think I see it in yon corner!"

Mal got to his feet. "Don't throw things at it Mammy, you might hurt it."

Mammy stood there holding up her skirt, her eyes flashing around the room for any sign of The Creature from the Black Lagoon.

Maybe mice were afraid of women's knees, that's why they showed them off as much, Mal thought. "It's a' right Mammy, wee Bertie cannae climb on to the table. Ye can drop yer skirt, ye are gettin yer stockings aw wrinkled."

Mammy gave him a look that would have frozen the Sahara in mid-summer. "Ye cheeky wee monkey, I'm no wearing any stockings!"

Now had been the time to leave, he having no wish to come second in the ten-yard dash to the door.

That is how he came to leave Mammy, now only to face a second front in the shape of his Granny. However, all had ended well. He had found wee Bertie safe and sound...if not his Mammy, who, forced by nature to abandon her refuge, had banged her head off the light bowl whilst in the midst of her descent. Once again, his backside would have stopped traffic had his Mammy had a mind to hire him out to the road traffic section after she had got through with him.

He was now at his Granny's door. He knew what was in store for him.

Granny opened the door. "Oh, it's yersel son. Come away in. Ye'll be fair wabbit efter humphin that bag frae yer Mammy's."

Granny sat him down at the table before a glass of orange and two pancakes. She delved into the shopping bag. "Noo, that's good o yer Mammy. If she had only put in wan or two wee things I need frae the Co-Op."

"Here it comes," Mal thought, sipping his orange juice.

"Ye'll no mind goin tae the Co-Op. fur me son, jist for one or two things? I'll write them doon."

He nodded. Usually his Granny's one or two things ended with him having a bigger list than the Titanic before it sank. "Aye Granny," he said resignedly.

Aye. All grannies were cunning.

Chapter 3

"Whit's all the hurry?" Mal's mother wanted to know as he dashed passed her into his room.

"Nothing," he called back, dropping to his knees and thrusting a hand under his bed for the cardboard box that held his cherished pistol complete with pearl butt. "That's funny," he thought pulling up the bedcovers to take a closer look. "Mammy! Where's ma kep gun?" he shouted, his head now half way under the bed.

"It will be where last ye left it," came the reply.

"No, it's no!" he called back, struggling to his feet. "There's only my fitba boots and dart board." Mal re-entered the kitchen, his face a picture of bewilderment. "Now I cannae go to Oor Bit tae play, I've nae gun."

"Take yer sword and shield, they're hanging up in yer cupboard," mother suggested holding the kettle under the water tap.

Mal's lips twisted in a contemptuous scowl. "Oh aye! I'll look a right wee eejit wi a sword and shield, when everybody else is playing cowboys and Injuns!"

"Well, take your bow and arrow, then."

"But ma gun's no there, Mammy! Where can it have got tae?"

"You are aye leaving things at your backside, Mal. Away and take another look."

Ten minutes, and several rummages later, Mal was back. "It's no in the hoose Mammy, it's lost."

Sitting at the table, a cup of tea poised at her lips, Mammy replied, "You've probably lent it tae somebody and no got it back."

Mal thought for a moment, wondering when he had last played with the toy, although certain he had not loaned it to anyone, for this gun was too precious. It had been a Christmas gift, one of the few given to him by his father.

Tearfully, Mal made his way back into his bedroom, and took his bow and arrows from the cupboard. Now he'd have to be an Injun. Whit a life! He turned, running to the door, for he would be late at Oor Bit if he didn't hurry; even miss the first attack. Then, remembering he'd be on the losing side for once, slowed in his tracks. Gees, it must have been rotten to have been an Injun, always getting beaten, just like his fitba team Third Lanark. Worse! The

Injuns had a least managed to win noo and then. Maybe Thirds needed a centre like Sitting Bull or Crazy Horse.

Shouting his farewells to his mother, Mal ran out the door and down the stairs, reaching the street at the same time as Calum, 'rode' by, slapping his thigh in time to his galloping music. Mal caught up. "Goin tae Oor Bit, Calum?"

"Aye." Calum turned in his saddle. "You goin tae be an Injun the day Mal? Where's your gun?"

"Don't know. You havnae seen it onywhere?" As soon as he said it, Mal knew it had been a stupid question to ask his cousin.

"Naw." Calum slapped his thigh harder, urging on his mount, not wishing to be late for them picking sides. "If I had, I wid have telt ye."

Mal nodded. It had been his last hope.

Mal was hungry. He passed Sadie's toy and sweetie shop, wishing he had a halfpenny for some sherbet dab.

What a gemme it had been at Oor Bit, it was definitely no good being an Injun. Five times he had been killed. Once, he'd been sure he'd only been wounded, but Jimmy Smith had declared he'd been deid, so that was that. The gemme had not been really fair. Even when his arrow had struck Sammy Quinn in the belly button, he had refused to lie doon deid.

Mal drew a finger along the tenement wall until he reached auld Coen's pawn shop. Ever since he could remember, the articles in the old man's window had seldom, if ever changed. Aye, there they were – a black case with a trumpet nestling in faded red velvet – a row of tarnished medals from the First World War – a broken rocking horse. Mal drew a finger along the dirty window. In the corner, under the wee light, there should be a box of conjuring tricks. He should know, for he had asked his Mammy if he could save up to buy it. Mal stopped, frozen in his tracks, the box had gone, replaced by another box, this one cardboard, the contents of which was a pearl handed toy pistol!

Instinctively, Mal knew it was his gun. He pressed his nose against the dirty window for a better look. Aye! There it was, the wee hairline crack along the butt. But how come? How had his gun come to be in Auld Coen's window?

Mal ran all the way home, crashing through the door. "Mammy!

Mammy! I saw ma gun in Auld Coen's windie!"

His mother looked up from her sewing machine at the table, calmly taking in this juvenile whirlwind. "Och! Ye've made a mistake."

It was the worst response she could have given her son. Immediate suspicion crossed his face. "It is ma gun! You know it is! You've pawned ma gun! Ma Christmas present frae ma Faither!"

Mother took the pins from her mouth, angry at being caught out and put on the defensive. "A present frae yer Faither is it? Well, let me tell you something boy, it was me who scrimped and saved tae buy you that gun, not yer precious Faither."

Mal's eyes opened wide. Why should he believe her? After all, she had lied about the gun, having him look everywhere for it and suggesting he had loaned it to someone, and her all the while knowing it was in Auld Coen's. "I dinnae believe you," he hurled at her, with all the hurt of betrayal in the sentence.

His mother pushed back her chair and got up and threw the garment she had been sewing over the top of the machine, her anger at being found out coming to the boil. It was time the wee sod learned the truth. She pointed stiffly to a chair. "Sit yer backside doon there."

Obediently, Mal did as he was told, anger waning before fear. The look on his Mammy's face resembling that of a clippie on her last tram run on a Saturday night. He sat back on the high chair his legs straight out before him, one sock snuggling his ankle, the other more respectably drawn up below his knee.

"Where do ye think yer precious Faither gets to noo and again? Eh?"

Puzzled by the question, Mal looked up blankly at his mother. "He's away fixin planes, that's the job the Air Force gave him efter the war ended, seeing as there is nae need for Bomber Pilots."

"Fixing planes! Mair like fixing drains, seeing as yer Faither's a plumber!"

Unable to understand what his mother was trying to tell him, Mal scratched at his knee. His Faither a plumber! How could his mother tell him such fibs? "Faither said he bombed places like Berlin, Ham...something or other and Flushing," he countered.

"Ye are right wi the last wan wee man, the only flushing yer Faither ever did was doon the lavy pan."

At the look of sheer bewilderment and frustration on her son's face, Agnes thought she had gone too far, after all, every boy wanted to believe his father was the best. And Mal had always believed his to be a war hero, which was not surprising after all the tall stories her husband had told the laddie.

Dropping bombs on the Gerries? More than once she had been on the verge of telling Hughie to stop filling Mal's head with such tripe. The only thing he could ever have dropped on the Gerries, would have been cisterns and lavy pans, and she fought back a smile at the thought of the dreaded enemy wearing a toilet seat for a collar.

"Whit dae ye think yer Faither is doing when he goes away for a month or two at a time?" she asked her bewildered son. Her bewildered son shrugged. "Well son, I will tell ye whit he`s doing, he's doing a month or two, that's whit he's doing."

Mal's lip began to tremble. His mother came round the table to stand over him, and take his hands in hers.

"Yer Faither's no a bad man, Mal, just likes a wee bit too much o the drink, that`s aw. Sometimes, when he has had a wee bit too much, he becomes a wee bit argumentative...hits oot at whit ever comes his way. Do you understand son?"

Mal tried to. "Where is Faither, noo, Mammy?"

"He's inside son, for a month."

His father in jail? He could not believe this of his war hero of a father. "Whit did he dae Mammy?"

"He put a man's bonnet through a pub windie. That's whit he did."

"A month fur putting a bonnet through a windie!" Mal cried in disbelief.

"Well ye see son," his mother explained, "the man was still wearing it at the time."

From believing one's father to be a former Bomber Pilot, to jailbird via plumber, was perhaps enough for one night, Agnes conceded, at the look of consternation on her son's face.

"Yer Faither has his guid points too, Mal. Mind the day we went ower tae Rothesay?" She laughed, giving her son's arm a tug. Mal smiled through his tears. "You had that wee boat, mind? Then, there wis yon day at Troon." Bad mistake Agnes, she thought, Faither had nearly skelped Mal black and blue for burying him in the sand while he was still sleeping. Sand everywhere, he had yelled...and that was after they were home and in bed.

Mal got up, knuckling his eye with his fist. "I think I'll go tae bed Mammy, I want tae get up early and go tae Oor Bit."

"Aw right son, but whit aboot yer supper? Will I bring something in tae ye? A slice of toast?"

Mal nodded. He reached his bedroom door. "Does Calum know?"

His mother shook her head. "Your uncles and aunts do, but it's something we don't talk about."

Mal closed the door behind him, his thoughts on how he had boasted about his father to Static. Static's father had died a hero. But what had his own father been? A plumber! A bloody plumber! And, at present, probably doing an inside job.

It was now more than a week since his mother had told him the truth about his father.

Sitting drinking his milk at the supper table, Mal watched his mother busy at her sewing machine. He was still angry at the lies his father had told him, and how hard his mother had to work to make ends meet. No one must ever know the truth about his father, especially about his being in jail. He got up and went into his bedroom, emerging into the kitchen again. "Here Mammy," he said, above the noise of the machine. His mother stopped for a moment. "It's ma bankie, Mammy. Maybe it will help tae pay the messages or something, or get ma pistol back," he said hopefully, holding out the wooden bank to her.

Agnes's eyes filled. "Oh, Mal, ye keep yer bank son. And don't worry, I'll get yer pistol oot o Auld Coen's in a wee while."

And, while his mother hugged him, Mal vowed he would never speak to his father again.

"Goin' tae the pictures the day, Mal?" Calum asked, pulling his 'bogie', his apple box on pram wheels behind him on this chilly October Saturday morning.

"Aye, the matinee, tae see Flash Gordon."

"How many jelly jars have ye found?" His cousin took a look into Mal's wooden go-cart.

"Mair than enough, I'll gie ma Mammy half the money."

"Yer Faither still away?" Calum drew his bogie alongside Mal's.

Mal eyed him suspiciously. "Whit dae ye mean away?"

Puzzled as to why Mal should look so angry, Calum explained, "I mean is he away fixin planes?"

"Aye. Ma Mammy needs the money 'till he gets hame."

His cousin halted at the kerb. "I'm away hame for something to eat afore I go tae the pictures. See ye there, Mal."

Mal confirmed the proposed meeting with a nod, and pulled at his bogie. For a moment, he had thought his cousin had known all about his father being in jail, by the way he had spoken, but obviously he had not. How long could he keep it from him and those at school he wondered? Each day, his anger had grown at his father's deceit.

Mal pulled his bogie behind him. Gathering speed, he let it run passed him, jumped on to the back and punted it with his right foot. He punted harder, the jelly jars rattling in the apple box as he hurled round the corner of the street, too late and too fast to miss the wee dog. Mal let out a yell, the wee dog a yap, as they collided with one another. Mal somersaulted over his vehicle and hit the pavement with a thud.

For a moment, he lay there dazed, the hazy figure of a woman in a feather hat somewhere at his shoulder – folks running up the street towards him.

"I think his leg's broken," he heard the woman in the hat say.

"Poor thing, they'll have to give him an injection and have him put down," he heard another voice say.

Mal panicked and tried to rise. No way were they going to have him put down.

"I'm aw right," he called out, struggling to his feet, and convinced, though his leg was bleeding it was not broken. "Nae need tae gie me an injection!"

"Not for you, you daft laddie," a man explained, pointing. "For the wee dog!"

Mal hobbled round. The wee dog lay on its side panting. "It just run in front o me," he tried telling them, rubbing his knee. "Will I hiv tae wait fur the polis?" Perhaps, he was about to make his father's acquaintance sooner than he had expected; even share the same cell together.

"No, it's all right," said the woman with the feather in her hat, "you better get away home and have your mother take a look at your knee."

Mal righted his cart, replacing what jelly jars were not broken, helped by the grownups kicking the broken ones into the gutter.

As Mammy was working in Woolies, it had been arranged that he should go to his Granny's for dinner on Saturdays, now, he would have to come to some financial agreement if he wanted to go to the pictures. He would cash in the jelly jars and give his Mammy the money. Borrow the picture money from Granny, with the understanding of paying it back at a later date. Aye, that's what he would do.

Three quarters of an hour later, Mal stood in the picture house queue, and slowly edged towards the pay box. At last it was his turn. "A half fur the front stalls please," he asked politely, pushing his two shilling piece under the grill onto the metal plate where his ticket would miraculously appear.

The cashier threw him a suspicious look, and swivelled round, intent on drawing Archie Martin the doorman's attention.

She must think I've done a bank job, Mal thought despondently.

Archie strode smartly over, dressed in his commissionaire's uniform with its gold braid and piping. "Do we have a little problem here, Miss Telfer?" he asked in a voice reserved for most evening patrons.

It's you that's got the problem dressed like a Japanese Admiral, Mal thought, watching him peer through the glass door.

Miss Telfer pointed suspiciously at Mal's coin. "Two bob." Cashier and commissionaire stared down at Mal's florin.

Mal looked at the offending coin, then up at the two bewildered employees, wanting to ask them if they expected it to do tricks or something?

"I see," said the commissionaire at last. "And how do you come to have a two shilling piece for a four penny seat may I ask, young man?"

Mal sensed the restlessness of the natives behind him. "My Granny gave it tae me, she had nae change…aw right? Dae ye think if I had robbed a bank, I'd be sitting watching Flash Gordon, in the Roxy, instead of half way tae Argentina, or somewhere?"

A few exclamations of disbelief rose from behind him. Nobody, but nobody, spoke to Archie Martin, like that.

"I'll have less o that cheek, ye wee monkey," Archie warned, pomposity now replaced by a straight down-to-earth, threat.

"A telt ye! That was aw the change my Granny had!" Mal exploded.

"Maybe ye need a lullaby fur havin the money?"

Mal swung round with the intention of informing the speaker that the correct word was alibi, and found himself looking up into the face of Basher Moodie. And Basher, the local bully, and all of seven years older than he, was not one, Mal decided, to whom one should attempt to correct one's grammar; especially without the assistance of one's front teeth.

"Away and let the wee bugger in, Erchie," Basher suggested, pushing passed Mal to the pay box.

For a moment, Mal thought the indomitable doorman was about to refuse, until thinking better of it signalled to the cashier to take Mal's money and let him pass. Mal waved his thanks in the foyer as Basher, with a laugh disappeared up the staircase to the balcony.

Mal found Static and his cousin in the front row as usual, just as the lights dimmed.

"Where hiv ye been?" his cousin whispered in his ear.

"A' wis late. Okay? So let's watch the picture."

"Sorry" Calum pouted, turning to warn the 'goodie' that the 'baddie' was behind him.

The cowboy picture over, the front row having behaved itself comparatively well with only two warnings and one sending out, settled down for the next item. It was Flash Gordon, the weekly serial, greeted with much enthusiastic cheering and stamping of feet. Suddenly, there was a commotion, and the intrepid Archie Martin was in the thick of it.

"Where did you come frae?" he challenged, hauling one of the offenders off by the scruff of the neck. "I'll teach you tae sneak in."

Seven minutes later, a second commotion, a second sending out by the scruff of the neck.

"This place is losing its class," Static solemnly informed his pals, passing them a wine gum. His comment having his cousins convulsed in laughter, as the lights went up for the end of the picture.

"Where are they aw coming frae? Static stood up, a bewildered expression on his face as he swept an eye around him.

Calum supplied the answer, "through the exit door. If somebody's leaving, sometimes ye can jist manage tae duck in, afore the door swings shut."

Mal looked along the front row from where he was sitting, to where Archie was busily trying to extricate another non-paying customer from his seat and being seriously informed that he had only moved down from the third row to be with his pals. Satisfied by the explanation, Archie moved along the row, flashing his torch, and, drawing to a halt at one seat, which appeared to contain a recipient without a ticket. "Where did you come from?" he asked the reclining figure. He leaned forward. "I didn't catch what you said. I asked you where you came from?" Again, the reclining figure appeared to mumble.

Mable, the usherette, moved forward to render her assistance to a fellow employee. "Whit's he sayin'?" she asked, chewing gum and flashing her torch in the unfortunate mumbler's face.

Mystified, Archie shook his head. "You try hen, I havnae a clue."

Switching gum to the side of her mouth, Mable leaned forward, to let out a cry and quickly stand back, her eyes wide in astonishment.

"Well!" Archie asked. "Did he tell ye where he came frae?"

Mable nodded, pointing upwards. "Aye, the balcony. Ye better get an ambulance."

From where they sat, Mal and his pals followed the pointing finger to where Basher Moodie stood grinning down at them from above.

Aye, it didn't pay to cross some folk, Mal thought, feeling weak and sitting back in his seat, just as the lights dimmed for the 'big picture' to begin.

It was almost a quarter to seven, time for Dick Barton, Special Agent. Mal drew closer to the wireless, eagerly awaiting the signature tune to finish and the announcer to relate what had happened in the previous episode...as if he did not already know.

"Have ye seen oor Calum, Mal?" The voice broke his concentration. Annoyed by the interruption, he looked up at the figure of his Aunt Jenny standing over him, arms akimbo.

"Aye, at school the day." Mal turned back in time to hear Snowy White, warn his hero that they were outnumbered by the baddies.

"I mean since then, Calum's run away," Aunt Jenny said, in a voice suggesting that her son's disappearance could be just that little bit more important than a wireless serial.

And I don't wonder, Mal thought, probably the only way he could get peace tae hear the wireless. He turned up the volume. "When wis this?"

Mal's mother leaned across and turned the wireless off.

"Oh, Mammy, I wis listening tae that. It's Dick Barton!" Mal wailed.

"That scunner! Noo listen tae whit your Aunt Jenny's telling you! Your cousin has run away!"

Agnes turned to her sister. "How dae ye know for sure, he's run away? Maybe he's only away playing with his pals?"

Jenny shook her head. "No efter whit's happened. I thought maybe he wis here wi your Mal, listening tae that Quit Fartin. But I might have known better, seeing as he took his case wi him."

"He's packed his case!" Agnes's voice rose in a mixture of surprise and concern. "Well he'll no get far haufin a case wi him."

"Och! It's just that wee case ye bought him when he wis wee." Jenny dismissed her sister's concern with a wave of her hand. "It's jist that he's packed a pair o pants, and they needed ironing. I don't want folk thinking he's frae some sort o hovel or something."

"Well, oor Jenny, if he has only taken that daft wee case wi him, he's either no meaning tae stay away for long, or he's heading for a warmer country." The relief in her sister's voice apparent.

"Where would you head fur Mal?" the runaway boy's mother inquired of her nephew.

Mal sat eyeing the wireless as if by some miracle it would switch itself on.

"Yer Auntie's talking tae ye Mal!" Agnes's eyes bulged at her son as she spoke, angry by his lack of manners and concern. "She is asking you, where would you go, if by some miracle you decided to run away?"

"America," Mal answered without hesitation.

"A' don't mean whit country, ye eejit!" Agnes blew out the words in exasperation. "Where wid ye go the noo?"

"Oh, the noo? Oor Bit. Where else?"

The simplicity of the problem, and the boy's answer hit the sisters at the same time, both echoing, "Where else!"

"Go and bring him hame, Mal," Agnes instructed with a flick of her thumb.

"Whit aboot Dick Barton, Mammy?" Mal whined.

"Ye can take him wi ye tae help, if ye like. Noo git!" Her jerking thumb offering her son no appeal.

Reluctantly, Mal headed for their favourite playing spot. It would

soon be dark on this cold October evening. He left the street, cutting
through the park until he reached the path skirting the woods,
footprints in the hoar before him. A cloud hid the moon in the steel
grey sky. Mal shivered, and not only from the cold. At last, he saw
the old gate post. Not long now. A pencil of light swung in his
direction, cutting through the eerie dusk. He walked cautiously
towards it.

"Who's there?" A voice, Mal recognised as that of his cousin,
asked.

"Calum! It's me." He drew closer, until he was looking down at
the boy sitting on the fallen tree. "Whit are ye doin here, Calum?
Ye'll catch it frae yer Mammy. She sent me tae bring ye back."

"No goin." The statement curt, final.

Mal sat down beside the runaway. "Whit are ye goin tae dae
then?"

"Goin tae China."

"Oh, I thought since ye've taken yer torch ye were headed for
darkest Africa, no China. Ye'll no get a bus for there at this time o
night." Mal nudged his cousin, squeezing out a laugh.

"Sno funny, Mal," Calum responded seriously, opening up his
case.

Mal sneaked a look. Auntie Jenny had been right, a pair of pants,
an apple and an orange, plus one and a tanner. Obviously, his cousin
thought China was just the other side of Blantyre.

"How dae ye expect tae live?" he asked, looking up at the sky and
absently counting three stars that had come out early.

"Work ma passage. That's how."

"Whit on?"

The reply came from one who had studied the problem in depth.
"On wan o thae Chinese boats."

"Junk."

"No it's no. I know whit I'm doing," Calum replied indignantly.

Mal gave out a sigh of disbelief. "No, I mean that`s the name o`
thae Chinese boats."

"Oh," said Calum, pleased that his edification had been somewhat
enlightened.

"Seriously though, Calum, whit caused ye tae run away?"

"It wis the rabbit."

"The wan yer keeping fur Leaky Tap?"

"Aye, the wan that wis the reason for breakin grandfaither's chiming clock."

"Dinnae be daft, yon wee rabbit couldnae reach up tae break yon clock on the wa."

"It didn't, but it caused ma Mammy tae nearly break her neck, when it ran below the sideboard...The rabbit, no ma Mammy's neck, afore ye go any further, Mal."

Mal made a face, indignant that his cousin should think such a thing. "Did Auntie Jenny trip ower it then?"

"Naw, she tripped ower me when I wis chasing it."

Mal scratched his head, and gave a shiver in the encroaching chill, while wondering what had happened in the episode of Dick Barton. "So how did the rabbit..."

"Joe," Calum informed him.

"Joe. How did it come tae break the clock, in the first place?"

Calum gave his cousin a look which implied that he must be daft. "Joe didnae break the clock, ma grandfaither did!"

Mal covered his eyes. This cousin of his meant tae run away? If dynamite were brains, he wouldnae have enough tae blaw his school cap aff. "So how did grandfaither come tae break the clock?"

"He hit it wi the claes pulley."

"Stupid fur me no tae know that," Mal nodded.

"The claes pulley was doon at the time. Grandfaither got aff his chair, just as wee Joe run between his legs. Grandfaither lost his balance, made a grab fur the pulley, and it swung and went through the clock. See?"

"Well, accidents will happen, Calum. Surely yer Mammy is no that angry at ye fur that?"

Calum nodded his head vigorously. "Naw, she wis a' right aboot that. It wis aboot the cat's broken leg, and Mrs Cathcart's new hat."

When's the first boat for China, Mal thought, I'll even help wi half the fare.

"Ye see," Calum endeavoured to explain. "When the pulley hit the clock it swung back and went through the windie."

"And?" Mal urged.

"It hit the cat sitting on the windie sill, whit fell, landing on Mrs Cathcart's heid, gless an aw." Calum gave a long slow sigh of despondency.

"So Mrs Cathcart's got a pane...in the heid...a windie

pane...smashing." Mal laughed.

"See you and your jokes, Mal!" Calum stamped his feet in frustration. "It's aw right fur you."

"But no for the cat!" Mal tittered, unable to resist a further swipe at his cousin.

"And tae cap it aw, I've lost wee Joe."

Mal leaned across and closed the case. "Come on Calum, a think I'll help ye tae run away."

Chapter 4

December 1947

It was a braw slide, three close mouths long, and it ran all the way to the end of the street forcing grown-ups to walk cautiously between it and the kerb, and have them mutter to themselves about not knowing what the present generation of weans was coming to.

Calum waited his turn in the queue of school pals for a 'shot' at the slide. He waved at Mal and Static, both out of breath having run from their respective streets for a chance at this superb slide, shining like glass in the sun of this frosty morning.

Mal slowed to watch the first skater hurl passed, lose his balance and polish the rest of the slide with his backside.

Static looked at him, his face flushed with excitement. "Some slide, Mal, we'll hit a hunner miles an hoor on it!"

Mal was not so keen. The skater, who had just completed the run bum first, was rubbing that part of his anatomy and trying unsuccessfully to stick a part of his breeks back into the lining. Should his own trousers finish in that state, he too would be rubbing his anatomy...and not from the effects of the slide.

It was his turn next. Suddenly, a large round shape emerged from the close mouth nearest to where he stood, carrying a shopping bag in each hand- Basher Moodie's Mammy! Too late she saw the slide.

Mal's eyes opened wide in admiration as the big woman proceeded to do several steps Ginger Rogers would have been proud of...and on ice...before shooting down the slide, to lose her balance two close mouths later, landing with a thud that registered a four on the Richter scale.

Instinctively, Mal shot a look up at the nearby tenement windows, fearing that the reverberations may have dislodged the odd flower pot or box, while Basher's Mammy's two shopping bags flew in different directions as she headed for the end of the street and Jamie, the milkman's horse. That poor creature, knowing he was outweighed by this human avalanche, took off as Joe, the milkman, was in the act of drawing out his tray of bread rolls from the back of his cart, letting out a yell, and going into his war dance routine, as the tray landed on his foot, spilling out their contents everywhere on the road.

Suddenly, the slide was forgotten as weans converged upon the trail of rolls, and hardly believing their luck of a 'scrammel' without a wedding.

From a sitting position, Basher's Mammy watched as the horse galloped up the street followed by a dozen yelling weans. All except wee Ian, who stood arms akimbo over the bewildered woman. "See whit ye've done!" he berated her, "you've dummied oor slide." And, with that, proceeded to join in the chase.

Spring 1948

Perhaps it had been this that had initiated Basher to commence hostilities against those playing in Oor Bit, Mal reflected. Four times now, the sixteen year old had wasted their game of 'kick the can'. But it was months now since Basher's Mammy had done her Cresta run. Why had he waited all this time?

Static looked at him from where he sat on the edge of the iron bathtub in Oor Bit. "Whit are we to dae Mal, that's two nights the gemme's been a bogie?"

"Aye," Calum agreed, "last night we had three in the den, and along comes Basher, kicks the can and sets them aw free. It's no fair. They knew Basher wisnae in the gemme."

As they spoke, their classmates converged on them.

Jimmy Smith was the first to reach them. "Kick the can the night again?" he asked, in a manner which would have expressed disbelief had any the courage to disagree.

"Aye, but if Basher is tae kick the can, the others don't run away, they have tae keep caught," Static said firmly. The rest nodded their agreement.

"Well that's settled then. We'll pick sides," Jimmy instructed. "The boundaries for the night, are...nae goin passed Broon Street, Morrison Avenue and the two main roads. Okay?"

So the boundaries had been reduced, Mal thought. Unlike other nights, such as going passed Belgium or Italy. All nodded. "Right. Who picks first?"

The game was well under way. It was almost dark in this April evening. Mal hid behind the police box in Inglefield Street, watching wee Ian and Calum who had been caught, heading dejectedly for 'the den', where they would have to wait until he, or someone on his side kicked the solitary tin can standing outside 'the den' which would set them free.

Cautiously, Mal followed the two prisoners, his eyes searching for any unseen foe that might suddenly leap at him out of the darkness of a close mouth and 'heid and tail' him; the procedure necessary to prove that he had been caught.

Both captors and captives left the street behind and began the long ascent to Oor Bit. Mal scanned the stretch of trees bordering the path for any hidden enemy. Suddenly, a cry of dismay, a yell, the swish swish of running feet on grass, shadowy figures running passed him.

Mal drew back behind a tree. A figure taller than the rest had caught someone and was twisting his arm first one way then another, as if unsure whether the arm was a right or left hand thread to unscrew it. "Basher," Mal whispered. "no again. And he's caught someone this time."

Turning the unfortunate victim around, Basher drew back his foot and kicked him on the backside, followed by another swift one for good measure to help him on his way.

"Oh no!" Mal watched as Basher headed back in the direction of the 'den'. Mal gave the older boy time to stay ahead before sifting his way through the trees. Having seen Sammy Quinn, and Leaky Tap capture wee Ian and Calum, Mal knew who the shadowy figures were in 'the den'.

Now in sight of his goal, Basher let out a cry of triumph at once again being in the position to waste the game and took a run at the shiny tin can, drawing back his foot as he reached it. Except this time, instead of the object of his anger soaring into the darkening night sky, as Mal had seen it do on several occasions, the can remained where it was. With a thud, Basher's foot came to a sudden halt, his cry of triumph instantly replaced by one of pain and shock.

From the surrounding trees and various hideouts, faint muffled laughs began to arise, as unseen spectators watched in fascinated admiration of Basher covering several yards of Oor Bit all on one foot, before collapsing onto his backside, where he commenced to rock back and forth hugging his injured foot with his outstretched hands.

For several minutes, Basher sat there rubbing his foot, then angrily grabbing a stick lying within range, proceeded to haul himself to a sitting position. Whereby using the stick as crutch-come-walking-stick, he slowly began to hobble his way home. The evening breeze that gently shook the trees, drowning out the curses and obscenities from the direction of the path.

Jimmy Smith was the first to show himself. "What happened to Basher?" The boy's voice held a mixture of surprise and delight.

Walking over to the can, wee Ian lifted it up and stared down at the tree stump hidden beneath. "Nae wonder Bashers got a sair fit! Who pit the can ower that?" The small boy's voice was full of admiration as he looked around at his grinning pals, who each shrugged their innocence.

"Well, he'll no be wasting oor gemme for awhile," Leaky assured them, plunging his hands into his trouser pockets.

"Are we having another gemme? Or is that it for the night?" another asked.

"It's getting late as it is, we'll be getting called in onytime noo," Calum pointed out.

"Aye, aw right. Same time the morrow," Jimmy suggested. And all murmured their agreement as they departed on their several different ways home.

"Are we fur pinchin Skinny Smart's apples or no?" Calum asked, rapidly losing patience with his pals who had lain stretched out the grass for the best part of half an hour.

"I don't think we should," Sammy Quinn, sniffed, turning up his nose to the weak sun. "Skinny's got a guard dug noo."

"How dae ye know it's a guard dug?" Static asked, chewing a piece of grass.

"Cause it wears a Busby and has Coldstream Guards written on the front," Sammy retorted with a sneer. The others laughed.

Static spat out his piece of grass. "I thought Skinny raced pigeons?"

"Aye, he did till his arms got tired." Calum let out a yell of laughter at his own joke.

"Did he ever beat them?" Mal joined in.

Rising to his feet, a note of finality in his voice, Sammy asked. "So we're no fur pinchin Skinny's apples then?"

"Nae point. They gie ye a sair belly anyhow," Static stated prosaically.

"Whit are we goin tae dae aboot Basher?" Calum asked, purposely changing the subject to that which was on all of their minds. "Dae ye think he knows who was aw there the night he kicked the can?"

"He knows I wis there, Calum," Sammy nodded, "for he caught me when I wis guarding the den. Twisted ma arm...the big..."

"I suppose he'll get tae know it wis wan o us, seeing as we aw play at Oor Bit," Mal said dejectedly. Now he was about to find out how Billy the Kid had felt, always on the run.

"I saw him yesterday," Sammy told them informatively. "He had his fit in stooky, and wis leaning on a crutch."

The others looked at one another, trepidation on each small face.

"That bad?" Calum swallowed. "Lord help us if he catches ony o us."

"Aye!" Sammy rubbed the side of his face. "He caught me once. Belted me on the heid that hard, ma heid was ringing that much, I thought I wis a fire engine."

"We could trip him up. Break his ither fit," Static suggested hopefully.

"Aye, and when that yin gets better, start again," Calum snorted. "I can jist see us still doin that on oor way tae collecting oor auld age pension."

"We could gang up and get him. Maybe efter that he would leave us alane?" Sammy volunteered.

Static shook his head. "Nae use. He'd get us wan at a time. Or get some of his pals tae dae it fur him."

With a sigh, Mal got up and stood beside Sammy. "Well, I'm fur hame and get ma dinner, nae use worrying aboot it the noo. At least no till Basher can run efter us.

"So we're no goin efter Skinny's apples?" Mal's question was more of a declaration. His pals shook their heads. "Okay, then," Mal nodded. "See yuse."

"I wonder who it wis that put the can ower yon stump?" Calum rose to join his cousin.

"Somebody wi a sense o humour and nae brains," Static laughed, joining the cousins.

"A lot of help that is, seeing as that could be ony o us." Sammy sighed.

A big lump came to Mal's throat, it came in the shape of Basher Moodie. Had Basher forgotten who had given him the broken foot? Unfortunately for them, the offending limb was now all healed.

Obviously, Basher had not forgotten by the way he had him by the throat.

Pinned against the shop window, Mal searched for a means of escape. To his left, the way was barred by a stack of banana boxes, to his right, a pram. No help there, unless the wean could grow up quick enough to help him fight off Basher.

Basher's fingers curled tighter around Mal's throat, a wicked gleam in his eyes.

"Who was it that put yon can ower the stump, Mal Moffat?"

Mal's heart skipped a beat at the realisation that Basher did not know. He tried to shake his head. "Maybe it wis an accident, Basher," he heard himself croak, above the noise of his knocking knees.

"Aye, that will be right!" The grip tightened on his throat.

A woman on her way into the shop had her intended interception of this daylight strangulation halted by Basher smiling reassuringly at her. "It's aw right missus, he's ma wee brother whose no doin whit oor Mammy telt him to dae."

The woman nodded her understanding. "That's aw right then. I didnae know he was connected to you."

Only by the throat, Mal thought, struggling in vain to wheeze out 'help', as the woman left him to his fate.

Basher took a half step closer until their noses were almost touching. "Who wis aw there, Moffat?"

Basher had always got right up Mal's nose, any closer and it most certainly would be true. "We wis aw there, Basher. But I don't know who put the can ower the stump. Honest I don't."

For a moment, Basher's hand slackened as he digested this admission. "Aw right then, but ye'll find oot for me," the bully demanded, re-applying pressure. "Won't ye?"

Mal croaked a "Yes."

Suddenly, Basher let him go. Mal sagged, rubbing his throat, and the bigger boy stood back, pointing a finger. "I'll be watching ye mind. So ye better find oot...and quick."

Mal thought life... and air had never smelled so sweet. He was free. Basher was not efter him, at least not to bash him up. He had a reprieve. All he had to do now was 'clipe' on his pals. That would be right; Basher would have to catch him first.

Basher walked to the lamp post where he had leaned his bike. Mal followed, keeping his distance from those tentacle hands, glimpsing Static and Calum peeking round the corner of Smart's, the ironmongers, both grinning wickedly. What were those two up to?

Mal returned to Basher who was throwing a leg over his bike. Then he saw it! The loose cable of the back break. Oh! No! Just when everything was getting better, his bawheid pals had to ruin everything. "Basher! Basher!" he shouted.

Basher was in the act of pedalling away when he heard Mal call out, and pulled on the back brake. Nothing! Panicking he pulled hard on the front one. The bike stopped, he did not, and he hit the road with a thud.

Mal did not know whether to take to his heels or not, though logic dictated that to run would only be seen as an act of complicity. "Are ye hurt Basher?" he cried, hoping that his voice carried genuine concern as he bent down to help lift the bike off the older boy. Basher glared up at him.

"It's yer back brake. Yer cable's frayed. That's how ye fell."

Basher rose unsteadily to his feet. Holding the bike between himself and Mal, he banged it down by its wheels. "If I thought ye had anything tae dae wi this, Moffat, I'd pull yer arse up through yer mooth," he seethed.

"How could I? Did I no save ye frae runnin into a lorry or somethin?"

Basher studied his bicycle saddle, the way a tennis player does his racket after a failed shot. "Aye, I suppose so. Thanks."

"Thanks! Mal could hardly contain himself. What a day! What had started by Basher almost introducing his head to his fist had ended in complete vindication of him having not been responsible for breaking his toes…And Basher actually saying thanks for saving him from injuring himself! What a day!

After Basher had cautiously ridden out of sight, the two instigators of bicycle sabotage crossed the road to meet Mal.

"Whit did ye dae that fur Mal, savin Basher?" Calum protested angrily.

"Aye, we could have had another month or two o freedom had he fell and broke his bum," Static growled in support of his pal.

"Yese nearly wasted it." Mal shook his head as if he had swallowed something vile. "Basher knew we wis aw there the night he broke his taes, but, he still disnae know who put the can ower yon stump. He's asked me tae find oot, so we're safe for another wee while."

"So, who are you goin tae say did it then, Mal?" Static asked, cleaning his nose on his sleeve.

Mal shrugged. "If Basher catches me again, I'll tell him I havnae found oot. Maybe by that time he will have forgot."

Calum shook his head. "No he'll no. He cannae, he has his reputation tae think aboot. He'll probably finish up bashing every wan o' us."

No me, Mal thought, but I better no tell these two, for that would be pushing friendship a wee bit too far.

Summer 1948

To Calum, the ultimate life of perfection was in having no homework or Highland Dancing to do, especially the latter.

He had lost count of how many times when, Mal, Static and the gang had been out playing football he had been confined to the front room to do his 'practice'. What a sight he must be, jumping up and down like some demented soul, in a far from perfect rendition of the Highland Fling, this was when he was not hopping around holding his foot, having banged his toe off his sword?

It was a family tradition, since his Aunt Maisie had started her dancing school, that one of the laddies should take up the art. Therefore, as 'quarter to three' feet were a distinct advantage, he had been nominated. Though the opposite applied to his beloved football, a fact quickly perceived by Mal asking if he was naturally crossed eyed as well. So he had started his many hours of torture. The endless double high cuts, entailing hitting the ball of his leg twice to one hop, repeating, and repeating it, until his bare legs were red raw, or cut and bleeding from the laces of his pumps.

The times he had tried to get out of his practice were endless, equalling his lack of talent. His attempted escapes always thwarted by 'Stalagfuhrer' Mammy's acute hearing from the depth of the kitchen...even whilst washing the dishes!

However, one escape in particular had almost succeeded. He'd wound up the gramophone to its fullest, tied a banister brush to the dog's tail, gave it a bone, and was out of the door like a shot, leaving the dog to thump the floor in wagging tail delight. The ruse would have worked he reflected sadly, had the dog's tail not gone into double quick time when it reached the bone's marrow. Next thing he knew was his Mammy standing arms akimbo at the edge of the fitba pitch.

Of course, he had tried to hide amongst the 'seven or eight hundred' sniggering players, or so there seemed to be when playing. Sometimes, there were so many playing it was twenty minutes into the game before anyone realised there was no ball. Perhaps, it had been his crimson face that had given him away to his Mammy. Therefore, short of dying with embarrassment at the thought of her infiltrating the game to haul him off by the ear, he had surrendered – a little later, so had his backside. Calum sighed. Aye, short of tunnelling his way out of his room, there was no escape.

Now came the worst time. The annual display of dancing, when Aunt Maisie's entire school would show off what they could do... or, in his case, could not do. Already he was earmarked for the Highland Fling and the Reel O Tulloch. His exclusion from the Sword Dance, was solely in the interest of safety for the first three rows of the audience. He was hopeless, yet his Mammy and his auntie insisted that he keep up the family tradition.

Next week was the dress rehearsal, and there was nothing for it, except to commit suicide. Though, he'd better make a better job of it than Sammy Quinn.

He had met Sammy, with just such an intention, when skirting the bog land next to what was locally known as the 'engine pond', for as legend would have it, a steam engine had once run off the rails on its way to the colliery, and had taken a dive into the nearby pond complete with fireman and driver. Sometimes, when the pond was frozen over, boys could be seen kneeling down to peek through the ice in the hope of catching sight of the engine and its two occupants, no doubt still standing by their stations.

"Where ye goin, Sammy?" Calum asked, catching up.

"Tae droon masel in the pond."

"Oh, aye," Calum nodded, acknowledging it had been a stupid question to ask, as drowning oneself at eight years of age was a natural action. "Whit fur?" he decided to venture, "it`s nearly tea time."

"I'm no goin hame fur mine. Cannae. My big brother will kill me. That's why I'm drooning masel."

"How? Whit have ye done, Sammy?"

"I've used my brother's new braces for a catapult. Now, he cannae go oot winchin his new doll."

"I didnae know it wis that serious. But, why the pond? It's stinking. Ye'll get yer claes aw soaked and smelly."

"Well, I tried hinging masel first, but the rope wis choking me, so I stopped. I thought droonin might be easier."

Calum nodded his understanding. "Can I watch?"

"Naw."

"How no? I could tell your folks how bravely ye drooned?"

Seeing the logic, Sammy nodded. "Okay."

The two boys sauntered along the narrow path towards the pond, Calum wishing Sammy would hurry up as it was getting near tea time, and he was getting hungry.

Several detours round a few bovine souvenirs later, Sammy left his pal and crossed to the sagging wire fence which gradually disappeared into the pond, until only the top of a wooden post showed above the surface.

"See ye again!" Sammy said with a departing wave of his hand as he levered himself along the fence.

"Sammy!" Calum shouted.

"Don't try and stop me Calum, my mind's made up," Sammy called back, slowly manoeuvring himself around a wooden post.

"I wisna tryin tae. I wis only goin tae ask, ony chance o gettin yer train set?"

"Naw, my pal Ian's gettin that!"

"Oh, aw right."

Calum stood back from the water's edge, his eyes fixed upon his pal. Soon Sammy would enter those murky waters. Doon, doon, doon. God knew how many miles until he reached the bottom. Maybe even bang his heid on the engine on the bottom.

At last, Sammy reached the last post, where, climbing on top of the wooden stake, he carefully balanced himself, before slowly drawing himself to his full height. Then, taking a last short stoical look at the cruel world, took a quick 'heider' into the murky depths.

Fascinated, Calum watched as his pal described a near perfect arc. First the head, then the shoulders disappeared into the water with a plop, until only a pair of 'guttified' feet were left kicking in the air, before collapsing sideways, only to have their owner re-emerge a few seconds later with the best sun tan Calum had seen in years. "Jings!" Calum cried in astonishment, "the ponds only up tae his bum!"

Though that had not been the end of Sammy Quinn, it had been for the reputation of the pond. Now that it was no longer the depth that every youngster believed it to be, Calum could not now consider it as a feasible means of escaping the Dancing Display, which had left him racking his brains for an alternative method of suicide.. Until, at last, he had come up with the idea of jumping to oblivion from a great height.

The washing house on the back green was too low, he'd only fall and hurt himself. Calum climbed the stairs of the adjacent close to examine the possibility of jumping from one of their landings, for try as he might he could not get the window open in his own close.

From the second floor landing, he looked down into the back green, where brightly coloured washing hung on clothes lines, and decided to climb a storey higher. Now he could see over the wall into the next green. Climbing onto the window sill, he heaved at the window, and to his surprise, though without some disappointment, felt it fly up with a jerk. He'd found the right window. He'd do it tomorrow.

Tomorrow came. Today was the day – his last on earth. He'd not done his homework. What was the point?

Mal came across the playground to meet him. "Did yer hamework, Calum?"

"Naw."

"How no?"

"Cause."

"We're goin tae Oor Bit efter school tae play Robin Hood, comin?"

Calum had always liked that game, maybe his suicide could wait until tomorrow? No, it was dress rehearsal tomorrow. Besides, he had not done his homework. It had to be today.

The bell went and both cousins received their usual 'belt on the heid frae the jani'. He would miss that, Calum thought sadly. What it meant to feel cherished.

Calum left school at dinner time. This way he'd get it over quicker, and also not have to face his teacher for not doing his homework.

Amongst the human stampede to get out of the front gate, Calum drew Mal aside. It was not exactly the way he had envisaged taking his last leave of his cousin, but under the circumstances he had no choice.

"Here's my plunker," Calum stated with all the mixed emotion of a smoker giving up fags.

"How come?" Mal asked incredulously. "Ye gien up bools?"

Calum stared lovingly at the green and white striped glass marble nestling in the palm of his hand; his jewel in the crown. "Maybe. If no, ye can gie's it back."

Mal's eyes gleamed as he took the proffered missive. "Aye, aw right then. See ye efter dinner." And, clutching the cherished gift, he bolted for the gate before his ba'heid of a cousin changed his mind.

Calum crossed the street and glanced up at his own window as he made for the next close mouth and, for a moment, imagined seeing the outline of his mother at the window, and felt a lump in his throat at the thought of never seeing her again. Serves her and his Aunt Maisie right, if they should feel rotten when they heard the news of his having taken a heider oot o the next close windie. He could picture them all standing around his grave greeting, and wishing they had not inflicted such a cruel punishment as Highland Dancing practice on him.

He also saw all his tearful pals from Oor Bit, standing there as they lowered his coffin into the grave. What would his folks put on the headstone he wondered? Something stupid, such as, 'Oor wee boy, sometimes a devil, sometimes cute'. Lord, give him another chance tae wear a parachute. Despite himself, Calum smiled at the ingenuity of his prose.

He heard the distinctive sound of a scrubbing brush on stone as he entered the strange close mouth, where a huge backside wobbled in rhythm to the swish swish of the brush, barring his way to the next landing. The backside straightened a little to ring out the cloth over the pail, the owner well aware of his timorous approach. The face swung round to glare at him like a rhinoceros protecting her young, instead of several pounds of potted heid guarding a pail and a few scrubbed steps.

The mound pointed to a sheet of newspaper laid out on one of the steps, the wetness already seeping through the headline, which he thought read, 'Man, who swallowed ten yo-yos, buried for the third time that day'. Calum nodded his understanding and started up the stair, carefully keeping to the sheets of paper, placed strategically on each step.

Reaching the landing, he hauled up the window, half hoping the sound would bring the mound wobbling up the stairs to see what he was up to. No such luck!

The would-be suicider ducked under the frame and got himself on to the ledge, his back pressed hard against the window panes. It was a lot higher from out here, he thought, taking a tentative look down. He lifted his head as though the screws on his neck had stuck, and stared across the back courtyard to the road beyond where men were emptying sand from a lorry, he'd wait until it was empty, then jump. No, it was too cold out here, he'd catch his death. Instead, he would close his eyes, count to ten, then jump. One...two.... He reached nine. Maybe he should make it twenty? He started again. Maybe fifty was a better number? After all, this was not something you could rush, while wondering as he did so, how many thousands there were in a million.

Calum never quite knew whether he slipped or jumped; only that he was headed for the black dirt of the back green. A clothes laden pram, a pair of hands and the top of a head came flashing up to meet him. He let out a yell. The head looked up and screamed at the damned Russians bombing them. Were they not supposed to get seven minutes warning? Useless of course, as the trams only ran every ten minutes from this street.

Calum flashed passed, hitting the pram belly first, forcing the hands to let go with a shriek, while his head, protruding over the hood, was in danger of having 'Made in Coatbridge' tattooed on his forehead from a rapidly approaching dustbin, this, compounded by the pram suddenly stopping in direct contrast to that of his body, which had already decided to complete the journey.

His wee brain still way back up on the window ledge, Calum struggled to his feet from the tipped over pram, and hastily tried to extricate himself from the mountainous folds of women's garments, as three Amazons advanced upon him, a look on their faces that would have curdled milk. Nimbly, he dodged to the side, as the first prop forward attempted to halt his run.

Love is a great stimulus, as well as the fear of having a blistered backside, should he have the misfortune to be recognized was the thinking of the schoolboy paratrooper as he quickly swung passed a clothes stretcher and around a clothes basket, and out of the back yard.

Only when in sight of the school did Calum slow down to contemplate on what a. b..terrible day it had been. He could not even commit suicide right. Now, he would have to face the dress rehearsal. More so, he had not done his homework. But way and above all, what was worse, he had given away his best marble, ...his cherished plunker to his cousin. Aye! What b.... a terrible day!

The fateful day had arrived. Despite his heider oot of the next close windie, he had not received as much as a skint knee. Of course, there was no way he could fake it. Mammies had their own built in x-ray equipment, it was called women's intuition. From as far away as twenty feet, a Mammy could point to a knee and state categorically, "There's nothing wrang wi that knee, it could play fitba if it wanted tae."

So here he was, walking by his mother's side on his way to the dress rehearsal, all dressed up in his kilt and plaid, doing his best to ignore the cat-calls of 'kilty kilty cauld bum', or 'away ye big cissie', from his so called friends, which had brought to mind what a Highland Dancing judge, standing outside one of the beer tents at one of the Highland Gatherings, had said to him after one of his poor showings in the Highland Dancing competition. "Never forget my boy," he had apprised, looking down several layers of brown beard at him, "Highland Dancing is a man's dance, it was never meant for daft wee lassies to point their toes and smile sweetly at judges to please their mammies, just to have medals pinned on their chests.

"Take the Highland Fling, for example." Here, the big man had halted to re-quench his thirst. "Those arms with the dainty fingers turned inwards are supposed to represent the antlers of a deer. Did you know that, wee man?" Calum shook his head. "There you are then. So what in the name of the wee man was all that jumping up and doon aboot? You did not even know what you were doing.

"Then, there is the Sword Dance," he pointed his whisky glass at Calum, "which is a dance of victory, when the conqueror put his blade over that of his enemy and did his dance of triumph. What did I get today when I was judging? Wee lassies with lip- stick doing pas-de-pas, which their teacher had measured to perfection. What in the name o some big hoose has that got to do with history?"

Calum decided that it was time to get out of there but instead found himself gripped by the gargantuan.

"The Reel O Tulloch? Why do you dance that one wee man?"

"Because my Auntie Maisie telt me tae," Calum shrugged, not really caring.

"Aye, but what does the dance mean?"

Again, Calum shook his head. It never had been his idea to enter this daft competition in the first place. He would have rather been away playing football instead of up on that platform, cocking his lug in a vain attempt to start a dance at the same time as the strange piper, and his even stranger tune.

"The Reel O Tulloch originated when a minister was late for the Sabbath service, and his parishioners started to dance to keep themselves warm until he arrived. Did I get one spark of that from any of the dancers here today? Not a sign."

The big man set his empty glass down on a trestle, broke wind and prepared to move off. "Therefore, be proud of your heritage wee man. Traditional dancing!" he mocked. "Only as traditional as last year's book they change the steps from. Ye never know, maybe next year ye will be dancing the Reel to Edmundo Ross and his Rumba band!" He gave a guffaw that sent waves escalating down his beard. "So long wee man. Mind what I told ye!" And, with that, he staggered back to the judges table.

Aunt Maisie had already started the rehearsal by putting up the 'wee ones' through a tap number in her tap dance section to pass the time until the piper arrived. Out of the blue, one of the wee ones stopped to take a look at the feet of the rest of her troupe and instantly realised she was on the wrong step. For a moment, she stood there sobbing, a small fist rubbing at her eye, while digesting the enormity of her blunder. Suddenly, the humiliation was too much for her, and letting out a wail reminiscent of 'the all clear' after an air raid, she howled for her mother, and was gently escorted off the stage by an understanding Aunt Maisie.

From his seat, as far away as possible from the stage, Calum watched the scene, while putting on his dancing pumps.

"Evening Calum." Mr Stewart, the piper, greeted him as he walked passed. "Going to show these lassies how it should be done?" The middle aged plump little man suggested, with a look which implied that we men should stick together.

"Evening, Mr Stewart."

"Dancers for the Reel O Tulloch!" Calum heard his aunt call out.

"God!" Calum thought, " D-Day already!"

Reluctantly, he made his way onto the stage, grateful that he was to dance from the outside of the foursome. At least, this way each time he cut the figure eight, he only had to return to the same position, whereas the centre two dancers would have to change with each other throughout the dance.

Mary Roberts brushed his shoulder as she passed. "Try and get it right this time, big feet," she smirked.

Calum looked out across the hall where everyone had stopped what they were doing to watch. It was then he remembered what the big judge had said that day at the Games. He would show them. Who did these lassies think they were? After all, the kilt was a man's dress.

Mr. Stewart, the piper, started up. Calum took up his position, and the first wail of the pipes filled the hall. Mr Stewart hit the bag under his arm, scolding it for making such a noise, his inflated cheeks almost matching his belly.

Calum pressed his lips together, he would do this dance as a man should, not like some lipsticked wee lassie; after all, he knew what this dance was all about. He bowed, turned and pointed his left foot. The pipes rang out. He counted the bars and started to cut the figure eight. This was when it usually started to go wrong. When the rest of the dancers were cutting the figure eight, he was usually cutting his own figure, either a five or a seven, but never an eight. He knew he was on course if he headed for Mr Stewart, standing at the corner of the stage, then turned right. He floated across the stage, and caught sight of his mother out of the corner of his eye, smiling proudly up at him. He swayed round his partner, changed feet and skidded, heading straight for Mr Stewart.

Too late, the old piper saw him coming, and his chanter dropped from his lips, the pipes dying with a strangled wail. In vain Calum tried to correct his balance, but only succeeded in accelerating towards the old piper. In desperation, he swung right, bumping into his oncoming partner, the collision sending him headlong for the open anti-room door, where he proceeded to fall headfirst down the steps, while his sporran continually hit his newly acquired nether regions, until he came to an uneremonious halt against the radiator.

For a moment, he lay there his eyes screwed up against the pain in his groin. Then, hearing the commotion from the direction of the stage, attempted to get up. Now he was for it! Both his mother and his auntie would kill him, not to mention Mr Stewart, who would no doubt strangle him with his pipes, or find a different place to stick his chanter.

"You poor wee soul! Are you hurt?"

Incredulously, Calum looked up into the worried face of his Aunt Maisie.

"Are ye all right, son?" his mother cried, rushing down the steps to his side. "Did ye hurt yersel? Let yer mother see, and she will rub it better."

Not on your life, Calum thought, edging away from her outstretched hands. Anyway what was this all about? No dunt on the heid frae the back o her hand? "I'm sorry Mammy. I did ma best, I don't know whit happened."

"It's all right son, don't ye worry, it wasnae yer fault. It was that daft wee lassie who wis greetin frae the tap dance number, that peed on the stage that caused you to fa'. Your feet just went from under ye."

Calum could not believe his good fortune. A ring of lassies helped lift him to his feet, uttering their sympathies, and one handed him his dented Balmoral with its feather all askew. Gingerly, he walked towards the steps leading back up to the stage, and to his surprise and above all delight, found he had hurt his hip. Now was the time for bravado. "Dae ye want me tae start again, Aunt Maisie?" he asked, with an exaggerated grimace. "My leg will be all right in a wee while."

"No son, we cannae take the chance. No more rehearsing for you. I know you will be heartbroken at missing the Display, but never mind, there is always next year."

Calum gave a solemn nod, wishing, he could find that wee girl and give her the biggest hug she'd ever had in her life. Besides a pair of dry knickers…

Chapter 5

As his mother was working late, Mal made for Granny's straight after school. He was to have his tea there and, as Granny always had in something special, he was looking forward to it.

Rounding the curve of the stair, he heard the swish of a brush and smiled in anticipation of Granny hard at work on the landing above. Instead, it was Mrs Devlin, Granny's next door neighbour who greeted him as he reached the stop step.

"Oh, it's you Malcolm! I was just hoping to catch you son. Your Granny's had a wee bad turn, she is in the Royal. It's nothing to worry your wee heid aboot. She'll be fine. The doctor's got her in for observation as they say," she hurried to assure him.

Mal stared at the woman, then in turn at her brush. It was inconceivable that Granny was not at home, even more so that she was in hospital.

"Your Mammy was here with your Granny, waitin for the doctor. She asked me to tell you to go to your Aunt Jenny's for your tea. Maist likely, your auntie will take you to see your Granny in hospital...if they will let you in."

Mal spun on his heel, all he wanted was to get away. Get to his Aunt Jenny's and find out what really was wrong with his Granny. He started to run down the stairs, Mrs Devlin calling out at his back, "Tell your Granny I'm asking for her, and I'll be in to see her at the end of the week. I cannae come before then as I'm expecting the coal man." Then, the distant shout as he neared the close mouth. "Then the rent man on Thursday. Tell her no to worry aboot the rent. I'll tell him she's in hospital and she will pay him whit she owes when she comes out!"

Mal knocked politely but impatiently on his Aunt Jenny's door, to have it opened by his cousin.

"Oh, hello, Mal – heard aboot Granny Findlay?" he asked, stepping aside to let Mal pass.

"Aye, I hope she is aw right."

"Come away in son," his aunt greeted him from the kitchen. "Calum! Sit yer cousin doon at the table. The chips will no be long."

"Ye mean tae tell us we're goin tae get short chips?" Calum

giggled, nudging his cousin.

"Don't get smart with me boy," Calum's mother warned above the sound of sizzling chips.

Mal gave his cousin a look of incomprehension. How could he joke at a time like this, when their Granny was in hospital, maybe dying? Then, he thought, again, not Granny Findlay, grannies were usually…what was the word he had heard indi…struct…able?

Mal finished his chips but had trouble with the pudding, which had his aunt commenting, "Don't worry Mal, Granny will be aw right, finish yer trifle."

"Maybe it's a trifle too much for him, Mammy?" Calum chuckled, spooning the last of his own into his mouth.

"Honestly wean, where dae ye get them?" his mother cried in exasperation.

"In the rubbish bin, if they are aw like that, Auntie Jenny," Mal suggested.

"Good for you Mal. That's telling him."

The woman got up to clear away the plates. "Ye better gie yer faces a wash afore ye go tae the hospital, the two o ye."

As both boys rose to do as they had been asked, Calum grabbed his cousin playfully around the neck. "So that's whit ye think o ma jokes, Mal Moffat!"

"Leave aff Calum! How can ye make fun when oor Granny's in hospital?" Mal retorted, feeling his temper rise, and wanting badly to take his fear for his Granny out on something, or somebody.

"Och, she will be aw right, Mal." Calum let go of the scrawny neck. "We will no let anything happen to her. Sure we'll no?"

Mal looked at his cousin, undecided whether to believe him or not. Too many people died in hospital. Still, she might be all right if she did not eat the food, having heard folk say they'd nearly died o eating it.

Having been instructed by his auntie to cheer up his Granny, Mal was unprepared for the sight which greeted him when he entered Granny's ward. Aunt Maisie stood by the bed, a hankie at her eyes, while Granny sat propped up in bed, quite unperturbed by what her daughter was relating. Spying her visitors, she held up her hand for her daughter to cease her snivelling. "Well, if it is no wee Mal and Calum come tae see their auld Granny," she called out cheerfully as they crossed the polished floor to her bedside. "Or, maybe it's picture money ye's are after?" she chanced with a false frown, amid both boys voicing their innocence and denial.

"Oor Agnes no here yet? Jenny inquired, leaning across the bed to give her mother a kiss on the cheek.

"She didnae want tae leave me, efter she came in wi me," Granny explained in defence of her daughter's absence. "I telt her just tae go back tae work. There was no use her biding here, listening tae me breakin wind."

"Aye, I thought she'd be back by this time." Maisie shoved her handkerchief back into her pocket, and glanced in the direction of the door. "Speak o the devil!" she cried nasally.

"Hello, mother, I'm sorry I'm late back, I just couldnae get away frae the last customer. How are ye feelin noo?" Agnes asked, out of breath, while the old woman received a second kiss from another daughter.

"No bad noo that they've finished giving me tests."

"I hope they weren't arithmetic wans Granny? I don't like sums at school," Calum interjected. "Did they expect ye tae pass at your age?"

"Oh, they expect ye tae pass aw right," Granny chuckled, giving her daughters a knowing wink.

"Have ye been behaving yersel at your Aunt Jenny's, oor Malcolm?" his mother asked, sitting down on the edge of the bed, her ungloved hand perilously close to her sons right ear, should the answer not be to her liking.

"Sure he has," Jenny assured her. "Haven't you?"

Mal nodded. Who was he to argue? To contradict might mean Granny having to move over when his mother had finished with him. Mammies! he thought.

"Have ye the cauld, Maisie?" Agnes had recovered from her rush back to her mother's side, inquired.

"She has just been telling me aboot last night's Dancing Display," Granny informed her, with just the slightest hint of disbelief in her voice.

"Oh! It was no that bad," Jenny attested.

Maisie's hankie made a swift reappearance. "No. It was worse!"

"Well, it wasnae your fault that wee lassie's tap shoe flew aff, and belted yon baldie man on the heid in the audience," Jenny comforted her sister sympathetically.

Maisie's hankie flew to her eyes. "And I don't suppose it wasnae your Jimmy's fault helping that wee lassie tae make her entrance, by hitting her that hard on the heid, her top hat went clean ower her een, and she fell ower the footlights and landed on the drums?"

"Well, it could have been worse, Maisie, she could have landed on the saxophone."

"Did ye hear that, mother?" Maisie exclaimed in horror. "Yer daughter thinks that's funny, and me wi no a reputation left. I'll be lucky tae have a pupil left after this. I'm ruined!"

"Och! Haud yer wheest, Maisie," Granny scolded, with an impatient look. "I'm sure the rest o the show was good."

"Good! Good! That was the best bits I was tellin ye aboot, tae cheer ye up!"

"Surely nothing else went rang?" Granny drew her bed jacket more closely about her, and gave the boys a sly wink.

"Nothing went right!"

"It's yer ain fault for booking that gormless Jockie Barr, for a compere," Agnes said, with an angry cutting motion of her hand. "Ye know how he likes tae hog the show. He thinks he's another Bob Hope."

"Nae Hope, mair likely."

"Tell me whit he did, Maisie." Granny smiled at the boys, offering them a sweetie she had found in her locker.

"And whit are ye two laughing at, may I ask?" their Aunt Maisie wanted to know, as the two boys tried to hide their faces beneath the level of the bed.

"Och, leave the weans alone. Whit aboot this Bob Hopeless, whit disaster did he cause?"

"Disaster is right. I asked him just tae tell a wee joke or two between turns, in order tae gie the lassies time tae change. And help ma Bob, I couldnae get him aff!"

"And he was rotten, mother," Agnes confirmed, screwing up her face.

"After all," Maisie said indignantly, "folk paid good money to see my dancers."

Forgetting her diction, but not her indignation, Maisie went on, "no some clown prancing up and doon the stage like somebody escaped frae a loony bin."

"I would have pulled doon the curtain," the old lady said,

searching her locker for another sweetie or two.

"Curtains for Jockie Barr, eh Granny?" Calum laughed, pleased at being able to contribute to the adult conversation and, in turn, received a look from his cousin that suggested he must have stolen that one from the derided compere. "Well, didn't Mammy say tae try cheer Granny up?" the junior Jockie Barr whispered in Mal's ear.

"Aye, cheer her up. No gie the auld soul a relapse," Mal whispered back.

"Ye were telling me aboot this Jockie Disaster chap," Granny reminded her daughter after her fruitless search.

"So I was." Maisie began again. "When he had finished telling a joke...that's a joke in itsel - he wid wander tae the back o the stage, tae gie himsel time tae think up another disaster, nae doot. Then, wid ye believe it, casually drift tae the footlights, as if he was giving the audience time tae calm doon wi laughter after his last joke? Calm doon!"

Again the soaking hankie made an appearance. "Maist o the audience were in a coma!"

"Maybe he was Perry Coma's brother?" Calum shot up from the side of the bed, his face beaming with success only to receive a slap on the side of his head to match the swiftness of his wit, which prompted him to sit down with a bang and a frown. Mal added to his discomfort by giving him a nip for good measure.

"So, I thought," Maisie went on, "next time he wanders to the back of the stage to where the backdrop has a wee hole in it...ye know, where I mean oor Agnes?" she asked of her sister. "Where it's painted wi a scene o chestnut trees, or something. Well, that's when I'll grab him!"

"And did ye, Maisie?" Granny asked, her eyes sparkling behind her spectacles.

"Yer no kidding I did! When the wee naiff backed tae the back o the stage, I shot ma hand through...right through tae the nuts."

"Oor Maisie!" Granny exploded. "No in front o the weans!"

Realising what she had said, Maisie's hand flew to her mouth. "No, I didnae mean it that way." She gave the nearest of her laughing sisters a playful shove. "I mean I put ma hand through to where the tree had nuts painted on it, and grabbed him by the tail o his jacket!"

"Aye, that will be right, Maisie," Jenny scoffed. "But wherever ye did grab him, it wasnae jist the audience`s eyes that were watering when he came aff."

"Served him right mother, considering what he did later," Agnes said in a tone implying the useless comedian had got everything he'd deserved.

"Don't tell me there's mair bad news!" Granny turned her eyes to the ceiling in disbelief.

"Yer telling me there is, it was nearly at the close of the show." Maisie searched her pockets for a dry hankie, the healthy blow she took at her nose, startling a few patients lying comatose for surgery. "There I was at the side o the stage, trying tae to tell the wee yins that was on the stage tap dancing, tae jump higher, when that eejit Barr, looks across at me shoutin at the weans and thinks I'm shoutin fire instead o higher, and belts on tae the stage wi a bucket o sand. Well, that was the best laugh he got aw night, prancing up and doon the stage shoutin where is it, I'll pit it oot!"

"It wis him that needed pit oot." Jenny clenched her teeth angrily.

Unable to decide whether it was appropriate to laugh or not, both boys looked at their Granny for guidance.

"At least, the audience saw the funny side," Granny laughed.

"Oh aye, maist o them, except, fur the mothers o the wee souls that was on dancing," Maisie choked. "How am I ever goin tae face them? It was as quick as I could get oot o there last night," she sobbed.

"Jist tell them yer in here wi a nervous breakdown," Granny suggested with mock seriousness. "Whit dae ye think laddies?" she asked, winking at her grandsons.

"I see you are enjoying yourself, Mrs Findlay." All heads swung to the tall distinguished man in the white coat, standing at the foot of the bed.

"Oh, I am, doctor." Granny gave the man a sweet smile. "Maisie here," she pointed to her daughter, "was just telling me all about the Dancing Display she held last night."

"And I bet it was a success too."

"Ye better no take up gambling," Maisie sniffed.

"Do either of the boys dance?" the doctor asked, attempting to draw the children into the conversation.

"Calum does," Mal said quickly, "his auntie teaches him."

"Then I suppose he will be a champ dancer?"

"Mair a damp chancer," Calum's mother suggested, giving her son a look implying that she was now not at all convinced his 'exit' from the stage at rehearsal had not been 'stage' managed, in order to avoid having to dance in the Display.

The doctor turned his attention back to his patient. "Well I should say we will know the results of your tests by tomorrow afternoon at the latest. Then, no doubt we will be in a better position to decide what to do with you."

"You'll have to shoot her, doctor, she's already three years older than Auld Nick, himself!" Jenny laughed, squeezing her mother's hand affectionately.

"Somehow, I don't think we will do that" the doctor replied good humouredly.

"However, it has been nice meeting you all." He gave them a polite nod of acknowledgement. "So, I'll leave you to what remains of the visiting hour."

"Is that the surgeon?" Agnes inquired watching the white coat flap its way down the ward.

"No, that's the second wan. The surd` yin will be along later."

"Oh, Granny!" Mal laughed, rising to give his Granny a hug. "You should have been on the stage instead of Jockie Barr!" The boy's exclamation followed by a hollow tin sound as Calum rose to duplicate his cousin's action.

"Whit was that?" Agnes exclaimed, lifting up the bedcovers and looking under the bed.

Granny gave Mal a hug. "Probably chamber music frae po-land. Eh? Calum."

"An I thought you were punny, oor Calum." His mother frowned at her mother's quip. "Noo I know who you take it frae."

"Whit else did the doctor say? Did he say anything aboot yer bad turns?" Maisie interrupted.

Before Granny could give a suitable or serious reply, the bell went for the end of the visiting hour.

"That time already?" Agnes snapped a look at her watch.

Granny's visitors stood up, each waiting in turn to give the old lady a hug or a kiss before making arrangements for the next day's visit. Slowly, they made for the door, each turning to give Granny a farewell wave.

Mal was the last to reach the door. Granny had pulled her bed jacket around her and, for a moment, he stood there looking at the frail little body lost in the white bedcovers, and was tempted to run back, tell her he loved her, and give her an extra big hug. Granny looked up, and gave him a wave and a reassuring smile, as if understanding what he was thinking. He smiled back, happy at having waited there for those few brief seconds.

That is how Mal always remembered her, for Granny passed away peacefully that night.

There never had been so many folk in Granny's house at one time since Ne'erday.

Mal wandered amongst friends, neighbours and relations, some distant, and to Mal the more distant the better.

Through the open door to the front room, he saw his father and uncles standing in serious discussion, beer glasses in their hands and, for some reason, he felt angry, wanting to tell them all to leave, that this was his Granny's house.

Someone he did not know sat in his Granny's favourite chair by the fire. A final affront – a declaration that Granny would not be coming home.

A sudden burst of laughter erupted from around the table set with sandwiches and cakes, where his aunties and mother sat.

"And then do ye mind the day we were coming back fae the toon during the war?" The laughter clear in his mother's voice as she asked the question of her sisters. "Mother looked doon frae where we were sitting upstairs on the bus at the newspaper posters, as we went passed. "Look, oor Agnes, the Germans are in Wishaw!"

There were knowing nods of heads from Mal's aunties.

"And what was it?" A puzzled neighbour wanted to know.

Agnes set her teacup down firmly in its saucer. "Mother had read it wrang, of course. It was Germans in Warsaw!"

Amid the ensuing laughter, Mal moved closer to the table. He was not really hungry, but he liked the look of those meat paste sandwiches.

"Come on son, have something to eat." His Aunt Maisie encouraged, drawing him closer. "Whit dae ye fancy? A piece o something?"

Mal nodded and reached out for the fancied sandwich as the reminiscences continued.

Mal moved on, squeezing passed knots of yapping people, some of whom took the time to ruffle his hair and offer a cheery, if to him a nonsensical word.

He pushed open the wee bedroom door and went inside, closing it firmly behind him. For a moment, he stood there at the window looking out over the back greens to the bus depot, with its orange and green buses all lined up in a row, remembering how Calum and he would play a game of trying to guess which bus would leave first. Now, there would be no more games to play from Granny's hoose. No more teacakes and chocolate biscuits, clootie dumplings at Ne'erday, shortbread, or Granny's homemade ginger wine. No more, Granny sending him for messages. There was only something inside telling him a chapter of his life had closed, and that things would never be the same again. This was his last time in Granny's hoose.

Tears came to Mal's eyes, blurring the buses. It was not fair. Why had Granny to die? He thought back to when he had seen her in hospital, now wishing he had run back and given her the biggest hug she had ever had, and told her how much he had loved her. To forgive him for all the bad things he had said and done to her. Now, of course, it was too late, Granny was in heaven. Now, she would be beside God whom she loved so much. He hoped she would put in a good word for him, and maybe even for Calum as well.

Aye, Granny would get on well in heaven. Maybe she would miss reading the Dandy or the Beano, for a wee while. Though, he could imagine after a while, when she got settled in, her wandering down to the Golden Gates, giving Saint Peter an icy stare and saying to him, " Ye think these gates are clean? See, gie me a duster!" Aye, Granny would get on fine, keeping the place tidy.

In the big car on the way to the cemetery, he had thought the world so cruel, so uncaring, going about their business as usual. Didn't they know his Granny had died? True, some had taken the time to doff their caps and stand for a moment or two to show their respects, but mostly others had just carried on. Mal sighed. Poor Granny.

Standing by the graveside, he had wanted to jump down into the grave, hoping that by some miracle he could bring his Granny home again, and that it had all been a mistake. But he knew, however hard he might wish it, it could never be.

Mal opened the bedroom door. Suddenly, he remembered he'd

not seen his cousin around for some time. The mourners were now well into their drinks and sandwiches. He passed the table and heard his mother say, "You can have the china set, oor Maisie, I know you always had your eye on it, but I want the wee set o drawers. Mother aye said I could have it when she was gone."

As he could not see Calum anywhere, he made for the lobby where Mrs Devlin was telling a neighbour how 'she was all ready to go and see the auld buddy on the Friday, never thinking she would have such a quick call.'

The front door was open, Mal saw his cousin sitting on the stair landing, chin cupped in his hands. "Have ye had somethin tae eat, Calum?" he asked softly, sitting down beside him.

Calum stared straight before him. "No hungry."

"It's awful noisy in there, all the big folk gabbin away, at, I don't know whit."

Calum nodded his agreement. "Can we no go somewhere, where it's quiet? We'll never be missed."

They stood up, neither having to say anything, for, was it not logical where to go in a time like this? Together, they ran down the stairs, heading for Oor Bit.

Chapter 6

Still Summer 1948

It was that time of the year again when weans howled with delight, school teachers sighed with relief, and mammies moaned with despair...the school Summer Holidays.

The day was especially hot...a good day for playing Tarzan. They were all assembled at Oor Bit again.

"I'm Tarzan, and Myra McClusky's Jane," Jimmy Smith proclaimed with all the authority of leadership.

Mal stared at Myra in her swimsuit seeing her in a way he had not seen her before. Somehow she was different from the laddies – a different shape.

"Aye, and Static can be Cheetah!" Wee Ian laughed in his strange wee cackling voice.

Static pushed passed Mal and Calum. "Yer asking fur it, Shaw!" he threatened, showing Ian his fist.

"I'm no feart frae you, Little," the smaller boy hurled back defiantly.

"I know that by the way you look me straight in the knees, when you tell me," Static spat out.

"That's enough, Static!" Calum held up his hands for peace. "Leave the wee keech alane."

The rest of the boys pulled the protagonists apart, each well aware of wee Ian's dislike for the bigger boy, and his hostility towards him having joined Oor Bit.

"Can we no get on wi the gemme?" The impatience in their leader's voice prompted them to follow him to the foot of the oak tree where the 'big rope' hung.

"Mal, seeing as ye've got yer kep gun wi ye, ye can be wan o the white hunters. The rest o ye can be the wild natives."

"And Shaw can be a Pygmy," Static snarled.

Exploding with anger, Ian tried to push through the semi-circle, his pals grabbing and holding him back amid shrieks of laughter at Static's joke.

"How can they be natives," Myra, 'Jane' McClusky, Tarzan's tree-top partner wanted to know, pulling at her swimsuit and sniffing, "when they are aw white?" Natives are aye black in the Tarzan pictures."

Calum made a face. "Well, they would be, seein as the pictures are in black and white!"

In the meantime, Ian had struggled free. "There ye go, then, Static can be a native, since he hasnae washed fur weeks."

"That's it!" Static stormed, making a dive at his tormentor.

At the anger in Static's eyes, the small boy knew he had gone too far. With a final defiant gesture at the 'native', the 'Pygmy' swung round and headed for the burn; or in today's case, 'the Amazon' closely followed by an angry native intent on murdering a Pygmy with a Glasgow accent, coupled with two white hunters with a similar accent who hoped to prevent an angry native from doing so.

Wee Ian ran up the side of the Amazon, swung right through the tropical rain forest, and into the pampas grass, and headed for farmer McGinty's 'coo park'.

The cousins finally caught up with Static who has stopped to regain his breath.

"Where's that wee scunner got tae?" Static gasped. "If he gets into the long grass, we're sunk."

"Especially if he hides ahint a toadstool," Mal giggled.

"Cut the comedy!" Static shot back, "this is serious business. There he goes!" Static shot out his arm, pointing to the diminutive figure scrambling over the fence of the coo park.

Once over the fence, Ian ran for the opposite side of the park, scattering cows in all directions, the denizens voicing their protests at the possibility of being made redundant over curdled milk.

Reaching the fence, the fugitive made a grab at the wire to haul himself over, and suddenly realised that the top strand was made of barbed wire! Trapped, he turned to face two white hunters and one wild native, the latter intent on making the world a safer place from cheeky Pygmies.

"Got ye noo, Shaw!" Static hissed, slowing down a few feet away from his quarry.

Wee Ian stood in a boxers' pose, fists at the ready, daring Static to come within range. "Come on, big yin! I'm no feart frae you. Yin step closer and I'll gie ye wan in the mooth."

"And who'll help ye up?" Static smirked, raising his own fists and slowly advancing on his opponent.

Calum took a hasty step forward and pulled back his pal. "Come on Static, leave him alane, he's only a wee shite. Kick him in the arse, and let's get back tae the gemme."

"That's right, Static, ye don't want tae hae a name o being a bully," Mal said in support of his cousin.

In the instant, Static was distracted from his opponent, Ian leaped forward, hitting him with an almost freshly baked 'cow pat' he had scooped up from the grass, green urine from the manure running down Staitic's face and on to his T-shirt.

"Ye dirty wee shite!" Static stormed, swinging round on a figure who was already half way to the gate at the opposite end of the field, shouting and laughing as he ran. "Listen tae who's callin a dirty wee shite, wi aw that runnin doon his face!"

Wrestling to get the steaming sticky T-shirt over his head, Static ran after the piston legs of Ian who, having now reached the gate was cheekily thumbing his nose at his pursuers, before dropping to the opposite side.

Angry at the prospect of his quarry escaping, Static launched himself at the gate at the same time as he heard the squeal of brakes. A few yards down the road a car had stopped, a small huddled shape lying beside the front wheels.

"Ian!" Static howled, vaguely aware of Calum and Mal by his side.

The three boys ran, gradually slowing down as if in mutual agreement at not wishing to be the first to see what lay hidden by the front wheel. Mal was the first to step closer. Wee Ian lay on the ground, a foot twisted at an awkward angle, his head cradled in the lap of a middle-aged man.

The man looked up, his face a mixture of grief and disbelief as he tried to explain.

"He just ran across the road, I hadn't a chance to stop!"

Ian lay motionless, his eyes closed and, as Mal drew closer, there was a hint of desperation in the man's voice. "We have to get him to a doctor, but I cannot leave the scene of an accident. You understand?"

Mal felt numb, he did not know what to say. The sound of a car drawing up and a younger man running towards them, came as a welcome relief.

"He ran out from nowhere!" the older man explained despairingly, staring up into the face of the young driver, searching for understanding, vindication. "I think it`s his leg that`s got it."

The other nodded quickly. "I'll go for help, and I'll phone for an ambulance as well. Will you and the kids be all right?"

The older man made some sort of gesture, "they're his pals." His voice was a little calmer, now that help would be soon be on the way.

The three boys had sat on the grass verge, waiting, not saying much, and, when they did, it was in a whisper, as if afraid to awaken wee Ian who still lay in the driver's lap.

The man had taken off his jacket and draped it over the legs of the still unconscious boy and, now and again, gently brushed back a strand of Ian's hair.

"Will he be aw right, Mister?" Static asked, looking across at the man and scraping at the grass with a stone.

"I hope so, son. He's just a wee boy, too wee to get hurt. But he should have looked where he was going! He was in too much of a hurry!" A little of the desperation in the man's voice had returned and the boys saw that his hands were shaking.

Static threw the stone down the grass verge. It was all his fault.

The police and the ambulance arrived almost at the same time. The three pals drew closer as they lifted Ian into the ambulance, though no one took the time to answer their question on how badly Ian was hurt.

A Police Sergeant, who came to take their statements, prudently stood up wind of Static, and was clearly relieved by their refusal of a lift home when he had finished.

"Do you not think we should see them home, Sergeant? They'll most likely be in shock, and it's getting late," the driver of the police car asked, passing the three boys heading for home.

"Obviously you did not get a guff of them McKinlay, for had we given them a lift, most likely you'd be for walking home, yourself. These tenement weans are all the same, frightened at birth by a cake o soap." He pointed out of the window, where the three boys had left the road to cut back through the fields. "Besides, they'll be home just as quickly by themselves."

They converged on Oor Bit as if by telepathy, drawn by news of the tragedy. Static saw them coming and hoisted himself off the iron bath. Hands deep in his pockets he walked towards the big oak tree.

"Static! Where are ye goin?" Mal called out, running after him.

Static kept on walking as if he had not heard.

Mal drew up alongside him. "Whit's the matter? Yer acting as if it wis aw your fault."

"So it was!" Static hurled back, his eyes drilling into his friend.

Startled by the statement, Mal stopped in his tracks. "How come?"

Static swung to face him. "If I hadnae chased..." he stopped, unable to bring himself to say wee Ian, "then he wouldnae have run across yon road."

"Och, that's daft, pal, Ian was cheeky wi ye, I'd have done the same masel." Mal laughed, attempting to make light of it.

"Aye, it's aw right fur ye tae stand there laughing, it's no your fault that, wee Shaw has lost his leg!" Static barked out. "And don't tell me they're no thinking the same." He threw a hand in the direction of his classmates gathered around the iron bath.

"If! If! My Faither says there's too many 'ifs' in this world. And really there's no such thing as 'ifs'."

"Whit dae ye mean?" Static's eyes blazed, fighting to control an anger which he had to let out at something, or someone.

"Well. If wee Ian hadnae hit you wi the coos shite, ye wouldnae have chased him tae the gate...right? If the driver hadnae waited tae gie his wife a kiss afore he left, he wouldnae have been there at the exact time. Ye see, it's just like my Faither says, ifs go right back tae Adam and Eve," Mal explained. "It takes a lot of things tae make wan thing happen in life."

Static nodded, astounded by the rational of it all. "Yer Faither must be a wise man, Mal." The boy's voice was full of admiration for a man whom he had never met. "Where did he learn aw that?"

"Oh, frae other folk, or just thinking by himself." Maistly his 'cell', Mal thought. "Come on Static, let's go and hear whit the others have got tae say."

Static followed his pal, wondering how Mal knew that yon driver had kissed his wife before he had left.

Wee Ian heard Mal talking to his mother at the outside door. Slipping the comic books under his pillow, he assumed his 'martyrdom' expression, and waited for him to open the bedroom door. He was getting good at this. So far, his expression had netted him three sherbet dabs and five comics.

Mal stuck his head round the door. "How's it goin Ian?" he

smiled nervously, before venturing into the room.

"No bad, Mal, except for the pain," Ian grimaced.

"Sorry tae hear that, Ian." Mal thrust the 'comics' at him. "Maybe this will help tae cheer ye up."

For a moment, the invalid's eyes gleamed at the sight of the glossy paper on top of Mal's bundle, until suddenly he remembered 'his pain' again. "Thanks Mal. I'll read them later, if the pain eases."

Mal tried to cheer him up. "That's the Eagle on top." He nodded at the glossy comic paper. "It cost us four pence, that's dearer than the Dandy or the Beano. Static, Calum and me pit the gither every week, but it`s hard tae divide three intae four pence. We tried tae get Static's Granny tae go a share, seein as she reads it when she thinks we're no looking, but she telt us tae go and bile oor heids. Static said tae her 'in this weather'?" Mal laughed.

Ian seized his opportunity. "I wouldnae know aboot this weather, seein as I'm never oot," he said dolefully, drawing the magazines over the bedcovers towards him.

"Ach! Ye soon will be." Mal did not know what else to say.

The boy looked around the small bedroom in the hope of spying some object which could engender a topic of conversation. The smell in the room reminded him of a hospital, and his eyes travelled to Ian again. "We would have come tae see ye in hospital, Ian, but yer folks said tae wait till ye came hame. No that we wisnae thinkin o ye mind." This last part was said in a rush.

Ian nodded. Then suddenly, his eyes gleaming he began to draw back the bedclothes. "Wid ye like tae see ma leg...or should I say...stump?"

"No!" Mal shot up from where he had been sitting on the edge of the bed.

Laughing at this sudden show of fear, Ian felt a hitherto unknown sense of power. "It's no that bad."

Mal swallowed hard, he felt sick, and ready to run should Ian pull the bedclothes higher.

"I think it's time for Ian to have his nap, Malcolm."

Mal had never been so glad to hear another human voice before. Nor, had he ever nodded his head so vigorously, not even when Myra McClusky had offered to show him her knickers. "Right, ye are, Mrs Shaw." Mal turned quickly for the door where he stood for a moment with his hand on the handle. "I'll see ye again, Ian, maybe

Calum will come wi me next time."

"That would be nice, Malcolm," Mrs Shaw agreed, standing a little behind him. "Thank Malcolm for coming Ian, and tell him to bring his pals next time."

"Aye, thanks Mal. See ye."

Ian's bed had been moved so that he could see out of the window. A few short minutes later, he saw Mal running up the street, no doubt heading for Oor Bit. Angrily he threw aside his 'comics'. What would he not give to be away playing with his pals? Even to be playing at Robin Hood, a game he never did like, but it would be better than lying here. Mal disappeared around the corner of Sadie's shop. Ian choked back a sob. That part of his life was over, he'd never play at Oor Bit again.

His anger mounting, he thought of that last day at Oor Bit. Every day since then he'd forced himself to believe that it was all Static's fault, even though deep down, he knew it was not. But he had to vent his anger on someone, then who better than a pockmarked semiliterate outsider like Static. It was unfair that Static should be up at Oor Bit playing with his pals, while he lay here a cripple.

Pulling the bedcovers up to his chin, Ian sank down in his pillow. He would make Drew Little pay for this, and very shortly, he vowed.

As the summer days grew shorter, so did the visits of Ian's pals. And, when they did bother to visit, the crippled boy would catch them stealing a look out of his bedroom window, eager to be away playing at Oor Bit. Even as the weeks went by, his anger at Static had not faltered or diminished. He was always careful not to blame Static outright for his condition, but would in conversation readily slip it in, as craftily as Big Nellie at the Co-Op did with the odd broken biscuit or two. So had he sown the seeds of anger and suspicion?

Of course, there were those such as Mal Moffat and his cousin Calum whom he dare not risk make such an accusation to. But there were others...especially Jimmy Smith, who was afraid of Static usurping his position as leader, and whom Static had humiliated on more than one occasion.

"Whit are we goin tae dae about wee Ian Shaw?" Bertha wanted to know, leaning against the iron bath in Oor Bit and scuffing her feet on the short grass.

"Whit dae ye mean? Whit are we goin tae dae?" her pal, Myra, asked, now 'resting' since her last role as Jane, Tarzan's mate.

"Well, could we no bring him up here and let him play wi us, or something?"

"Well, he couldnae play Tarzan for a start, could he?" Leaky Tap sniggered, sniffing.

"He could play a kangaroo. Hop aboot on wan leg!" Bobby Jackson laughed, holding one foot up behind him.

"That's no funny, Bobby," Calum said solemnly, staring angrily at the boy.

"Then we'll play Treasure Island, and wee Ian, can be Long John Silver!" Jimmy Smith guffawed.

"No. That will no dae, Long John Silver had a widden leg," Myra said loftily, having read as much in her big brother's book, the one with the dirty pictures hidden in it.

Jimmy grinned evilly. "They say Static's good wi his hands, havin made aw those model planes an everything, so let him make wee Shaw a widden wan. It's the least he can dae."

Jimmy never knew there could be so many stars in the Galaxy, especially at two o'clock on an August afternoon. Before he could consider a recount from his seat on the grass, Static was on him again, swinging a fist at an already bloody nose. Punching the leader's face and kicking him with all the energy he could muster in a size five rubber shoe. All the while shouting at the near catalytic figure on the ground 'to take it back'.

At first, lassies started to scream at the ferocity of the attack, accentuated by the blood spouting from Jimmy Smith's nose. Then, after awhile, wholeheartedly enjoying the challenge of trying to out-scream one another, while the laddies stood back, alarmed by the curl of the lip and the look of destruction on the face of the diminutive Benny Lynch as their semi-circle grew rapidly wider.

"That's enough Static! Dae ye want tae kill him?" Mal shouted, running forward and grasping a fist in the act of descending once again on an unprotected face, while Calum grabbed Static's other hand.

Gasping for breath, Static stood back, glaring down at his erstwhile antagonist, while the coterie lapsed into silence, all now clearly shaken by Static's frenzied attack.

"Ye'll no say that again Smith!" Static seethed at the moaning leader, who was holding his nose, and being helped to his feet by

Sammy Quinn.

"Watch it, Static!" Jimmy said, trying to stem the blood from dripping down his T-shirt, and fighting to string together letters that left his brain in the correct order, but somehow had got lost on the journey to his mouth. "Yer heid in the ba'. Yer no playin here again. Swee!"

It took another twenty minutes for the news to reach wee Ian, who after his harbinger of good news had left, lay back on his pillow, smiling a smile of triumph. "So, Little, if I cannae play at Oor Bit, now neither can you."

Autumn 1948

All heads were down in the classroom. Some scratched busily at their jotters, while others scratched at their heads in despair. The door opened slightly. Heads came up, some grateful for the respite. For a few suspense filled seconds, all eyes stared at the narrow space of the empty doorway before the space widened to give them their first glimpse of the sorrowful figure leaning on a crutch.

A gasp arose from the otherwise hushed classroom, broken by the voice of the headmaster sternly ushering the crippled boy into the room from behind. "Come on Shaw, no need to be shy, you know all of your classmates."

"It's Ian!" someone called out. Miss Sprinkle's glare at the 'impudent' child sufficient to pacify the headmaster.

"Come on children, let's behave in front of Mr Watt," Miss Sprinkle ordered, her voice a little less harsh than usual as she took in the pitiful sight of wee Ian struggling into the room.

"Drew Little! Take Ian's desk for now." She pointed to where Ian's desk stood three rows back. Ian! You take Drew's seat in the front row." She saw the crippled boy's tortured expression, and hastened to explain. "It's no reflection on your academic qualities young man, but perhaps you might find it a little...easier than climbing to your own desk at present."

"A good idea, Miss McFadyen," the headmaster agreed, though the tone in his voice left his teacher and her class in no doubt as to who was in charge. "I'm sure when you get a little stronger, Shaw, your teacher will give you your own desk back."

Ian looked up at what seemed a great height at his tall headmaster. "I can make the steps now, Sir. If you please Sir, I want my old seat

back."

Headmaster and teacher exchanged glances. With a slight nod of his head, the headmaster gave his approval.

"Very well, Ian," Miss McFadyen said, not unkindly. "Can I get someone to help you? Or can you manage by yourself?"

"I'll be all right, Miss. I can do it by myself."

Ian passed the front row of desks, and took his first step up the narrow aisle, his eyes fixed on his own desk, or more precisely on its recent occupant. All eyes of the class now alternated between Ian, struggling up the passageway, and Static, the scene similar to a tennis match in slow motion. All awaited the moment Ian would reach his desk, and the inevitable confrontation.

Still a few feet away from his desk, Ian halted to draw breath. Static rose and stood aside to let the crippled boy passed. As Ian started again, his crutch seemed to slip and Static shot out a hand to steady the smaller boy, who in turn tried to shake himself free of his rescuer. "I don't need your help, Little!" he exploded, regaining his balance and dropping into his seat.

Hastening to defuse a situation she did not fully understand in front of her senior, Miss McFadyen took a few steps forward, clapping her hands together for attention. "Now children, don't you think it would be a good idea if we were to welcome Ian back?"

From the opposite side of the street, Static and the cousins watched their classmates skip and dance around wee Ian on their way home from school, some stopping to buy him cinnamon stick, or sugar lolly from Sadie's.

"Ye wid think he wis that wee wan wi the crutch in yon Christmas story," Static said bitterly.

"He's enjoying the attention, especially frae the lassies," Mal agreed.

"So wid you, if you went through what that poor wee bugger's been through." Calum turned away as the peals of laughter reached him from across the street.

"Are ye's fur a gemme at fitba in Broon street?" Static turned his head away to look at a shop window. For a reason he could not understand, he felt uneasy at what was going on across the street.

The cousins stole a glance at one another, neither wishing to tell their pal they had already agreed to play with the rest of their class at Oor Bit.

"No the day. Too much homework to do."

"Same here, Static," Calum added. "You better get yours done as well."

Static nodded. "Maybe yis could come roon and help me wi mine?"

Calum almost choked. "Naw. Ye'll mind it longer if ye can work it oot for yersel!"

"Oh well, I thought I might ask," Static sighed.

Jimmy Smith kicked his football in the direction of the three pals. Mal stopped it as it dribbled over the playground towards him.

"Good goal ye scored last night up at Oor Bit, Mal," Jimmy praised, while his gloating eyes searched Static for any sign of a reaction.

Crimson faced, Mal glanced at Static. Jimmy kicked the ball away from his feet and, as he turned to dribble the ball away, called out over his shoulder, "Yer no a bad goalie either, Calum!"

"Well?" Mal challenged as Static, glared at him, "whit if we did go to Oor Bit, we've aye played there. Haven't we Calum?" Mal solicited his cousin's support.

"See if I care." Static started towards the school shed. "Only next time, don't tell me any lies. Okay?"

Miss McFadyen had mistakenly taken the look of happiness throughout her class to be the result of her dogged persistence in the pursuit of perfect education. At last her seedlings had began to germinate. In other words, they had learned the capitals of the world, all with the exception of Drew Little, that was, but then again miracles did take a little longer, when in fact the reason for this radiance of happiness was, Jimmy Smith, having announced in the playground that they were going to take wee Ian, who had been cast to play Long John Silver, in their game of Treasure Island, to Oor Bit.

After school, while some ran home to change and acquire the appropriate costume, others stayed behind to help Ian up the path to Oor Bit, most of the former having returned before a quarter of the journey to their favourite playing area had been completed.

"See, Ian, I've borrowed my auntie's stuffed budgie, ye can stick it on yer shoulder and kid on, it's a parrot, jist like Long John Silver," Myra McClusky spouted proudly. "Only the gemme will have tae be ower before my auntie wakes up, and sees it's no in its cage."

Leaky Tap turned up a runny nose in contempt. "Whit does yer auntie keep a stuffed budgie in a cage for? The thing's deid."

"Don't know," Myra admitted, screwing up her face. "But she loved the wee thing. One week, she'd buy it a wee ladder, hoping it wid speak, then another week a mirror, and hope tae hear it say, 'who's a pretty boy', then, or something. She'd buy it something new for its cage every week. Then, it died." Myra sighed sadly.

"Did it ever speak, or say something afore it died?" Beryl Wright asked, close to tears.

"Aye," said Sammy Quinn, with a howl of laughter, "it said, ony chance o gettin somethin tae eat, aroon here!"

Tam Speedie drew level with wee Ian as he struggled up the uneven path. "I'm a pirate, Ian. I stole ma auld grandfaither's hankie. See." He pointed to the red and white chequered handkerchief tied around his head, bandana fashion.

Ian nodded, wincing at the pain. He was not going to make it. Never had he realised that the path to Oor Bit had been so long and rough. Already, some of his pals were growing impatient at his slow progress. He looked up, remembering the last time he had played here, and felt a lump in his throat. If only he could go back to that day and eradicate what had happened.

"Jist go on, I think I'll hae tae turn back. It's too far the day."

Jimmy Smith threw him a look. "Can we no help?" His tone brusque at losing so much valuable playing time as it would be dark soon.

"Come on Ian, it's yer gemme, yer the star!" Bertha anxiously coaxed the crippled boy.

"Aye! Come on Ian, it's no that far," Beryl encouraged him, her eyes on Ian's empty trouser leg.

Ian shook his head.

"Oh well then," Jimmy cried, already moving away, "maybe ye can come up the morn. We can aye play Treasure Island again. Okay?" Without awaiting an answer, Jimmy led his band of pirates away up the path to Oor Bit, with only a few taking the time to look back.

"Come on Ian, we'll see ye hame," Calum said softly, putting an arm around the smaller boy's shoulder, aided by Mal on the other side.

"Thanks." The gratitude in the crippled boy's voice was also mixed with disappointment at the callus attitude of his classmates.

From behind a tree, Static had watched the scene unfold, and felt an affinity towards his adversary, for no one knew better than he, what it felt to be an outcast. What it meant to have folk laugh at you in class when you gave the wrong answer, or lassies making fun of your appearance behind your back. Static sighed a deep sigh of understanding, for all his faults, he knew wee Ian deserved something better.

After three weeks, there were not so many school pals taking the trouble to see Ian home. Neither were there any so keen to buy him sweeties from Sadie's. In fact now that the novelty was over, most found Ian Shaw's presence a cumbersome embarrassment.

For Ian's part, he knew even when pals like Calum or Mal walked him from school, they too were anxious to get home to get changed and be back at Oor Bit. He could now climb the stairs from his close mouth to his landing a lot better than he had ever done, but, once within the confines of his room, he was all alone, with nothing to do but look out of his bedroom window at his pals running up the street to Oor Bit.

Mal looked across the aisle at Calum. "Where's Static?" he mouthed, while Miss Sprinkle's back was turned. His cousin shrugged his ignorance, turning to stare out of the window as if hoping to catch sight of Static in the playground on his way back to class.

Static had been at school until the afternoon interval, or as it was better known, 'playtime', but now that they had returned, Static was absent.

Miss Sprinkle turned from where she had been writing on the blackboard to survey her minions. "Now children, hands up those who can give me any word ending in 'ing'. There was a flurry of hands, all anxious to please. Miss Sprinkle pointed her chalk. "Calum Muir, have you been paying attention?" she queried, her eyes narrowing in the way they did in prelude to extracting 'tingle' from her desk.

Calum shot Mal a look of helplessness as he had been too busy staring out of the window in the hope of catching sight of Static, and had not heard the question. "Yes Miss," he lied.

"Then, young man, you should have no trouble in giving me a

word ending in ing."

Calum shot Mal a furtive look, who in turn mouthed him a word out of the corner of his mouth.

"Well! I'm waiting Calum Muir!" Miss Sprinkle demanded impatiently.

"Please, Miss.... Inging" Calum returned, relieved.

Instantly, the class irrupted in laughter. Mystified by the reaction to his answer, Calum threw his cousin a look of disbelief, who winked back, whilst joining in the laughter. Calum's unprintable reply to his cousin drowned out by the noise of his peers.

"Inging! Inging!" The indignant teacher exploded. "The word is Onion, Muir! And does not end in 'ing'. Come out here this instant. Obviously, you have not been listening!"

After 'six of the best', Calum red faced, and even redder handed, returned to his desk. "I'll get ye for this, Mal," he vowed, blowing on his cupped hands.

Mal made a face. It was nice to get your own back on your cousin now and again.

The bell rang, they scrambled 'in an orderly fashion' to the door, waiting there for their teacher to dismiss them, before rushing headlong down the stairs to the front door and so to the gate.

Ian Shaw reached the door at the same time as his teacher came back into the room.

"Are you managing all right, Ian?" she asked, cocking her head a little to one side in an act of sympathy.

"Yes Miss," Ian replied hitching his schoolbag a little higher on his back.

"Good. Then don't forget to do your homework. I'll see you in the morning." The teacher patted him gently on the shoulder as she passed on the way to her desk, but not in a way as to suggest favouritism.

Mr. Wilson, the janitor, looked up at Ian's slow progress down the stairs, and swithered whether to go up and help him or not. No, the boy would have to learn to stand on his own...he almost thought two feet. Poor wee bugger.

Usually, the playground was deserted by the time Ian reached it, except, today a crowd had gathered just outside the main gate, as when a fight was impending. Ian drew closer, wondering why, if it was a fight there should be lassies there. A few turned at his laboured approach, falling back to make room for him to pass, whispering his name as they looked at him, then to something partly obscured by the crowd.

A cheer went up. Suddenly, everyone was shouting his name, and guiding him towards the railings. For a moment Ian stood there mesmerised by the sight of the 'bogie', the name 'Ian's car' painted on its side.

Mounted on a pram chassis, the car had a seat made out of an old motorcycle side car, a plywood bonnet and dashboard, complete with painted instrument panel, real car sidelights (although dysfunctional) at front and rear. And to everyone's amusement and delight, a genuine steering wheel.

"Come on, Ian, ye'll get booked fur parking!" someone shouted.

Then it seemed to Ian as if everyone was laughing and helping him out of his schoolbag and into his new car. For a moment, he sat there unable to comprehend what to do next.

"There's a place fur ye tae put yer crutches!" Mal thrilled at his shoulder, guiding his crutches into a stand, close to the 'nearside' wing.

"And we're the engine!" Calum and Sammy shouted together, seizing the rope by the front wheels and pulling, the bogie starting off amid a roar from his schoolmates, and some good-humoured wisecracks, as they helped him on his way.

Ian was overjoyed. Whoever had made such a vehicle must be a genius. Even the front wheels responded to a touch from the steering wheel. "Where we goin?" he called out to the backs of heads pulling his 'car'.

"Where dae ye think? Where else but Oor Bit!"

"To play racing cars. The iron bath is oors!" Jimmy Smith shouted, running by his side.

Oor Bit! Ian thought to himself, his heart leaping, never having thought to see it again. And to be actually playing there! "Thanks pals!" he shouted

"Fur whit?" Mal asked, breathing heavily by his side.

"For making the bogie," Ian answered, feeling slightly embarrassed.

"We didnae make it. We couldnae even if we wanted to," Mal gasped.

"Then who did?"

"Only wan person I know who can dae this wi his hands, Ian."

Ian sat silent. The one whom he had blamed for his accident, even although he knew within himself it was not true, as he only had himself to blame. Static!

Ian came into the classroom. This morning instead of making for the passageway that led to his desk on the third row, he swung awkwardly towards the front of the class, and stopped in front of Static's desk. A hush descended on the class, each pupil sitting apprehensively in their seats. Static looked up as wee Ian clumped towards him.

"Did you make me yon bogie?" Ian asked, jerking a nod over his shoulder.

"Aye. Whit aboot it?"

All awaited the likely angry response from wee Ian, who had drawn closer. He stared directly into the bigger boy's face. "Thanks," he said simply. "Can ye show me how tae drive it properly?"

"Aye, nae bother," Static answered.

Ian turned for his seat. "And jist so everyone knows," he announced to the class at large, "it was ma ain fault whit happened tae ma leg, so I think Static should get tae play at Oor Bit again. Do yis no think?"

It took the appearance of Miss Sprinkle to silence the subsequent cheering to wee Ian's remarks.

Chapter 7

It was almost a month later when Calum, accompanied by his cousin, were headed for their Aunt Maisie's, each scarcely able to contain their excitement, to find that lady in her Friday night ritual of washing her hair and cutting her toe nails. One of the little objects pinged passed Mal's head into the coal pail as he opened the door.

"Oh, it's you two, Laurel and Hardy!" Their aunt greeted them, putting down the offending weapon.

"Aunt Maisie?" Calum sang out her name as he hitched himself into a chair at the table, "Mal and me were jist thinking..."

"And aboot time too, I thought the baith o ye wid never start," Aunt Maisie responded, splitting a kirby grip with her teeth and inserting it in a rebellious strand of hair.

"Oh! Aunt Maisie, this is serious business we've come to discuss," Mal interjected, coming to his cousin's aid.

Aunt Maisie looked up from where she had been coiling a towel round her wet hair locks, a look of apprehension on her face. "Didnae tell me, ye've broken a windie, and ye want a lend o the money tae pay for it afore yer folks find oot.?" Two heads shook, simultaneously. "Worse?" She moaned. Two heads shook again.

"No auntie, we wis wondering, could ye run a concert fur wee Ian Shaw's leg?"

"How can wee Ian's leg no run wan fur itsel?" she asked deadpan.

The boys looked at one another, hurt by the callus remark.

"Ach, never mind me," Aunt Maisie apologised. Adding to herself "It's that time o the month again."

Mal picked up the near whisper. He nodded sympathetically. "Got the gas bill again, same as ma Mammy," he sighed.

"And just as welcome," Maisie smiled with amusement. "Well, whit's aw this aboot running a concert, eh?"

"Well ye see Aunt Maisie," Calum started eagerly, "we heard at school that wee Ian wanted tae take up the accordion, but doesnae have the money, so we thought that if we could hold a concert, we might be able to gather the money fur it."

"And seeing as ye are good at holding dancing displays, ye would be the wan tae help us oot," Mal supported his cousin.

"Whit kind o concert have you geniuses thought of?" The boys' eyes clouded over. "I mean whit sort of acts are ye visualising?" Aunt Maisie sighed, and extricated her curlers from a pouch. "Right. First, I can gie ye some of ma dancers. Who else have ye in mind?"

The boys shrugged. "I thought ye'd know somebody," Calum said softly, reaching across the table and opening one of his auntie's curlers.

"When had ye this Command Performance in mind? Remember, ye have tae let the King and Queen know well in advance, in case it clashes wi their laundry day."

"Aunt Maisie," the boys moaned.

"Right. Leave it wi me, and I'll hae a meeting wi yer mammies, and see whit we can come up wi."

Overjoyed, the boys rose. "Jist wan thing Auntie." Calum's expression grew serious. "We don't want wee Ian tae know. It's tae be a surprise."

"Oh, it will be a surprise all right," their aunt assured them. "Ye can baith be assured o that."

Two weeks later, the three sisters, accompanied by their respective off springs, sat around Aunt Maisie's table.

"Well. We've just aboot done it!" their hostess proudly announced. "The Sons and Daughters of Scotia have agreed to come along for a small fee. They will be oor star attraction. They will open and close the show wi their singing and country dancing. My lot will provide the Highland Dancing bit."

"Great!" Calum's mother slapped the table. "And it's definite, the Co-op will let us have their hall for nothing, provided we tell everyone aboot it."

"How aboot the tickets? We'll need tae get some printed with the price and, date," Mal's Mammy reminded them.

"Already been taken care of, Agnes," Maisie assured her sister. "Adults, two bob, weans a tanner."

"Is that no a bit steep?" Calum's mother queried, turning up her nose.

Maisie shook her head. "Mind we have the Sons and Daughters of Scotia tae pay. They want a fiver."

"How many sons and daughters have they got? I thought it wis Sons and daughters of Scotia, no Sons and daughters o the hale o China?"

"A fiver's no bad in this day and age, Jenny," Maisie gently rebuked her sister.

"Who else hiv we got, Aunt Maisie?" Calum asked, sipping the orange drink the grown-ups had given them to keep them quiet.

"Well. Ye can have four o ma best tap dancers; they're good for a turn or two. And, just tae give the show some class, shall we say, we've got Percy Smart, tae gie us a tune or two of classical music on the piano."

"Very good." Jenny nodded her approval.

"As long as it's no too long, Calum moaned. "Mister Watt, oor heidie, asked him tae play wan day during oor school play festival. He played three sympathies. It lasted wan day!" Calum said, still horrified by the memory. "Missed playin at Oor Bit, we did."

"Oh, that's a shame," his mother mockingly consoled. "And the word you are after is symphony, no sympathy."

"No if ye were there," Calum chuckled.

"We were discussing turns," Maisie reminded the company impatiently. "Besides Mr Smart, I got Sybil Jamieson."

"The contortionist?" Jenny asked in astonishment. "The wan that was going tae hiv a career on the stage, until she took that bad turn?"

"A sad twist o fate," Maisie laughed, looking around the table for approval of her joke.

"Whit does she dae noo?" Agnes asked inquisitively, choosing to ignore her sister's wisecrack.

"She hauds a high up position in the Co-op," Jenny informed her, nondescript.

"Well, she would, being a contort..." Calum sniggered, nudging his cousin under the table.

"That's enough oot o you wee yin," his mother glared.

"It's settled then." Maisie rose. "Time for a cuppa." She pointed a stern finger at her nephews. "So it's up to you pair tae sell as many tickets as ye can at school."

"It's no use!" Maisie burst through her sister's door like a whirlwind gone mad. "They Scotia folk cannae come, seems it was something they ate at their last doo!" she cried disconsolately. "Noo we've nothing tae open and close the show wi!"

"When did this happen?" Jenny asked, who had just happened to call in for a cup of sugar and a bob or two, if her sister Agnes could spare it.

"Two days ago," Maisie replied, sinking into an armchair by the fireside.

"Och! That's no sae bad, oor show's no 'till Friday, maybe they will have got ower it by that time," Agnes suggested hopefully.

Maisie shook her head. "We cannae take the chance. Whit if they did come? Started tae sing and dance tae The Floors o The Forest, and half way through, had tae go into the Dashing White Sergeant, and belt aff the stage?"

"Aye," Jenny agreed, seeing her sister's point of view, "and ended up singing, We're no Awa Tae Bide Awa frae the lavy!"

All three sisters roared with laughter, which left Mal wondering, if it was this grown up sense of humour during a crisis that had got them through two World Wars…or maybe it had been the reason for starting them.

"So, whit are we to do aboot it?" Their host left the table to fill up the kettle under the tap.

Jenny blew cigarette smoke up at the ceiling. "It could be worse."

"It is." Maisie rose from her chair by the fire. "I wis hoping tae spare ye the news, but we've lost oor other turns as well."

"But we've selt ower fifty tickets at school, Aunt Maisie!" Mal howled in horror.

"Fifty tickets, is that all? An ye expect tae buy that wee laddie wi the leg an accordion? Lucky if we hae enough tae buy him a moothie when this is aw ower," Aunt Maisie bit back, wishing she had never heard of wee Ian or his leg.

Agnes set the kettle on the gas ring, and asked without turning round, "Whit happened tae oor ither turns, then?"

Maisie sat herself down at the table and gave her nephew a look inferring that it was all his fault, and it would have been better had he sold raffle tickets to avoid all this trouble.

She turned to face her sisters. "First, Percy Smart knocked on ma door." She hesitated. "Let me see…This is Tuesday…the concert's on Friday…so it must have been Sunday night. Aye…that's right, Hughie," she referred to her husband, "has his bath on a Sunday night. He's a joiner you know," she explained.

"I thought Hughie was an engineer?" Jenny feigned surprise.

"No ma man, ye eejit…Percy, he's a joiner. Seemingly his chisel slipped, and he cut maist o his fingers. That was whit he came tae tell me. I asked him if he could still play the piano, and he said no unless I knew a concerto fur thumbs. So he's oot."

"In that case, who else have we got?" Jenny mused, watching the effect the smoke from her cigarette was having on a fly coughing its wee lungs up on her sister's ceiling.

Maisie hesitated, slipping in the name as one does a swear word. "There's aye Danny Clarke."

"The magician? Or so he likes tae think he is," Jenny choked, snuffing out the remains of her cigarette in an ashtray displaying a solitary picture of the delights of Troon. "He should dae wan trick, and disappear. He's rotten!" she declared adamantly.

"He's no that bad," Maisie defended. Though she knew within herself that she had scraped the bottom of the barrel, which the unfortunate magician had also done on his last performance while trying to get out of a trick performed by the Great Houdini. The result of which the audience had given him three hearty encores while awaiting the Fire Brigade and when that stalwart body of men had arrived, half the audience had refused to tell them where the hapless magician was.

"I suppose he's better than nothing," Jenny sighed.

"I'd rather watch nothing," Agnes said solemnly. "It's mair interesting."

"Well, when it comes doon tae it, I suppose I better gie ye wan mair o ma dancers." Maisie consulted a sheet of paper she had extracted from her handbag. "But it will no be easy, seeing as there is so much jealousy amongst the mothers."

"We've still got Sybil Jamieson the contortionist, though," Agnes said cheerfully.

Mal saw his Aunt Maisie shake her head. "Oh no we haven't."

"How come?" Jenny quizzed, setting out the cutlery.

Maisie explained. "Sybil's sister came tae the door just afore I left. It seems Sybil was practising wan o her positions...well tae cut a long story short, if the doctor wants tae talk tae her face tae face he will have tae stand on his heid, if ye take my meaning."

Agnes made a face. "Whit a shame, and Sybil always bent ower backwards tae be obliging."

"Well maybe this time if she hadn't, she'd still be in the show," Maisie said bitterly.

"Bertha Mollings!" Jenny cried, slapping the table, as if having found the solution to all of their problems.

"To sing? You cannae be serious?" Maisie challenged. "She uses mair keys than a Barlinnie Jiler."

"Oh, I don't know. It's her style of singing. She has a very wide range."

"So has the Lone Ranger, but he cannae sing either."

Unabashed, Jenny went on. "Ye must admit she throws herself into every song."

"Then let's hope she sings Old Man River." Maisie made a moue.

Letting out a low moan, Mal slid down in his chair. He had seen Bertha's wide range, it was what she sat down on in the church choir. God! Was she a big wuman! It always looked as if she had two Rowntrees jellies stuck up her jersey when she sang, while at the same time someone was grabbing her by the backside and making her scream for help.

Maisie reached for the tea pot. "Wid she be able tae make the show, Jenny, I thought she had a job away oot at the Bellahouston roundabout?"

"I thought the fat bauckle wis the Bellahouston roundabout," Maisie laughed.

Ignoring the frivolity, Agnes sat down at the table and stared dejectedly at the tea pot. "So whit do we do noo?" she solemnly inquired of the company.

"The weans will have tae help," Maisie decided, thumping the table with the flat of her hand.

Mal's head jerked up, his expression asking if his aunt was mad, and she returning the look as if to say she wasn't. "Ye said ye had school plays. Well then? We could fill up the show wi a play or two. Could we no?"

"Great idea, sister o mine," Agnes waxed enthusiastically. "That's a sure way tae sell mair tickets. Do ye no think so, Mal?"

Mal studied the table, and wishing he was under it. School plays! That would mean Mr Watson, auld Cecil B DeMille himself, getting involved. And quite frankly after the school Summer Festival of Plays, he had had enough, which he was sure had most of his fellow 'thespians'.

"Well, can ye no ask at the school the morro?" his mother shot at him.

"I suppose so," Mal replied slowly and dejectedly.

His Aunt Maisie had been right, they should have tried to sell raffle tickets after all.

Mal has said they had wanted to keep the concert a secret from wee Ian and his folks, now he wished he could keep it a secret from all of those who had bought a ticket. It was going to be a disaster. He and Calum would have to shoulder the blame. And for how long? Probably they would still be refunding money from their Old Age Pensions, he thought, miserably.

However, by some miracle, his Uncle Hughie had contrived to get The Caledonian Accordion Band along for the price of one hired bus, they having heard that wee Ian wanted to take up the instrument. So, at least they had one respectable act.

All too soon, the fateful occasion arrived. Calum, who would have been conscripted into taking part in the Highland Dancing; and who would have died in front of the entire school had he been forced to do so, had gained a reprieve on the grounds of having to help with the tickets, and arrange 'other things', beside taking part in his school play of Dick Turpin, which, Mr Watson decided, was an excellent idea, considering the play would be cast by the guest of honour's own classmates

Jimmy, Calum's father and their Aunt Maisie's husband, Uncle Hughie, were assigned to collecting tickets at the door, aided by the parents of the boys classmates who had been roped in to help.

The boys made their way into the foyer where Isa Robb and her pal Myra McClusky had set up a stall.

"Whit are you two selling?" Calum asked inquisitively, approaching their table.

"Lucky charms," Myra responded proudly. "We thought it might help raise a bob or two."

"Good," Calum nodded. "How many have ye selt?"

"Nane," Isa answered despondently.

"Nae luck then," Mal countered with a snigger, which had the affect of both girls suggesting a warmer place for him to go.

The cousins reached the entrance to the hall.

"Jings! There's hardly anybody here!" Mal gasped, running an eye over the rows of empty seats in the big hall which now appeared to be even larger.

"It's early yet. The seven o'clock bus hasnae arrived," Calum reassured him optimistically.

They went backstage, which in contrast to the auditorium was in a state of flux.

"Dancers! Come and get yer make-up on!" Aunt Maisie was shouting at her pupils, amid squeaking accordions and the band attempting to arrange their music stands.

Jenny drew back from where she had been sneaking a look through the curtains at the respective audience. "Nice o them tae come on the same bike. Ye wid think they might at least sit the gither and help save the cleaning up."

Maisie captured a Highland Dancer who was making a charge for the anti-room, and spun her round to powder her face. "Aye, there's mair up here than there is doon there. We might hae tae take turns at sitting wi the audience to help fill the hall."

The cousins gave each other a look of dejection. It was going to be a disaster which led Mal to wonder what age he had to be to join the Foreign Legion.

"The hall's fair freezing," Agnes shivered. "They wee weans in their dancing frocks are blue wi the cauld."

"Come on Calum, I've an idea." Mal grabbed his cousin by the arm and led him through the anti-room and down the back stairs to the boiler room.

"Whit are ye two doing doon here?" a stubby middle aged man in overalls wanted to know, stepping out from behind one of the boilers.

The boys drew up. Calum threw his cousin a nervous look.

"The heid bummers sent us doon to see if ye couldnae heat up the hall a wee bit. Folk are dying up there wi hypochondria." Mal drew himself to his full height, trying his best to sound important.

The man scratched at his nearly bald head. "Hyper...whit?"

"Somehow I don't think that's the right word, Mal," Calum whispered. Adding nervously, "Whit are we doin doon here, anyhow?"

Ignoring his cousin, Mal faced the man. "Well they're aw nearly blue wi the cauld," he explained.

Angrily, the man turned to the gauge on the side of one of the boilers. "See this?" he asked, pointing. Neither being short-sighted the boys nodded. "Well, I can only turn the heating up as far as this." He indicated the green markings between that of white and red. "If I shovel mair coal into that, the place will heat up considerably." He stood back, feeling as important as the chief stoker of the Titanic.

"And whit if it reached the red?" Mal asked, stoking the man's ego.

"Ye would be fair roasted up there," he replied adamantly. "But there is no chance o' that I can assure you."

"How come?" Calum wanted to know, and still at a loss as to why Mal was here in the first place, and asking all of these strange questions.

"Because you are getting the hall for nothing. And I have also been told to keep the dials down as well as the cost of fuel." Mal looked at him, wondering why it was that people spoke so politely when they felt important. The man returned his look. "All right," he conceded, "I'll put a wee bit more on. But, after that, you'll just have to jump up and down...no more coal, right? And my shift finishes at eight. So after that...hard luck."

Mal nodded. "Thanks mister."

Outside, Static had almost reached the hall doorway. It was raining, the wind strong enough to blow dustbin lids up the street. A private bus drew up, and above the noise of the wind, Static assured the driver that this was in fact the Co-op hall, and was equally quick to get out of the way of a dozen or so passengers running for the shelter of the hall, before he was trampled in the stampede.

"Hello, Mr Muir!" Static said cheerfully, addressing Calum's dad on the door.

"Hello Static. Just the wee man I'm looking for. Try and find yer pal's Auntie Maisie, son. Ask her tae haud up the show for a wee while until the seven o'clock bus arrives. Besides, it bringing Ian Shaw, and his Mammy and daddy, there might be a few mair on it. Okay?"

"Okay!" Static nodded, starting to thread a way through bewildered looking passengers from the private bus.

His message delivered, Static headed for the back stage where he found a harassed Mr Watson haranguing the entire Greek army from the Siege of Troy. "What do you mean, this is it Mr Watson?" he exploded. "This!" He pointed a shaking finger at an object in the stairwell. "This is the wooden horse in which the Greek soldiers are supposed to hide? This is a rocking horse!"

"Please Sir, we know Sir," the nearest boy pleaded, pulling down the short white kilt bought from material from Marks and Spencer he was forced to wear as a Greek soldier, and now knowing why auld

Scotia had never been conquered by the Romans, as they were too busy breaking icicles off their Togas in the winter, or waving off midges in the summer, to have any strength or hands left to fight with.

"Where then is the original horse? The one used in the school play." The exasperated teacher howled.

"We broke it up, Sir."

"What moron told you to do that?" He bawled at the 'company' and to the spokesman in particular.

"You did Sir. You said burn it as a symbol of our atrocious acting."

"Never mind Sir," another ventured to suggest, "we can use it in the same way as we did in our school play."

Defeated, Mr Watson stared at the floor. "At least there is one consolation," he sighed, "we still have Dick Turpin to rely on."

Aye, and ye have as much luck there, as catching the Loch Ness Monster in a chip poke, Static thought, with a chuckle.

Mal's mother had decided to take another quick look through the curtain, where a drunk man was soliciting customers for chiropody by standing on corns and bunions on his way to his seat in the fifth row, while two rows back that entire row seemed to be in some sort of turmoil at something or other.

Maisie ran to join her sister at the curtain. "Is that wee Ian arrived?" she asked hopefully.

"Naw. Jist a drunk man fell aff his seat," came the reply.

At last, Ian and his parents arrived, Mal and Calum proudly showing them to their seats in the front row. The boys' trepidation at the show's expected failure momentarily forgotten.

The curtain opened amid strains of the Caledonian Accordion Band in full swing, and Maisie wishing she could close the curtains right there and then while she was still winning.

Five acts later, things still seemed to be going well, despite the drunk man standing up and cheering mid way through every act, then having to be helped to look for his false teeth.

"Only three mair turns tae the interval, Calum," Mal said, with a hint of trepidation. "Ye better start setting up the orange drinks stall. And make sure that Sadie Clark and her mob are ready tae sell the raffle tickets. I'll be back in a wee while."

On his way to carrying out Mal's orders, Calum encountered

Static in the anti-room. "Hi, Static! How's it goin?" he asked cheerfully.

"No bad. I'll be glad when this is aw ower, though."

"Whit are you worried aboot.? Aw ye have to dae is bang they coconut shells the gither, like ye did in the school play. Easy!"

"I hope ye think so!" Static said nervously. "When are we on anyway?"

"No 'till the second half."

"Good," said Static, "so I've still time for a keech?"

Calum winced at Static's choice of words. "Nae bother. In fact, ye have time for diarrhoea, if ye hurry." And he continued on his way in search of Sadie Clark and her helpers.

By the time the interval had arrived, the hall was almost full. The commotion in the seventh row had also calmed down, somewhat. Sales of raffle tickets and orange drinks rose, as did the temperature in the hall.

"It's fair roastin in here." Maisie blew out scarlet cheeks, and wiped her brow.

"I telt ye. It's wi aw they folk in noo," Jenny replied, combing one of the young dancer's hair.

Maisie crossed to the anti-room wall where she consulted the sheet of paper showing the order of acts. "Oh my Lord! I had forgotten aboot him. He's on efter the accordion band, at the start of the second half!"

Jenny left the dancer and her hair to peer at the list. "Who dae ye mean?"

"Charlie Higgins," Maisie said flatly.

"No him wi the musical saw?"

"Aye. I booked him when I thought aw the rest couldnae make it," Maisie moaned.

"Well, the puir soul tries. At least he tells ye the name o the tune afore he starts," Maisie pleaded, while at the same time trying to convince herself of the wisdom of her decision.

"Yer right there. Jist like the last time. Did nine numbers, then sawed through the piano for an encore. The double bass was next if they hadnae stopped clapping!"

"Yer exaggerating, oor Jenny," Maisie laughed, giving her sister a friendly nudge.

The second half commenced with the accordion band in full

swing. Backstage, Mr Watson was getting his junior Lawrence Oliviers ready. "Dick Turpin, first!" he announced, gathering his perspiring cast together. While, on stage, Charlie Higgins went into his similarly sounding third tune, to finish with subdued, but polite applause.

Bowing his gratitude, Charlie adjusted his bow tie in his over large evening suit, and announced with his best professional smile, " now for my next piece..."

"Make it a jam wan, ye wee scunner!" the drunk man shouted up at him, amid some embarrassed laughter. "An bugger aff. Musical saw? I've heard better music frae a hammer and chisel!"

Cut to his spats, Charlie gave a polite but hurried bow and exited stage left.

Mr Watson appeared next, announcing, "Ladies and Gentlemen, we now proudly present an abridged version of two of our school plays. The first of which is Dick Turpin, Highwayman. We open...and close..." He gave an nervous laugh; waiting for a reaction that never came .... "where Dick and his band are waiting to hold up the coach."

The teacher gradually exiting in the same direction as had the failed saw musician, while the curtain rose amid cheers and catcalls from his pupils in the audience.

Jimmy Smith, dressed as the intrepid highwayman, opened the scene, with Calum continuing with his line of, "Hark I hear a coach approach!" His eyes were on the wings where Static should have been standing rapping the coconut shells on the tiled wall to impersonate the sound of galloping hooves.

Shrugging, Jimmy gave his fellow thespian a look that strongly suggested he'd rather be away playing at Oor Bit.

Nervously, Calum repeated his line. Still no Static. No coconut shells. No galloping hooves.

On the opposite wing, Mr Watson threw a hand dramatically to his brow, fearing his career as an up and coming Hollywood director had 'gone with the wind'.

For the fourth time, Calum repeated his line.

A shout went up from the hall. "Ye've got better hearing than us Calum!"

Glaring through the footlights at Stevie Wright, who had shouted the comment, Calum was sorely tempted to bunch his fists at him, instead he tried again, promising to put the heid on Static the next time they met.

Suddenly, there was the sound of pounding hooves. The drunk man leading a chorus of cheers from the pupils, and shouting, "It's been held up! Maybe it got stuck ahint the seven o'clock bus?"

Jimmy Smith, Mal's kep gun in hand, moved to the edge of the stage, letting the curtain partially hide him. "Stand and deliver!" he shouted at an imaginary coach. Slowly, two men and a woman passenger appeared from the doomed coach.

"Put your hands in the air," Dick commanded, adding with a polite bow to the lady, "pray, not you madam."

"You are too kind, Sir," the lady replied with a slight courtesy.

"May I ask the name of the beautiful lady I have the privilege tae rob?"

"Ye know her, Smithy. It's big Maggie. The wan ye snog ahint the bike shed!" Stevie shouted again.

A red faced Dick Turpin ignored the interruption. It was important to get the next part right.

Suddenly, one of the passenger's hands flew to the inside of his coat. Jimmy raised his pistol and fired. Nothing. The percussion cap had failed to go off. But, what was worse, the passenger now lay 'dead' at his feet. At a loss as to what to do next, Jimmy looked first at Calum, the passengers, then across to the wings where Mr Watson was slowly sinking to his knees. Again, Jimmy tried to fire the pistol. Still nothing.

"Never mind Jimmy ye got him the first time wi yer silencer!" Stevie bawled up at him, amid uproarious laughter.

Jimmy had had enough. Stepping to the edge of the stage, his eyes searched out the heckler. "I know where ye live, Wright," he called out, pointing the pistol, which now having recovered from its stage fright discharged itself with a bang. And the closing of the curtain.

From the passageway close to the front row, Mal had watched his classmates perform and, although the scene had been a 'dramatic' disaster, it had gone down well as a comedy with the audience, who had called enthusiastically for an encore.

In an aisle seat, Mrs Mackay puffed out her cheeks at Mal and rapidly loosened her fur stole.

"Feeling the heat, Mrs MacKay?" Mal asked sympathetically.

"Here, fan yersel wi a programme."

Taking the proffered sheet of paper, she did as Mal suggested, while he held out his hand. "That will be tuppence, Mrs MacKay."

"Away and raffle yerself," the lady retorted angrily.

"I already have. I hope ye bought a ticket?"

"Cheeky wee monkey!"

Not to be outdone, Mal persisted. "All right then, a penny, seeing as the shows nearly ower. It's all in a good cause." Mal received his penny as well as a few words, even he had not heard before.

Having risen to the occasion, as well as his backside off the floor, Mr Watson plucked up enough courage to announce the second play, finishing with a flourish of "I give you The Siege of Troy!"

In the school version it had not mattered that 'Helen' was an overweight Muriel Bradshaw, a spoiled brat who believed Santa Clause was for life and not just for Christmas, and who just happened to be Mr Watson's niece. The curtain rose. 'Helen' appeared.

"In the name o the wee man!" the drunk man choked. "Is that supposed tae be the face that launched a thoosand ships? Mair like a face that munched a thoosand chips! Or sank them. Wi a build like that she could launch the Queen Mary...wi a shove!"

Unperturbed, by the uproarious laughter from the audience Helen plunged on, either too much the Thespian or too thick to notice, until her part finished she exited the scene. At the sight of the rocking horse being pushed on to the stage, the laughter increased, fuelling more fire to the drunk's wisecracks, "That the Greek's must have been a race o midgets," while the Greek soldiers did their best to give the impression of dropping out of the horse.

Suddenly, there was a bang, shaking the curtain and backdrop, and pieces of plaster dropped on to the stage.

"Run chaps! The Trojans are using heavy artillery!" the drunk shouted, collapsing into his seat and nudging the woman next to him, at his humour.

None too soon the curtain fell, opening again after a few seconds delay for the finale. The entire cast, headed by the Caledonian Accordion Band finishing with a few rousing Scots songs; whereupon the audience, lead by the drunk and some riotous school pupils, stamped and cheered, until silenced by Mr Watson, who, on behalf of the cast, stepped forward to thank all of those involved, especially to the audience for turning out on such a wild night. With the somewhat recovered 'director' concluding, by stating that the show whatever its artistic shortcomings , had been a financial success. And how through the generosity of the accordion band, Ian would get his accordion...second hand though it may be."

"Well, thank the Lord that's ower." Backstage, Maisie gave a sigh of relief, putting a powder puff into her makeup box.

"But it went doon well. Did it no?" Jenny gave her sister a gentle slap on the back.

"I thought for awhile, yon drunk man wis goin tae cause trouble." Agnes curled a lip sourly.

"It was yon lot two rows further back that had me worried," Hughie admitted, lifting up a suitcase. "Your pal's fault again, Mal."

Mal knitted his brows. "How come, Uncle Hughie?"

"Static met them ootside gettin aff some private bus. He telt me a wee while ago, he thought they had said they were looking for the Co. Hall. Instead, they were looking for the Gospel Hall. He said he couldnae have heard right, for the wind and rain!"

Laughing, Agnes shook her head. "That's Static fur ye. At least he selt a few mair tickets."

Hughie agreed. "The poor souls must have wondered what they had walked into, and me charging them two bob. Nae wonder they nearly left before it got started. Still, when they learned it was for a good cause, they stayed. I think they fairly enjoyed themselves in the end."

"Come on, it's roasting in here. Nearly everybody is away." Picking up a bag, Jenny started for the stairs.

"And that bang!" Maisie blew out her cheeks. "The janny was caud back frae his hoose, he said it wis the boiler."

Calum drew closer to his cousin. "I don't suppose ye had anything tae dae wi that Mal?"

Mal made a show of ignorance. "Me? Still, we did sell a lot more orange juice than we thought." He delved into his trouser pocket. "Must have been this lucky charm a bought frae Myra McClusky," he grinned, dangling the trinket in front of his cousin's face.

Chapter 8

Mal did not mean to listen, he was in too much of a hurry to get to Oor Bit, but the door stood open and he saw his Aunt Maisie standing in the kitchen, her back against the sink, an elbow cupped in her opposite palm, an eye half closed against the smoke rising from her cigarette. He drew back quickly into the lobby before he was seen.

"So yer telling me that soadie heid of a man o yours has been away for three weeks and you no saying a word tae ony o us? Why no oor Agnes?" she was asking sharply of her sister.

"Och! He's been away afore. He only went oot for a bottle o`milk. Whit dae ye think I should dae, Maisie?" Mal heard his mother say.

"Besides sending oot for another bottle o` milk?" Maisie could scarcely believe her sister's folly.

"He's no inside. He would have got word tae me if he was. I think he's got himsel anither wuman!" Agnes drew the cup of tea across the table towards her.

"He'll be back once the guide dug gets jealous," Maisie proclaimed, dropping into a chair opposite her sister.

Mal slid down the wall and drew his knees up to his chin, Oor Bit temporarily forgotten. He remembered the last time he had thought his parents had found someone else. He sighed. That had been before Granny had gone to heaven.

With his schoolbag in one hand and, in the other, his wee case containing everything he would need for the weekend at Granny's, Mal waited on the landing until his mother had locked the door behind her.

"Noo, ye are sure you've got everything? All yer toys? A clean hankie?" Impatiently, his mother started on her list, and Mal quickly reminded her he had a second pair of everything at Granny's.

It had been a long time since he had seen his mother so agitated. The last time had been when she had made that ham soup, which proved to be off.

"Here's a sixpence fur the pictures."

Mal took the proffered coin as they ran down the stairs, unable to fight off a lurking suspicion that there was something fishy in the air, and it wasn't flying fish either! Although this sixpence could well be a red herring.

At the junction of Brown and Wilson Street, Mal got ready to say his goodbyes to his mother when she hauled him from the side of the kerb.

"There's someone I think you should meet, Mal."

Mal looked up into his mother's sparkling eyes, mystified as to why she should be so happy. She didnae do the fitba pools, so it couldnae be that. Or back horses. And for the life of him, he could not see his mother gathering jeely jars, to make a bob or two.

His mother swung him round. "Look!"

Mal saw a scraggy figure wrapped within a blue striped suit walking towards them. His heart leaped. Mammy had a boyfriend!

Despite his anger and disappointment at his father, he had never envisaged anyone else taking his place.

"Come and meet him," his mother urged, pulling him by the hand.

Angrily, Mal pulled back. "No, Mammy!"

The figure was almost on them. Mal kept his eyes firmly fixed on the pavement.

"Yer acting like a wee wean!" his mother voiced angrily. "Say hello to...."

"It's aw right, Agnes. The wean doesnae have tae speak tae me if he doesnae want tae."

At the sound of the familiar voice, Mal looked up, up into the face of his father.

"Hello, son. Long time no sea, as the auld blind sailor said."

Mal drew back. This was the man who had betrayed him. The man who had made him ashamed to tell what his father had done during the war. When his pals played at Oor Bit at being their Faithers during the war; some even bringing caps and helmets, what had he been expected to do? Either pretend to be a bomber pilot, or tell the truth and turn up with a ballcock and spanner.

"It's nice tae be hame son. Whit have ye been doin since I went away?"

Mal shrugged. Obviously Mammy had told Faither about him knowing of his 'exploits', in and out of the 'service'.

His father looked so thin in a suit and shirt several sizes too big for him, that he fully expected him to slip through his shirt collar at any second.

"Did ye miss me?" his father asked, kneeling down beside him.

Mal felt a lump in his throat. Why, he did not know. Whether it was because of what his father was, or had pretended to be. Or could it just possibly be, because he was his father? A father so thin and worn out.

"See! I brought ye this, Mal." Erchie delved into the paper bag he had been carrying. "I made it when.....well I made it while I wis waitin tae see ye again." He looked up at his wife and gave her an apologetic smile, "waitin tae see ye baith again."

"Well, Mal, can ye no gie yer Faither a hug, and say thanks?" his mother chastised him.

Mal looked up at his mother. Then, throwing his arms around his father, beamed at the present he had made for him. The model of a Spitfire aeroplane.

Maybe, just maybe, everything was going to be all right after all.

It had been all right, Mal sighed, at least for the first few days, until once more he had to seek sanctuary under the bed, or doon at Granny's, his Faither having resorted to thinking himself a drummer in the Orange Lodge and using his backside to practice on.

Mal returned to the conversation in the kitchen.

"Erchie was no always that gowkit looking." His mother was defending her husband with an aggressive stirring of her tea. She tapped the rim of the cup with her spoon, shaking off any drips that had the strength left to cling to it. "I mind the first time I saw him." The woman gave a wee chuckle of amusement, reliving the moment once more. "I wis working in McNamara's at the time. He wis hiding ahint a row of ootsize frocks we widnae be able tae sell till the camping season. Wee Betty gave me a nudge. There's a pervert ower there in amongst wumens' wear, she says."

"Wis that yon wee Betty wi the squint?" Maisie interrupted.

"Aye. Poor wee soul. Had a goggle eye. Couldnae look ye straight in the face. Wid have made a good politician," Agnes confirmed, while deciding to give her tea another stir. "Spent mair time goin roon wi the shop's revolving door than she did wi her boyfriend."

"Whit ever happened tae her?" Maisie wanted to know. Now more interested in the unfortunate shop assistant than in her sister's matrimonial troubles.

Agnes gave an impatient flick of her hand, annoyed that her romantic reminiscences had been overshadowed by a wee fat bauchle with a squint, who she had almost entirely forgotten about. "Transferred her tae alterations of all places, wid ye believe. Took her the best part o a week tae thread a needle."

"That's management fur ye." Maisie shook her head sadly.

Agnes sipped her tea. "Didnae last long though. There wis a rumour whit hit it on the heid, wis the day she was fitting a bride tae be fur her goon. Seemingly, she was kneeling on the floor doin the alterations and didnae realise she had pinned the goon tae her ain dress, until the poor lassie started tae walk tae the changing room. And there wis wee Betty waggling efter her on her knees. Seems the goon ripped. Turns oot wee Betty had tae borrow a pinnie tae get hame."

"That would put the hems on it so tae speak," Maisie chuckled. "Did she get her books?"

Agnes broke a chocolate biscuit in half. "Naw. But wid ye credit it? They moved her tae the restaurant as a waitress. Word was she got her books for pouring a pot o tea in tae a wuman's handbag, instead of her cup."

"A simple mistake," Maisie commiserated.

"Anyhow," Agnes sharply reminded her sister. "Ye were goin tae gie me advice aboot whit I should do aboot ma man."

"I wasnae!" Maisie denied, drawing the tea pot across the table towards her. "But if I was, ye'd only get the jile, if ye did take ma advice."

Agnes watched her sister help herself to a chocolate biscuit. "Yer supposed tae be on a diet, oor Maisie," she reminded her, drawing away the plate with the three chocolate biscuits she had planned having whilst listening to Woman's Hour on the wireless. "It's Mal, I feel sorry for. Him havin tae think he only has a Faither oot on loan. If Erchie had been a lemonade bottle, I'd have made a fortune on the returns."

Maisie eyed the retreating biscuit plate longingly. "Well, maybe next time soadie heid comes hame ye should stamp non returnable on his foreheid. Do ye think he will come back? He always has before."

Agnes poured herself another cup of tea. "Could do, he's aye come back mair times than yer average boomerang. Only this time..." she vowed angrily. "If there is another wumman..."

Another wumman? Mal did not quite understand. How could his Faither get drunk with two women? Was it no bad enough tae get bashed ower the heid by wan woman? But as his mother had said, perhaps this time Faither was staying away for good. And he did not know whether to feel sad or not at the news. At least if he did, it would give his bum time to heal.

Mal drew a finger along the linoleum. When he was small, his father had been good fun, especially when he came home drunk. He would play games with him, tell jokes, turn his mother's scowls to laughter. But then, as he grew up, his father was less inclined to play with him. And he would find himself on the receiving end of a good smacking should his father be in a bad mood. Normally, this was initiated by his mother's wrath at her husband wasting so much money in the pub, when there were so many things needed for the house, so that a Saturday night soon became something to dread, instead of something to look forward to.

Mal sighed at the prospect of his father never coming home. Poor Mammy would have to do even more sewing to make ends meet. Now there was no chance of him hearing Dick Barton on the wireless, for the racket. Whit a scunner! Aye, Mal thought sadly, Faither had never taken into consideration the pain he wis inflicting on him, when he wis away staying with another woman. No Dick Barton!

"Ye were telling me aboot the first time ye met his nibs. It wis in amongst women's frocks, was it no?" Mal heard his Aunt Maisie prompt his mother.

On the other side of the wall, Agnes gave a little chuckle. "Oh, so I was." She took a sip of her tea. "I mind saying tae wee Betty, 'I'll away ower there and see whit this juker wants'. So bold as brass I says tae him, can I help ye sir? Wis his face no red oor Maisie. Quick as a flash he says, 'I wis looking fur something in a blue skirt.'"

Agnes gathered chocolate biscuit crumbs together with the edge of her hand. "It wis on the tip of ma tongue tae say, will I do? But, instead I says, whit size does sir take? Well, Maisie, ye should have seen his face!"

"Wis it red, Agnes?" Maisie put a hand to her mouth in wonder.

"Beetroot it wis , Maisie!" Agnes threw biscuit crumbs into the fire. "I wish I hadnae said it though," she sighed. "Oh, it's no for me. It's fur my sister" he says. Well tae cut a long story short. I finished up wi a date, and he finished wi a SLX , and a twenty two cup. Some shape of a sister that!" she laughed. " Of course, efter the first date, I took them back tae the shop, for it turned oot he didnae hae a sister."

"No offence Agnes, but I never did know whit ye ever saw in Erchie. It's no as if he wis pure dead handsome."

"Maybe no, Maisie. But he did have a sense o humour," Agnes replied, slightly hurt by her sister's remark, though determined not to let it show by confirming with a chuckle. "I mind lying in bed on oor honeymoon, sayin tae him, 'where's thae big broad shoulders of yours noo?'" And him answering, 'hanging up in the cupboard beside they big boobs o yours!"

While out in the lobby, Mal wondered what both women were laughing at.

"I only met Erchie's mother wance. That wis at the weddin. Smoked like a chimney, she did. I'd heard o chain smokers, but she wis the missing link!" Maisie reminded her sister.

Agnes nodded. "I mind the first time Erchie took me hame tae meet his mother. I nearly missed her, and that wis in her ain hoose. Ye couldnae see across the room for smoke." Maisie laughed as her sister went on. "His mother had this knack o letting her fag hang frae the corner o her mooth. She could sook tea and eat a piece wi it still hanging there. It aye fascinated me the way the ash used tae creep closer tae her lip, and just when I thought it wid fa' on the table or something, oot wid come this ashtray frae nae where."

Agnes rose abruptly, drawing her sister's cup and saucer together with her own, hoping her sibling would take the hint and leave as she had to get on with her sewing. Instead, Maisie appeared to be more engrossed in her in-laws' history. This, and the fact it was a good twenty minutes before the next bus. "Erchie's Faither wis killed in the First World War, so I believe?" she inquired of her impatient host. "In the battle o the Somme." She shook her head sadly. "An awfy thing the number o young men lost in yon battle, and yer man's Faither jist wan o them."

"Lost is right," Agnes spouted indignantly, setting the dishes down on the bunker. "Got blown into a shell hole and, when he came too in the dark, started walking in the wrang direction. The only sojer tae get captured by his ain regiment."

"Then wis he no killed?" Maisie asked in astonishment, now that her brother-in-laws family tree had been uprooted.

"Oh, he wis killed aw right." Agnes, turned on the tap. "But that wis in Shawlands Road with a horse efter a skin full...Erchie's Faither I mean, no the horse," Agnes explained.

"Whit a shame, efter goin through aw yon," Maisie commiserated. She rose, lifting up her coat draped over the back of her chair. "Well, I better away. Catch the next bus."

Pushing her chair under the table Maisie asked suddenly, "How long wis you and Erchie merrit, afore the hostilities commenced?"

"Jist a month."

Maisie furrowed her brows. "That cannae be right. The war didnae start 'till 1939."

"Oh, that war! I thought ye meant the wan between Erchie and me."

Agnes turned from the sink, making an elaborate show of looking at the clock. "That time already and no a hands turn done!"

Sensing the history lesson to be over, Maisie edged towards the door. "I better get cracking masel. Get the mince and tatties on. At least that's wan thing ye'll save yersel the trouble of, if yer man disnae come back, Agnes."

In the lobby, Mal also got to his feet. His Aunt Maisie was right about saving, for he could not remember ever having seen his Faither without a bonnet, or a heid fu o mince and tatties.

Things were changing, they would never be the same again, Mal thought.

Their class had broken up. Some, like Calum and himself, who having passed their Eleven Plus, were now at the High School. While others, such as Static who, having failed had remained in their old Primary School, in what was elaborately called The Advanced Division, until they were of age to leave.

They still had Oor Bit of course. But it was not the same. Some of the original class, who were now at the High School had brought along new pals, Mal sighed. Bad enough as this was, what was even worse, a few like his own bawheid of a cousin had found themselves a 'doll', and had elected to spend more time 'stoatin' up and doon the street holding hands, rather than play a good gemm o fitba at Oor Bit.

Now that the original denizens attended two different schools it was becoming increasingly difficult to organise the next day's events for Oor Bit, especially by a leader more renowned for his physical attributes than his mental ability, such as Jimmy Smith. And, with so many boys 'winchin', it was sometimes hard to get up a good gemme of fitba, Mal moaned, unable to comprehend how anyone could forego a good game of their national sport in exchange for holding hands in Cathcart Road. Even some of the 'hard men' had been reduced to jelly, and had gone as far as to give up swearing and the odd drag at a fag. A condition which had a bewildered Static solemnly declaring it to be 'a catastrophe of such great magnitude.' to which Mal had expressed his surprise at his pal knowing words of such 'great magnitude'

Aye, Mal sighed, things were changing. Things would never be the same again. They were all growing up. Soon, the place that had meant so much to them in their lives would soon be a thing of the past. No more Oor Bit. With worse to come…work!

Chapter 9

Winter 1954

It was Wednesday night. Mal turned the corner as Jimmy Smith and his cronies were coming the other way.

"Aye, Mal! Where are ye headed?" Jimmy asked cockily, hands deep in his jerkin pockets.

Mal shrugged. "Tae meet Static."

"Ye'll no have far tae go." Jimmy nodded to where Static was crossing the street towards them. "How's it goin then Static?" their former leader asked, a broad smile on his face as if the very sight of Static was hilarious.

"No bad," Static answered, acknowledging the rest of the company with a nod. "Aye Mal."

"Static." Mal nodded back.

"We're jist goin roon tae the cafe for a coffee or something. Comin?" Jimmy asked.

Static and Mal looked at one another, neither relishing Jimmy Smith's invitation, or his company. "Come on," he urged. "It's just roon the corner."

Reluctantly, the two pals allowed themselves to be led by the others.

"I think I'll gie it a miss, Mal," Static decided, drawing up outside the cafe door. "I've some things to dae at hame."

Smith knew it was a lie. Had not the two pals arranged to meet?

"Come on. It's my shout. I'm quite flush, Okay?" He smiled condescendingly at Static, urging him through the door. Reluctantly Mal followed.

"What's it to be lads?" Jimmy asked, as the company shuffled towards their respective tables while he made for the counter.

"Make mine a milk shake, Smithy," one called out as his other three pals expressed similar wishes.

"And you two?" Jimmy inquired of Static and Mal. "I'm having a coffee, masel. The same fur yuse?" Both pals nodded, lowering themselves into their seats.

Jimmy gave his order, winking at the prim waitress behind the counter, an amused smile playing on his lips as he watched her set out the cups.

"Want a photo?" she scowled, catching him watching her.

Amused by the witticism, Jimmy turned to lean back on the counter to survey the almost deserted cafe. Taking a comb from his inside pocket he drew it assiduously through his hair. "We're fur the pictures efter this. Fancy coming?" he asked the two pals, sliding the comb back into his pocket.

Beside him, Mal felt Static stir uneasily as Jimmy made an exaggerated show of extracting a one pound note from his wallet.

"Naw. But, thanks aw the same, Smithy," Mal said, convinced that this eejit had been watching too many Yankee pictures and believed himself to be James Cagney, or something.

The drinks came. Jimmy added to the two pals discomfort by pocketing the change without bothering to count it, and leaving a three-penny tip on the tray.

"You working yet, Static?" Jimmy's question implied interest in his former classmate's welfare.

"Naw. But I went for an interview yesterday."

"Where to, Static?" one of the company asked, putting down his milk shake.

"The filters," Static answered blandly.

Oh, no! This is it, Mal moaned, wishing his friend had kept his mouth shut.

"The filters?" another laughed. "You mean up at the sewerage works? That`s a shite joab!"

"You don't fancy that do ye Static. You'd be browned off efter the first day.!" A third added, and pretended to choke on his coffee.

Smithy banged his cup down in his saucer with exaggerated hilarity. "Do ye get tae take yer work hame wi ye Static?"

Mal saw Static's face turn a bright red, a clear a warning as any traffic light.

He rose, kicking Static's foot under the table. "I think we better away Smithy and let yuse get to the pictures."

Perhaps this is why they had been invited into the cafe in the first place? Or more precisely, why Static had been invited, and that by humiliating him he might just lose his temper, and with the odds against him, Smithy might...just might get a little of his own back for all the thumpings Static had given him at school.

"Aye, maybe yer right, Mal," Static said, draining the dregs of his coffee as he stood up.

They were outside and a few steps away from the cafe before either spoke.

Mal was acutely aware of his pal's anger. "Never mind them Static." He kicked out at an empty cigarette packet on the pavement. "Smithy's always wanted to be the big cheese. He's a bigger bum than ten arses as they say in the army."

Walking, shoulders hunched, hands deep in his pockets, beside his friend, Static did not answer. His thoughts were on his friend's circumstances, and how it was all right for him to talk, with his mother working part-time. Whereas, his own mother could not get anything. They were only just surviving.

Static felt the dry anger in his throat. It was all his fault, of course, being as bright as an unlit candle. Who would employ him? He had put his name down for labouring, but what chance had he at fifteen, when there were plenty of full grown men available?

"Do ye fancy grocery, Static?"

The unexpected nature of the question took Static by surprise. He walked on, visualising lassies in white coats serving behind counters. Grim faced Brylcream-haired men, wearing tight collars and even tighter ties. To become one of them? "Don't know?"

"There's a place in oor shop," Mal informed him. "They are taking me off the message bike and promoting me to weighing tatties and bagging sugar."

"You mean, your joab?"

Mal kicked out at the cigarette packet that had blown passed him. "Aye, you'd be on the message bike. The pays no that great, but it's a start. Then there's the tips. Of course, you'd have tae work Saturdays. Miss goin tae watch the fitba."

"The message bike? Then I'd no be in the shop aw day?"

Mal nodded, more than surprised that Static should even consider such a way of earning a living. "Yer legs and bum will get sair at first, but ye will get used tae it."

"How much did ye get in tips?" Static asked, trying hard to cast aside the vision of going home after having been bent over a bike all day, like yon hunched back French eejit he had read about at school.

"Five, or six bob."

Static's heart leaped. If he was to give his mother all of his pay, he could keep the tips for pocket money! Suddenly, the prospect of becoming that rich negated missing the odd football match he could afford to go to. "How do I get tae know aboot the job?"

"I'll talk tae Mister Simpson the morn. If he thinks yer okay, ye'll likely start on Monday. Wear yer best claes. He's a hard man, pal. He's done mair sacking than yer proverbial Viking."

The cigarette paper blew past again, this time Static beat his pal to the kick.

Static started on the following Monday. Leaning the big black bike, with its even heavier basket, against the wall, he went through the door that led into the back shop, where he found Mal shovelling potatoes into paper bags.

"That bike's killing me." Static rubbed his backside.

"Aye, they say cycling aye gets ye in the end!" Mal laughed at his pun.

"And the saddle's far too low."

"There's a spanner in yon drawer. I'll show ye." Mal dropped his shovel.

"And where you think you are off to, Moffat?" Mister Simpson suddenly appeared in the doorway that led into the front shop.

"I wis only goin tae show Sta...Eh, Drew," he hurriedly corrected himself, "Where the bike spanner was."

"Then don't take all day. Get on with it. We need more tat...potatoes in the front shop," the manager nipped, turning back into the front shop.

"Is auld diarrhoea bum, aye like that, Mal? Does he aye cry ye Moffat?"

Mal shrugged. "Sometimes he calls me Malcolm, if he is in a good mood."

The spanner found, Mal escorted Static out of the back door to the bike.

"It needs new brakes as well," Static proclaimed, pressing the tyre of the front wheel with his thumb. "I nearly run ower an auld wuman and her dug."

"As long as ye didnae break the eggs," Mal replied, adjusting the saddle height.

"Or the yokes on me, Eh! Mal!" Static tittered, looking through the back window at a white-coated female entering the back shop. "Hi! Ye didnae tell me Sarah Chapman worked here!" Static stuck his head round the door. "How's it goin, Sarah ?" he asked cheerfully of the astonished girl.

"Oh! No you, Static! Don't tell me, you've started here! Well that should see us shut by the end of the week. And it's Miss Chapman to you," she reminded him haughtily.

Static laughed at the girl's mock dismay. "Och! Come on Sarah, admit ye are overjoyed tae see me."

Mal tugged at his pal's sleeve. "Come on, Static. That's yer bike ready. Take the spanner jist in case. Ye've a lot mair rounds tae dae."

Saturday night arrived. The door had finally closed behind the last customer. The two pals ready for a night at the pictures.

Mal was standing at the sink washing his hands when he saw Static coming into the back shop, his lip curled in the way it did when he was angry or annoyed, the lassies saying their goodnights as they left.

Static crossed to the sink. "I'm a half croon short!"

"In yer pay, Static?"

"Aye. I don't mean in brains exactly," Static hurled back. "You telt me the pay was one pound, seven and six. I've only got one pound five bob." The boy shook his head in despair, having already visualized the surprise and pleasure on his mother's face when he presented her with the full one pound seven and six. "And another thing. I only made one and nine in tips. You said I'd make five, or six bob!"

Mal rinsed his hands and stooped to dry them on the towel hanging beneath the sink. "So you will, wance they get tae know ye better. How many jam jars did ye get?"

"Nine," Static reflected sourly.

"See! Ye'll get mair next week!"

"How aboot ma pay?" Static inquired, convinced that his boss was pocketing the full half crown for himself, as he had the feeling the man had not liked him since the moment of his interview, and had been surprised when offered the job. Now, he had a sneaky feeling he knew why this had been so. "I bet auld torn face is keeping that half croon fur himsel. I think I'll maybe jist go and ask him. Better in ma pocket than his." Static crammed the two ten shilling notes, plus the few coins into his paper bag which served as his pay packet.

Mal shot up from the sink, for he knew that tone and look only too well. "Ye better watch whit ye say, Static. Ye jist cannae go aroon accusing folk." As he was sure that, in this frame of mind. His pal was likely to put the heid on dear Mister Simpson's coupon. "Say ye thought your pay was one pound seven and six, and had he by some chance made a mistake. Or, had the half croon slipped oot the packet. Something like that."

Static stood repeating what Mal had said, like an actor learning his lines, before heading for the front shop.

Mal watched him go, and for a moment wondered whether he should go with him for moral support, then thinking better of it, reached for his jacket hanging on the peg. Could it be that 'Head Office' was paying Static what they thought he was worth, on auld Simpson's recommendation?

Mr Simpson looked up from his accounts as Static entered the front shop. "Well young man, how did you find your first week?" he asked, with the merest hint of a smile.

"No bad," Static answered, in no mood to trade pleasantries until the matter of his pay had been resolved. "I wis coming tae ask you..." He had already forgotten what Mal had told him to say. "If ye haven't paid me a bit short?"

Manager glared at junior staff. "What do you mean, a bit short?"

Static shrugged. "Mal...Malcolm said he started wi one pound, seven and six when he wis on the messages. You've only paid me, one pound five."

"Oh, I see." Mr Simpson replied, regaining his composure. "Of course, this is so. However, Head Office has decided that this shall be your wage until you have learned the rounds, when you will receive your increase." Then, at the look on the boy's face, hurried to assure him. "Of course, you will also receive an increase on your sixteenth birthday, which I understand is not too far away."

Static nodded, though puzzled as to why Mal had not mentioned this to him.

"Sorry to interrupt you Mister Simpson," Static apologised.

"Then you quite understand?" Mr Simpson smiled.

"Yes thanks." Static tried to return the smile but found his lips did not trust the man any more than his brain did.

They were outside before Mal ventured to ask his pal, "What did his nibs say then?"

Static shrugged, his face sour with disappointment. "He said I'd get the rise when I had learned the rounds like you had."

Mal was not exactly sure what his pal meant, but had a sneaky feeling it would be better not to ask. "It's aw right, then?"

"Aye. I suppose so."

A month had gone past. It was Monday again. Mr Simpson caught Static putting away his brush and pail, which he had just finished using before starting on his message rounds.

"Drew! Martin, from the butcher's next door, has asked if I would consent to your showing his new message boy how to wash the windows, to which I have agreed."

"You mean the noo, Mister Simpson?" Static stood the brush inside the toilet door where it was kept.

"Yes, the noo...the now. So hurry up. I don't want you late for starting your rounds." Mr Simpson swung on his heel.

"Promotion, eh, Static?" Sarah Chapman beamed, giving him the thumbs ups.

"Away and bite yer bum, Sarah," Static retaliated. After all it was Monday morning.

Static found the next-door message boy nervously waiting for him on the pavement, a bucket full of soapy water and brushes at the ready. Static looked him over. Puir wee soul, drooned in his blue striped apron, no quite five feet with his hands up.

"Nae need tae worry, wee man. Jist watch whit a dae," the expert encouraged. "First, soap the windie. Where's yer soap?" The wee boy held up a cake of soap for his instructor's inspection. "I'll show ye how it's done. But ye'll need a stool tae stand on fur the morn, tae reach the top windie."

The striped apron nodded.

Static commenced to show him how it was done. "First, soap the windie. Then dip yer brush in the water. Scrub up and doon. See! There's nothing tae it. When ye've finished, take yer bucket and throw the water at the windie tae clean aff any surplus water." Static was proud of his use of that word, and continued in his best English in order to impress this underling. He lifted the bucket to demonstrate. "And mind tae keep a firm hold of the bucket while doing so." He was enjoying this. He let fly with the bucket, the water cascading down the window. "Got it, wee man?"

The wee boy nodded.

"Then I'll leave you to it. I've my message rounds to start."

Static turned in his own shop doorway. "Whit's yer name by the way?"

"Michael," the wee boy replied, in a voice barely audible behind a bus ticket.

"Michael?" Static mused. "Then ye can call me, Mister Little."

Static entered the shop, picking up an empty banana box on the way and carrying it into the back shop before returning for a second one, whereby narrowly missing the pyramid of tinned beans standing centre floor.

"How many times have I told you to watch where you are going, Little?" the manager voiced angrily from behind the counter.

Static was about to express an insensate apology when he heard the crash, and knew instinctively that it was the butcher's window. Mr Simpson glared across at him before starting quickly, if however apprehensively for the door. Static waited a moment or two before following.

"Whit's happened?" Mal peered over Static's shoulder, while behind him the remainder of the staff crammed one another for a better look.

"I think wee Michael has had a smashing start to his day. Puir wee bugger."

"Wheest! I cannae hear whit's goin on," Sarah Chapman chided him with a sharp elbow to his ribs.

"I should have known better than to have asked for your assistance, Simpson!" they heard Martin the butcher say. "All that...person." Martin gulped. "Had to do, was show my new apprentice how to wash a window, but not both sides at the same time!"

"It was not my messenger's fault, Martin," Mr Simpson relied indignantly. "Andrew would have shown him the correct way to do it. All my staff are completely trained."

"Aye, completely trained eejits!"

"There is no necessity to take that attitude, Martin, especially when I was doing it as a favour to you."

"Favour! Favour! I've got a woman member of staff in there, near hysterics.! And so would you be if you were suddenly hit on the head by a pun o link sausages!"

"Come, come, Martin. Surely link sausages cannot injure you?"

"They can, if they are still in a bucket, and your standing in the back shop at the time!" Martin exploded.

Mortified, Mr Simpson took a step away from his irate neighbour. "I'm sure Andrew would have told him to take a tight hold of the pail, before he threw the water at the window, that is how he was trained here. So, if there is no other way in which I can be of assistance, I have a business to run!" With which, the irate grocery manager turned on his heel.

It was an unusual occurrence for Mal and Static to go to the pictures on a Monday night, however, on this occasion they had scraped up just enough for the stalls.

"I didnae think there wid be a queue the night, especially in this weather," Static moaned, turning up his coat collar.

"There's nae seats at aw. No even fur the balcony,'' Mal shivered.

"Oh, aye, and we could afford the balcony! Whit dae ye want me tae dae, gie ye a dummy and sit ye on ma knee, cause that's the only way we'll ever see the balcony," Static retorted.

An optimistic busker came dancing passed, mouth organ at the ready. "He'll be lucky," Static commented.

The commissionaire trotted down the steps to the pavement. "One at ninepence for the stalls. Two at one and six for the balcony!" he announced to that entire side of the city.

"Jesus!" Mal swore, as the human foghorn disappeared back up the steps. "Did he no used tae sell coal? Where did they get him? Had I known he could shout that loud, I d have waited at hame until there was a seat!" Behind Mal, a couple lit up the dreary evening with their laughter at his quip.

"Whit charisma." Static turned to include the same couple in his sigh.

Mal turned to give his pal a bewildered look. "Where did ye get that word?"

"Frae Sarah Chapman. She said I wis fu o it!" Static announced proudly.

"Are ye sure she said Charisma?"

"Sure. She said I could have a loan o the word, but she wanted it back on Thursday."

"Talking aboot charisma, whatever happened to yon wee juker, Archie Martin, that used tae throw us oot o here when we were weans?" Mal reflected.

"Him? He's working in the lift at Lewis's. Got an elevated position, so tae speak." Static chuckled.

"Goin up in life, is he?" Mal quipped.

"And doon."

"Can ye imagine yon wee chancer, dressed in his gold braid, announcing, second flair, women's underwear, knickers and over shoulder boulder holders. Men, third flair, drawers simmits and gallouses!" Again the couple behind joined in the pals' laughter.

The busker now had his 'moothie' (mouth organ) at full blast, floating up and down the queue to his music.

"Whit did Mister Simpson say tae ye aboot the butcher's windie Static?" Mal breathed warmth into his cupped hands, ignoring the free show.

"Whit?" Still being on the third floor of Lewis's it had taken Static time to realise his pal had changed the subject. "Och! He jist asked me whit had I shown wee Michael. He thought maybe I hadnae telt him tae haud the bucket tight when he wis scooshing the windie."

"And did ye?"

"Aye…Although on second thoughts, maybe I should have telt him tae dry his hauns, before he let fly."

"Oh Static!" Mal moaned. "Sometimes I wonder."

The busker, now cap in hand, was slowly moving up the queue thanking those generous enough to have donated a coin or two. Absently, Mal watched him draw nearer, asking of his friend, "Yer Mammy said you made yon sideboard that stauns in front o the windie. She says ye made it up oot o yer ain heid and that ye had enough wood left for a cupboard. Is that right?"

"Very funny." Static made a noise with his lips.

"Seriously though, Static, that's a good piece o` workmanship. Yer wasting yer time at the grocery."

"That's whit I think Simpson`s trying tae tell me."

Impatiently, Static stamped his feet on the wet pavement. "When the hell, are we goin tae get in? We've missed half the wee picture already."

The busker reached them, his cap half full of coins. "Thank you

Sir," he said to Static in anticipation of his generosity.

Static gave him and his cap the full measure of his generosity. "Bugger aff!"

"One seat in the balcony at one and six!" cried the commissionaire, striding purposely down the steps.

"Here!" shouted the busker, emptying his cap of coins and running up the steps.

"Well wid ye credit that!" Mal burst out, a look of incredulity on his face.

Static leaned his shoulder against the wall, unable to restrain himself from laughing. "Well, that's charisma fur ye!"

It was Saturday night, another week over.

"Happy Birthday!" the lassies cried as Static entered the back shop. "See, we have bought ye a cake!" Sarah Chapman sang out. "With a candle for each brain cell!"

"Very funny!" Static sneered, eyeing the fairy cake with the two candles perched on top.

"Well, there's gratitude for ye!" another voiced in fake offence.

"Never mind Static. Happy Birthday, anyhow." A third ventured forward to peck the boy's cheek. Hesitantly the others followed suit, each searching for a stretch of skin that did not resemble an aerial view of the landscape around Rotorua, to snap a quick kiss.

"Yer in luck the night, Static. Must be yer Birthday," Mal teased when the lassies had left. " No goin tae cut the cake then? Goin tae keep it aw fur yersel?"

"See you, Mal. Yer as funny as them." Static crossed to where the cake sat on a small table used during tea breaks. "Tell ye what, I'll half it wi you. Here you can have the candles."

Laughing, Mal shook his head. "Okay, you win."

Mal was the first to break the silence on their way to the pictures. "I'm glad ye don't have a birthday every day pal, if this is how it affects you. Was the lassies' kisses too much for ye? Cheer up fur any favour."

"Sorry, pal," Static apologised. "It's jist that auld Simpson hasnae paid me the money he owes me."

"Did ye no get yer rise then, seeing as it's yer birthday?"

"Aye. But no the half croon extra he said I would get back when I had learned ma roons. I will have tae see him aboot it on Monday."

And so he will, Mal thought, sensing trouble.

Monday came. Static finished his second round and, before Mal could stop him he had made his way into the front shop determined to confront his manager as regards his wages. Fortunately the shop was almost empty of customers.

"Can I have a word with you, Mister Simpson? Static asked in his best English.

The manager's head appeared around the 'fruit' scales. "Not just now, Drew, I'm talking to Mister Classen, our inspector," he answered in a tone designed to impress his superior.

"It's all right, Mister Simpson, I can wait. Perhaps what the lad has to say is important," the inspector suggested.

Mr. Simpson nodded his consent.

"Mister Simpson," Static began, "Ye said I would get a rise when I had learned the roons on ma bike, then another wan on ma birthday?"

"But you have. I distinctly remember putting your rise in your poke, on Saturday."

"I know. But no the half croon extra I should have got. I know the roons noo Mister Simpson. In fact, I have been doing them in near half the time fur the last three weeks." Static went on unabashed.

"I don't think this is the time or place to discuss these matters, Drew. Why don't you come and see me after the shop closes?"

"It's all right Mister Simpson, I can go over these accounts while you deal with the lad," the inspector endorsed, drawing a long narrow book towards him.

"Maybe ye have jist forgotten tae tell Head Office aboot it Mister Simpson," Static consoled, seeing the angry scowl on his manager's face.

At the mention of Head Office, Mr Classen's head swung in the speaker's direction. "What about Head Office, young man"? he asked, his curiosity aroused.

There was not a boning knife sharp enough in the shop to match Mr Simpson's expression as he stood aside to hear his message boy tell his inspector of how he had been paid two and sixpence a week less until he had learned all of his rounds on his bicycle, and now that he had done, had still not received his half crown a week rise, only his birthday one.

"There must be some mistake, Mister Simpson, I have not heard of this arrangement before," the inspector queried of his manager. "I shall phone Head Office, and find out how this has come about. In the meantime young man, I suggest you get back to your work."

"Yes Mister Classen. Thank you Sir." Static gave a slight bow of appreciation as he headed for the back shop.

"Noo yer fur it, ye wee crawler," Sarah Chapman declared as he strode passed her.

It was almost closing time. Mr Simpson drew Static aside. "Mister Classen phoned Head Office before he left, Little. It appears there has been some slight mistake. There never should have been a reduction in your wages, so you will receive all of those half crowns in your back pay this coming Saturday. All right?" And, as Static nodded his understanding, there was a slight twinge of colour on the manager's cheeks as he went on to deliver his warning. "And never approach me again in the front shop over a personal matter while we are open, especially in front of the inspector. Do you understand?"

Mal who had been standing close by, saw Static's cheeks outmatch those of his manager's. Oh, no, he thought, Static's goin tae pit the heid on him! He stepped forward, halting almost between the two standing vis-a-vis. "Shall I close the front doors Mister Simpson?" For Mal knew should his manager consent, Static would be obliged to bring the wooden gate from behind the shop to the front door.

Mr Simpson's head turned slightly in Mal's direction. "What? Oh, yes do that Moffat, if it is time."

"Come on Drew," Mal urged his pal, "and help me get the gate."

Next morning, Mal was bagging tatties in the back shop as usual, when Sarah Chapman seized her opportunity to speak to Mal alone. "I know ye will no say anything Mal, but I think ye ought tae know," she began. "Yon wis a lot o cods wallop Simpson wis givin Static aboot Head Office." Sarah popped a potato into Mal's bag. "Mister Classen telt his nibs, Head Office had paid Static the correct amount every week and there never had been any reduction for his learning the rounds." Sarah spoke politely as if repeating Mr Classen's words verbatim. She gave her listener a little nudge on the shoulder. "Ye should have seen the look on Simpson's coupon! Crimson it was. Then bold as brass, he says, 'of course now I know how the mistake has come about, I have mistakenly deducted the half crown from Little's wages for the laundering of his white coat and apron, which I also do for the other male members of staff. How stupid of me, as the lad does not wear the whites as yet."

Mal put down his shovel. "Surely ye're no goin tae tell me Classen fell for that wan, Sarah?"

Sarah shook her head. "I dinnae think so, Mal. However, he said it was a simple mistake to have made." Sarah let out a grunt. "He must think we're aw simple tae believe that wan."

"So the bold, Simpson got away with it?" Mal said angrily.

"...I'll need a half stane bag!" Sarah announced over loudly, quickly changing the subject as one of the male staff entered the back shop.

"Right ye are, Miss Chapman," Mal answered politely.

Sarah leaned closer to Mal. "Noo, mind whit I telt ye. No a word tae Static. If he wis tae find oot, he'd maist likely pit the heid on bugger lugs."

Fearing Sarah was right, Mal nodded his agreement.

Mal suspected that his pal would not last long after 'his wages' incident. In fact, he had thought of not remaining there himself. How could anyone be so devious as to try to swindle a half crown a week out of someone who had a widowed mother to support? He would have told Static and let him put one on his 'nibs's' chops if it was not for fear of getting the boy into further trouble.

"Last roon the day, Mal?" Static called out cheerfully to him as he wheeled the big heavy laden bike passed the open back shop window.

"Good fur you, Static. Saturday night again! Two cowboy pictures on at the Roxy...Calum's comin. Ye want tae come tae, as usual?"

"Try and keep me away, especially since ye owe me a tanner, ye wee keech," Mal heard him say as he trundled out of sight.

Static reached Hynds Street, which to him was an aptly sounding name for the fifty-seven varieties of folk who lived there, dismounting in front of number nine.

Old Mrs Kerr, who lived in the semi-detached, and who had a brain to match, would not let him bring his bike up the garden path to her front door for fear of him dirtying her 'flags' as she called her paving stones. And who would, on occasions, chastise him for the odd footprint he may have left on her beloved squares on his way to finding out if she was at home, before returning to his bike for her precious 'messages' leaving Static to seriously consider the possibility of doing handstands to her door, if he thought she would not inspect her flags for fingerprints.

Static knocked on the door and stood back a pace or two. After what seemed to be an eternity, he heard the rattle of the letterbox, and a pair of eyes staring out at him.

"Who are you?" A voice belonging to the eyes challenged, squinting first right then left. "I'm waiting for the message boy. Away and no dirty ma flags!"

"I am the message boy!" Static politely assured her.

"No yer no. The message boy is no as tall as you."

"I've grown taller waitin fur ye tae open the door, ye daft auld wumman!" Static shouted back, bending down to stare at the eyes through the letterbox.

"Whit did ye call me?" the voice shouted back.

"I said have ye been waitin for me comin?" he lied. The shop would be closed if he had to wait here any longer.

Silence. Static stepped back, thinking "She's deid. Died of auld age. Jist like me if I have tae wait here any longer."

A click. The door opened, and the small drooping frame of an old woman appeared in the doorway. "Mind ma steps!" A crooked finger pointed at Static's feet.

"Steps," Static muttered.

"Whit did ye say? Ye came frae Stepps? Nae wonder it took ye aw day tae get here wi the messages!"

Giving up, Static turned on his heel in time to see the figures running away from where he had leaned his bike against the hedge. Letting out a curse, he started off in hot pursuit.

After covering almost half of the street, the nearest of the two boys Static was chasing spun round, throwing one of the eggs from the brown paper bag he was holding at him, hitting him in the chest.

"Ye bad bugger! They're auld Missus Kerr's eggs!" Static bawled out at him, to receive another egg for his pains.

"So whit, knuckle heid? The yokes on you, as they say!" came the reply.

On the opposite side of the street, his partner in crime roared with laughter. "Does broon sauce go wi eggs dae ye think, eejit?" he asked, holding out a bottle at arm's length. "Aye, maybe no," he decided, letting the bottle drop to the pavement with a plop.

Static calculated that the distance between himself and the bottle dropper was too far for him to catch, but not so his pal, the egg bearing thief, on this side of the street. Before he had time to digest what was happening, Static had covered the short distance between them, wrenching the paper bag from out of his grasp and using it in a fair imitation of a fly swatter around the unfortunate boys head, followed by a few quick punches. "Who's the yoke on noo, kaki heid?" Static barked angrily at the egg dripping figure, and hit him again. "Next time I see ye it will be yer brains I'll scramble, no the eggs. Noo bugger aff!" His warning instantly carried out.

Still angry, though dejected, Static started back to where he had left his bike, his mind on how he was going to tell the old woman what had happened to her groceries. And because of this was only vaguely aware that the machine was not where he had left it. Static bent to pick it up aware that the basket was almost empty, and heard the laughter in the semi-darkness from the opposite direction from which he had chased the two boys.

So that had been their game, get two to act as decoys while the rest of the gang stole the rest of the groceries. Static fumed. His only alternative now was to make his way back to the shop, and face whatever auld stinky bum Simpson had to say. But could it not have happened after he had been paid his back money?

Keeping his eyes from the old woman's door, Static straddled his bike and felt the rims hit the kerb. The buggers had let down his tyres! He grabbed for his pump and realised after a few minutes of furious pumping that both tyres had been slashed. Now there was nothing left to do except push the bike back to the shop. He was going to miss the pictures.

By the time Static got back, only a few lights still shone in the shop window. Lifting the basket off the bike, he trundled with it to the front door, and knocked. A few second later, Mal's face peered out at him from between a gap in the blind.

"Don't ask!" he warned his pal as he brushed passed him on his way into the front shop.

Mr Simpson looked up from the corner of the counter where he had been going over his books, as Static sat the basket on the floor. "You are late Little! I have a home to go to as well, you know!" he spat at him.

"Aye, a dog's home," Static muttered under his breath.

The manager slid Static's pay packet along the counter. "It's all there, including your back money," he grudgingly informed him.

Static`s hand shot out, curling around the paper bag. At least, he had his wages before auld stinky bum found out about what had happened. While from the doorway of the back shop Mal winked at him, before making a discreet exit.

"What kept you?" Mr Simpson asked, putting on his coat.

"I wis attacked," Static replied solemnly.

"Attacked! What do you mean you were attacked?"

Briefly, Static related to his manager what had happened. When he had finished, Mr Simpson rounded the corner of the counter to stare into what was left of the groceries in the basket. "Then, what has happened is entirely your own fault. You should not have left your bicycle unattended."

"What else could I do? Auld Missus Kerr will no let me bring ma bike up ower her flags!" Static choked.

Ignoring his junior's explanation, Mr Simpson pointed disbelievingly at the contents of the basket. "Is this all that remains of Mrs Kerr's order?"

"Aye. They stole the rest."

"Then it will cost you for your carelessness. It will have to come out of your pocket," Mr Simpson apprised with all the power of a grocery manager, and what it entailed.

"That will be right! It's you that should be paying me for the damage tae ma jerkin," Static fumed pointing to the eggs stains.

The manager made a chopping motion with his hand. "I have spoken. Consider the matter closed. I shall begin by deducting the damage, from next week's pay. So, let us not have any more of your insolence. Now put your bicycle round the back and bring the gate to the front. And let us get off home."

Static bunched his fists by his side. He'd had enough for today. "Pit it roon the back yersel, ye auld shite! I've jist aboot taken aw I'm aboot tae take frae the likes o you!"

Static knew as he spat out the words he had just said goodbye to his job. However, there were limits to what a message boy could take.

Static's manager stood in a state of shock. "Do you know who you are talking to?" he asked, specks of foam appearing at the corner of his mouth.

Static nodded confirmation. "Aye. Were ye no listening? I said an auld shite." The angry boy had no reason to retract his words now that he had gone this far.

Static swung on his heel and, with a last defiant gesture, aimed a foot at the pyramid of beans standing in the centre of the shop floor.

The noise of the pile of beans clattering to the floor brought Mal rushing back to the scene of a manager striving to balance, like some learner ice skater, amongst tins of beans rolling about the floor, while Static stood crimson faced, fists clenched by his side.

Static swung to face his pal. "Come on, Mal, I've had enough of this grocery gemme." He swung back to an aerobatics manager whose face matched the bashed tins of beans scattered on the floor, to add as a final insult, "...And don't forget, by the way, to take auld Misses Kerr's messages to her, she'll be waitin. And don't dirty her flags! OK"

Chapter 10

Mal heard his mother talking to someone at the door. Looking up from where he was sitting at the table, his mother preceded a beaming Static into the room.

"It's Static come tae pay ye a visit," she told her son, happy to see the boy. "He's got something tae tell ye."

"Hello, there, Static. Won the pools have ye?"

Static's beam widened. Was that you that did that fur me, Mal?"

"Did whit?" Mal inquired, feigning ignorance.

"Ye know whit I mean, it wis you that sent Mister Scobie roon tae see me. Or mair precisely, tae see yon cabinet I made."

"Oh, that!" Mal replied, as if suddenly remembering something so insignificant. "Well? Whit did he say?" Although by the expression on his pal's face, there was no need for him to ask.

"He wis impressed. He asked me where I last worked, and why I left."

"And whit did ye say, son?" Agnes interrupted, lifting a dirty plate off the table.

"The truth, Mrs Moffat, jist in case he asked auld stinky Simpson aboot me."

"Good for you," the woman approved with a nod of her head.

"So, whit's the story?" Mal urged.

"He's giving me a try oot. I start Monday."

"Well! That calls for a celebration!" Agnes cried happily. "Wid ye like a drink, Static?"

At this unheard of offer, both boys looked at one another in amazement.

"If ye like, Mrs Moffat," the would-be carpenter replied nervously.

"And wan fur ye Mal, tae drink yer pa'`s good fortune?"

Mal almost choked. "That wid be nice, Mammy!"

"Good." Agnes swept towards the cupboard. "Yous baith take sugar and milk?"Agnes heard the groans of disappointment at her back.

It had been a long time since Mal had seen Loch Lomond. Now, he thought he would like to see it again, and had suggested as much to Static, who had suggested camping, as he only had to work a half day on a Saturday in his new job at the joiners, and, as he, himself, was due some summer holidays, he had persuaded Mr Simpson to let him have a Saturday off in two weeks time. Now, the only drawback was to find Static a bike.

Leaky Tap had told him Bobby Inglis had an old bike he never used and would most likely lend it to him, should he ask.

At Mal's knock, Bobby invited him into his home. "Leaky says you would like to borrow my old bicycle?"

So, this is how a Co-op manager lives Mal thought as he followed Bobby down the hallway of his parents' bungalow. "Aye, if it's no too much trouble."

"It might be a bit rusty, I have not used it in years."

Mal focused on the back of Bobby's head as he turned right. Bobby had always counted himself that wee bit above the rest in his High School class, academically as well as socially. Maybe it had been a mistake to have come here in the first place. It might only give Bobby the impression of doing something good for the 'peasants.'

To his surprise, Mal found himself in a bedroom, where his host stood aside to introduce him to the figure sitting in bed propped up by a pillow.

"I would like you to meet Liz, my cousin. She has an allergy, and I was reading to her when you called."

Mal swallowed, his eyes fixed on the occupant of the bed. Although her eyes were red and swollen, to Mal she was the most beautiful girl he had ever set eyes on.

"Pleased to meet one of Wobert's friends," she sniffed, pronouncing her 'rs' through her cold as a 'w'.

"Same here," Mal spluttered.

"I`ll leave you two alone for a minute until I haul out that old bicycle from the shed." Bobby turned for the door. "Shan`t be long."

"Oh, take yer time, I'm no in a hurry," Mal politely suggested, his eyes still on the bed's delectable occupant.

The girl smiled up at him. "Have a sweet, Mal"

Mal looked at her in puzzlement. "You mean a sweetie. Aye. Okay." He held out his hand.

"No. A sweet!" she laughed, gesturing to him to take a seat by the bedside.

"Oh, sorry," he apologised, sitting down, his face red, and

thinking whit a start. Eejit!

Still smiling the girl went on to ask, "So you are one of Wobert's fwiends?"

Mal shook his head. "No, not weely...I mean not really." He apologised again. "We used tae go tae the High School the gither. That's all. I jist came the night tae borrow his bike for a pal." He was trying to talk posh, and failing. "That's a terrible cauld... I mean ...cold ye've got."

"Yes. It's what is known as an allergy...I'm allergic to some peculiar things."

"Same as me. I'm allergic tae getting up in the morning." That's better Mal thought as the girl gave a little laugh, and put her hankie up to cover her mouth.

"As you can see I have a little twouble with my speech."

"Something else we've got in common. Except yours will get better. With me, it's terminal."

"Yes, it's all diffewent from Inverness."

"So you're a Teuchter!" Mal cried in mock surprise.

"I beg your pardon, Mister Moffat!"

"Only kidding hen."

Mal felt more relaxed. She was a wee smasher. Talked different too, despite her cold. "How long are you here for?" Mal asked, hoping she would say for life.

"Oh I'm at college at present."

Mal felt relieved, yet strangely uncomfortable at this revelation. Bang went his chances of asking her out, unless he took a brand new course on how fur tae speak English in the next few days...and passed.

"What do you do?" she asked, cocking her head to one side, as if expecting him to confess to something exciting, such as an undercover worker in a bed linen factory, who needed her cousin's bike to make a quick getaway should his cover get blown.

Mal hesitated, for some reason he was ashamed to admit to this girl that he worked as a grocer. "Me? I serve the public," he ventured, letting his gaze drift across the room, away from the girl's eyes.

"Then you are a Swivil Swervant." She blew her nose.

"Very civil." Mal frowned.

"How many work there?" The girl's interest aroused.

"Aboot half o them." The girl laughed. That's better, Mal thought.

"The bicycle is around the back, Mal." His host's head appeared around the door. "Although, I think it may require a few repairs."

"Ach. That's all right. I'll fix it." He stood up disappointed by Bobby's quick return.

"It wis nice talking tae ye Liz. I hope yer cauld gets better. Maybe I'll see you aroon the college some time."

Liz smiled up at him through her red rimmed eyes. "That would be nice."

Mal turned as he reached the door. "Did ye hear the wan aboot the dog that couldnae bark?"

Liz shook her head.

"It had something wrong with the woof of its mouf!"

Liz laughed. "I suppose my allergy reminded you of that one."

Not amused, Bobby stood aside to let Mal passed. "It's this way Mal, out the back door. Should you not get the cycle to work, I may have a few bits and pieces lying around that may help."

You sure will pal, Mal thought, if it means another chance to see your cousin.

Mal returned next day with the excuse he had broken one of the wing nuts on the rear wheel, and could not get another one to fit it. Unfortunately, Bobby led him to the garden shed instead of to his cousin's bedroom.

"How is Liz, the day Bobby? Is her cauld gettin any better?"

"If you mean her allergy, no, I had to stop reading to her just before you called," Bobby told him coldly, rummaging through a tin box.

"Does she like books?" Was Mal's next question.

"Yes. Surprisingly for one who is studying foreign languages, she likes detective stories, especially American ones. Ah! Perhaps this is what you came looking for?" Bobby held out a slightly rusty wing nut.

Not really pal, not really, Mal muttered under his breath.

Mal gave it two days before he made his next visit to the Inglis household. This time he came prepared for all contingencies. Watching the house from behind a tree across the street he waited until Robert B. Inglis…snob, had left. And, a few breathless minutes later, he was knocking at the Inglis door, where a woman in her early forties answered.

"I'm sorry to suppose…I mean impose," he started nervously,

"but I think I've just missed Robert." Mal hastened to alleviate the woman's bewildered expression, by explaining. "Bobby...eh...Robert has given me a loan of his bike. And I met his cousin..." He hesitated as if not quite sure of the name, "Liz? When she was ill." A flicker of understanding crossed the woman's face, encouraging him to go on. "She told me she likes books. He held up a paperback. "I just wondered if this one would help to pass the time?"

The woman held out her hand. "That is nice of you...Mister....?"

"Mal...Mal Moffat," he said with a smile, making no attempt to part with his Greek gift.

Mrs Inglis smiled. "I'll see that she gets it…Mal. Thank you again."

Reluctantly, Mal handed over the book. "Tell her I was asking for her." He pretended to turn away. "I know whit allergies can be like. I was...quite worried about her. Anyhow I hope she has not read that one." He nodded at the book. "Cheerio. Nice tae have met you Mrs Inglis." If all my charms and good looks hasnae worked, I better start taking lesson frae Static, he thought as he started down the steps.

"Just a minute. Perhaps Liz would like to thank you for the book herself."

That's mair like it missus, Mal thought. "Only if you think it will no disturb her too much?" The boy affected an apologetic tone.

"I'm sure it won't. She's beginning to feel much better now. She will be up and about soon," the woman assured him, ushering him into the house.

Liz was sitting up reading, when Mal entered the bedroom. Having made the introductions, but careful to keep the bedroom door open, Mrs Inglis left them alone.

"I brought you this." Mal held up the book, the jacket displaying an American Private Eye, holding a scantily clad female in one arm, and a smoking revolver in the other hand. "I hope ye havnae read it?" He would have been surprised if she had, considering he'd found it under a pile of magazines announcing the death of the Kaiser, whilst waiting in the dentist's surgery a few months back? Well perhaps not quite.

Liz took the proffered book and its well thumbed pages, and read the title 'Peter Pistol'.

"The Scottish version is the Bum wi the Gun," he joked, sitting down by the side of the bed. "I see yer able tae read by yersel. Is that a sign yer feeling better?"

"I hope so. I'm enjoying this one." She held up the book. "But my eyes are beginning to water again."

"Wid ye like me tae read it tae ye?" Mal hoped that by doing so he would get to spend more time with the girl.

"How nice of you, Mal." She handed him the book, and settled down to listen.

Mal studied the open page and began, affecting an American accent. "The two detectives heard an ear piercing scream. They both turned. Behind them a sign in a shop window read, 'Ears pierced while you wait'. They looked at one another and nodded. "I'm going to smoke out that good for nothing sun of a gun from the other side of the street" said the first dick. He took a draw of his cigarette. "Cover me partner."

"Okay" said his partner throwing a blanket over him. "But you do not have to risk getting yourself shot, when we have put a tail on him. He'll be easy to find, they cannot be many men going about the street at this hour wearing a tail." His partner dropped his eyes, his partner stooped and picked them up. Yes he said..."

"Enough! Enough! That is the greatest load of rubbish I've ever heard. There is not a word you've said , printed in that book!" Liz sat back laughing.

Deadpan, Mal held out the book to her, affecting an aggrieved look. "Do ye no` believe me? It's all here in this book."

"Mal Moffat!" Liz scolded him.

"Aye. Maybe ye are right. Anyhow, I thought it might help tae cheer ye up."

"Oh, it did!" Liz chuckled.

They sat talking for a while until Mal heard a door opening further down the hallway. He rose. "When dae ye think ye will be up and aboot?"

Liz wrinkled her nose. "Most probably by the end of the week."

Mal`s heart leaped. "If ye are? Fancy goin tae the pictures? There's wan right up yer street. Buphrey Gocart, in a gangster wan."

She laughed at the mispronunciation of the star's name. "I'd like that."

"Then I'll get back tae ye by the end of the week. See if ye are a right. Then if ye are...." He heard the footsteps in the hall, and moved reluctantly to the open door.

"Then we'll go and see Buphrey Gocart," she laughed.

After an eternity of uncertainty, Saturday night came. Liz was up and about and had agreed to meet him in Woolworths' doorway.

He had tried to reach Static to tell him he would not be going to the pictures with him as usual, but his pal had already left to play a game of football now that it was summer and there no more matches for him to watch. Neither was his mother at home.

In the back shop's tiny toilet, Mal washed his face and combed his hair. Now he was as ready as he would ever be. He said good night to his manager, and closed the door behind him.

Weather-wise it was a fine night, too fine a night to sit in a stuffy picture house, and he hoped Liz would agree.

"I thought ye would never come oot!" Static emerged from out of the butcher shop doorway.

Mal let out a moan. It was just as he had feared. "Hello Static. How's it goin?" he asked, trying to appear cheerful.

"A lot better if we hurry up. I don`t fancy standing in a queue, and missing half the picture."

This was it, Mal decided, facing his friend. "Look Static, I wis trying tae get haud o ye, tae tell ye I`ve got a date fur the night." There. It was out. He had said it.

Much to Mal's surprise, Static gave an indifferent shrug "It's a' right, she can sit between us."

Mal rolled his eyes heavenwards. Surely even Static could not be this thick. "Ye don't get ma meaning, pal. Two's company, three's a crowd."

Slowly, it dawned on Static what it meant to have a date. Three`s a crowd would not mean Mal getting rid of the lassie. "Ye mean ye want me tae bugger aff? Go by masel`?" Static's complexion deepened.

Suddenly, Mal hated himself. After all, how many friends did the poor bugger have? There were few who took the time to look passed his pal's disfigurement to the real Static, a person, who unlike himself would not do anyone a bad turn. "Aye, maybe for this wance, pal...Ye see..." He tried to soften the hurt he saw in Static's eyes. "She has been ill. She comes frae Inverness, and doesnae know many folk doon here."

"Oh well," Static twitched a lip, "I'll maybe see ye the morra."

"Aye. Maybe the morra," Mal agreed, hating himself for this

further deception, as he knew should Liz agree to meet him next day, he would more than likely do the same again to his pal.

Mal hurried across the street. He would have to get a move on, and he felt his heart miss several beats at the thought of Liz thinking he might not be coming.

Static was now halfway down the opposite side of the street. A lonely hunched figure on a busy street on a bustling summer evening. For a moment, Mal stood on the kerb, feeling more ashamed of himself than he had ever done before. Even more so, than the day at school when he had put that dead frog down Beryl Wright's knickers. He sighed. Well, that's life, and the quicker Static faced up to it the better. Face? That was the trouble. The only thing going for his pal, was the certainty of never having to be asked to take part in a Police line up. Poor Static! But what the hell!

Liz was waiting for him in Woolworth's doorway and all too soon his pal was forgotten.

It was Wednesday before Mal saw Static again. Static was out the back green, fixing the bike he had borrowed for him from Bobby Inglis. "Hello, Static," he greeted him guardedly, unsure of his pal's reaction.

"Mal," his pal answered without looking up.

"Ye got the bike goin?" Mal knelt down beside him.

"Jist aboot." Static adjusted a nut on the back mudguard. "But whit's the point, noo that ye've got yersel a doll?"

Mal helped hold the mudguard steady, while his pal tightened the nut. "I thought we were goin tae Loch Lomond on Saturday?" Mal tried to inject a note of surprise into his voice, as though the mere thought of not keeping his promise was abhorrent to him.

Static turned his head to see if his pal was serious or not. "The tent only hauds two. Unless ye were expecting me tae sleep ootside?"

"Whit dae ye mean? They'll only be the two o us. Who else were ye expecting?"

"Oh, I thought ye might have asked yer doll, seein as she disnae know anybody doon here?"

Mal chose to ignore the sarcasm. "Naw, there will be jist you and me, pal."

"And the rain," Static smiled up at him.

"When will we know we're near Loch Lomond?" Static moaned, easing himself off his bike saddle.

"When ye see a big dod o watter jist lying there."

"Awfy funny. Are ye sure we are on the right road?"

Mal steered his tent laden bike around a dead hedgehog which had most probably been run over by some Roman's chariot on the way to watching a game of football in the Highland League.

He searched the hills to his right, the way he had seen Indian scouts do in the cowboy pictures. "We'll pedal tae the top of this brae; see if we are on the right road frae there."

Once at the top of the hill, Static threw his offending machine down in a heap. Drawing back his foot, he aimed a kick at it, then thinking better of it stopped himself in time. "I'd kick the bl...thing if it wasnae lent," he fumed.

"On ye go then, Lent is no until next year." Mal made a face as he dismounted.

Disgusted by his pal's good humour, Static began to climb the dry stane dyke behind him.

"Where are ye goin?" Mal inquired.

"Where dae ye think?"

Mal sat down on the grass verge by the side of the empty country road. "Okay! But don't pee long," he ended with a laugh.

Static made a gesture. "As far as I'm concerned, ye can go and sh..."

"Now! Now! Static," Mal grinned, flopping down on his back, and lacing his hands behind his head.

Mal was not aware of having dozed off, until he heard the cry of alarm. It had come from his grocers' shop. Mr Simpson had been standing at the counter patting marg, but Marg had not liked it. He became fully awake. Static was scrambling down the hill as fast as his legs would carry him, closely followed by an almost newly born lamb.

Mal broke into uncontrollable laughter. "Dinnae tell me ye're feart frae a wee lamb, Static?" he burst out.

His face beetroot red, lungs bursting, Static jerked a thumb over his shoulder. "No frae the wee lamb, but here comes its daddy!" For over the brow of the hill, head down came a charging ram. "Don't jist lie there! Help me ower this dyke!" Static cried out, a leg already in mid air, as he launched himself over the top.

"Nineteen feet," Mal stated prosaically, turning on an elbow.

"Whit are ye on aboot nineteen feet?" Static asked irritably, lifting himself off the grass verge and wiping bits of grass and twigs off his trousers.

"Nineteen feet. Ye haud the record on this road fur, the hop, step and chump."

Static stuck his tongue out at a departing father and daughter, trotting back up the hillside, no doubt anxious to tell future generations of lamb chops of how they had chased a strange creature, half man, half kangaroo, clean over a four feet high dry stane dyke.

The athlete turned to face his pal. "See you Mal!" He made a gesture of despair.

Suitably censured, Mal sat up and spread out the map on his knees.

"Sure you've got it the right way up, fur I`m buggered if I'm goin tae push this damned thing a' the way tae Ostrilya!" Static flopped down beside his bike.

"Australia's no on this map. Fort William is as far as it goes. Besides, I've tae be back at the shop on Monday," Mal replied, deep in map study.

"New Zealand, here we come!" Static sighed resignedly.

His decision made, folding up the map, Mal stood up. "I'm no sure this is the right road, so, I'm goin back doon the brae. Maybe we should have kept on goin instead of turning up here. If this is the right road, I`ll come back up. If no, I'll shout and ring ma bell."

"And if this is no the right road, I'll shout and ring yer neck" Static assured him, settling down on the grass to wait.

Mounting the bike, Mal free wheeled until nearing the first bend, where he gently touched the front brake, also out of the corner of his eye the humped back bridge several bends away at the foot of the brae.

Nearing the next bend, he again touched the brakes. He heard a ping, and a brake cable almost hit him in the face. The rider let out a yell and threw his body to one side to counteract the cycle now plunging around the bend, and at the same time pulled on his one remaining brake. The change of speed was imperceptible. He pulled harder...nothing.

Mal flew around the next corner on the wrong side of the road, his face twisting; probably with the 'G' force he thought nervously.

For at this speed he would assuredly hit the humped back bridge at the rate of knots...his bike probably a few minutes later.

He fought to clear his brain. Gripping the handlebars tighter, he aimed the cycle at the grass verge in an attempt to arrest his speed. However, his bike, disliking the idea, careered along the verge and back onto the road.

It was now or never. Either he jumped off the bike now, or aimed it at the verge and into the ditch. Discarding the first option, he put the second into operation, believing for a fraction of an airborne second that his plan had worked until the bike leaped out of the ditch and back on to the road. Perhaps, he should have entered The Grand National.

Now desperate, the humped back bridge drawing ever closer, Mal decided on giving it another try. Wrenching on the bars, he steered it for the ditch at a more acute angle, this time plunging across the ditch to the other side, his yelling, scaring birds and small animals as he flew towards a bush. Twisting on the bars, he swung left, squeezing between two trees, his bike succeeding but not the protruding tent slung on the back. With a yell, he flew up into the air, thinking as he did so, that he must tell Static that they were on the right road after all for he could see Loch Lomond from away up here, hanging there for what seemed an eternity before re-entering the earth's atmosphere to land with a crash of breaking limbs, thankfully of fauna and not his own, amongst the bracken.

Mal lay staring up at the sky. There was a dull throbbing in his hip. Gingerly he got to his feet, brushing twigs and bits of bush from off his clothes. Flexing his legs, he heaved a sigh of relief that they or nothing else was broken. Now, he knew how Static had felt after his recent fall.

Surprisingly, the bike had remained upright, still wedged between two trees by the protruding tent poles. Mal hobbled over to it and, taking the saddle in one hand, the handlebars in the other, succeeded in pushing it free, hearing Static's laughter before he saw him.

"Whit's so funny?" Mal hurled at him, pushing the bike through the bushes to where his pal stood on the road.

"You should have been where I was, tae see whit I saw!" Static held his sides in mirth, tears running down his cheeks.

"Whit dae ye mean I should have been where you wis?"

"It was so funny! You zig-zagging doon the brae. Then doing yer ski jump on wheels!" Static gulped in great lungfuls of air!

Now, it was Mal's turn to be in no mood for hilarity. "Yer standin there laughing, and me nearly broke ma bum. Some pal you. Well Mr droopy drawers, at least I found oot we're on the right road."

"How dae ye know? You didnae go that far. Ye canna see the loch frae here?" Static choked.

"Ye can frae up there!" Mal pointed skywards.

"Through the clouds an a'?" Static cleared his throat of laughter. "Away and sh..."

"Now now, Mal," Static chided. "Where's your sense o humour?"

"Right noo in ma right fit!" Mal responded angrily, taking more than a playful swipe at his cheerful friend.

A quarter of an hour later, Static sat at the top of the brae watching his friend endeavouring to straighten out his buckled front wheel. Chewing a piece of grass, he bent closer to the mechanic. "Ye know, Mal, watching you tryin tae straighten oot that wheel is like watchin Rembrandt at work." Mal's face lit up with pride at this unexpected compliment coming from one as gifted with his hands as Static. "Aye," Static concluded, "Rembrandt couldae straighten wheels either." He got up. "See, and I'll fix it."

His ego deflated as his tyres, Mal threw down the spoke key. "And when yer at it, O genius O the pump, ye can fix ma brake as well."

"There it is. I knew we were on the right road!" Mal cried out triumphantly.

"How's aboot a rest then?" Static threw himself down on the grass verge, unimpressed by the sight of the Bonnie Banks.

"Sure. But let's get aff the road, and doon by the loch side."

Reluctantly, Static got to his feet. "Where we goin tae camp?"

"Don't know. Someplace."

Eventually, they found a spot, a green banking, and sat down, Mal now quite content to recover from his first flying lesson; which had given a whole new meaning to the term...and the bicycle, Flying Scot. "Is this no great?" Mal filled his lungs and gazed admiringly at Ben Lomond across the blue waters of the loch. "Jist look at that scenery! Ye cannae whack it!"

Static dwelled on an old couple sitting on deck chairs a little distance away, totally at peace with the world. "Beats me how folk can jist sit and look at scenery. I mean, ye sit here as if expectin it to dae somethin, which is no likely, since it`s been here fur yonks."

Mal made a clicking noise with his teeth to express his disgust at his soulless friend. "Look at a they different shades o trees, and different colour o bushes." He waved a hand to encompass the vista.

Static turned his head away so that Mal did not see him grin. "Ye've got me there pal. Who am I to argue with someone who has studied such matters at close quarters, such as yourself?" Before Mal could answer, Static cupped his chin in his hands. "I'm starvin, how's aboot a drum up?"

"We'll pitch the tent fist."

"Where?"

"Ower there, amongst yon trees."

"Would we no be better on this side of the road, jist in case it rains?" Static asked anxiously.

"It'll no rain. Jist look at that sky. No a cloud tae be seen. Naw. We'll camp doon here. Then we can get watter frae the loch. Maybe even go fur a dook," Mal proclaimed optimistically.

Static lifted up his bike. "Better get the watter first, before ye pit yer smellies in there," he commented drily.

Their spot found, tent pitched, evening meal over, the boys sat back awaiting their tea to brew in the syrup can. Static leaned forward giving the Primus stove another pump.

"Tea's nearly biling." He broke a match letting it float in the can as this was an old way of keeping the tea leaves to the bottom, and at the same time gave a swipe at an elusive insect, and asking of Mal, "Are ye sure it was us that beat the English at Bannockburn, and no the midgies?"

"Aye. Maybe they had a hand in it," Mal agreed drowsily.

"Midgies dinnae hiv hands," Static reflected, stirring the tea with a twig.

A ring appeared around the broken match in the can, followed by a hiss, then another then another.

"Too nice a day fur rain? Pity ye didnae say anything aboot the night." A large slice of sarcasm in Static`s voice.

Mal wiped a spot of rain off his upturned face. "It will no come tae much."

"That's whit they said aboot the war," Static replied dejectedly.

"Merely a passing shower," his friend assured him.

"Merely a passing shower!" Static mimicked. "But how long will it take tae pass?"

"Quite a long while!" Mal bawled, shooting up as the first of the deluge hit them. "Quick! Into the tent!"

"Whit aboot the stove, and oor tea?" Static cried, lifting the can up by its makeshift handle.

"Pit the stove oot and bring the can into the tent," Mal quickly ordered, already beginning to crawl inside.

Two hours later, it was still raining, for it was here, according to Static, that Monsoons were born before emigrating to India, and other such places.

"I'm frozen, Mal." Static's teeth began to chatter.

"The temperature has dropped," Mal said wisely.

"So has ma spirits," Static sulked. He nodded in the direction of the loch. "Ye know, if that big puddle oot there rises, we'll hiv an indoor swimming pool in here."

"It will no rise that high."

"We're no talking aboot the Jags noo, ye know."

By 2a.m. it had still not ceased. Lonely, with only the smell of wet canvas to keep them company, Static suggested, "How's aboot lighting the stove?"

"A bit risky in the tent, Static."

"Aye, that's whit a' the lassies say," Static added to keep himself cheerful.

"But for all intent and purposes let's risk it."

Not fully convinced it was a good idea, but willing to try, Mal drew the stove towards him. "You open the can of tomato soup, Static. I'll light the stove. You haud the pot above it, so if it flares up, it will no catch the tent. O.K?"

The plan succeeding, Static lowered the pot of tomato soup onto the blazing stove. Mal laid a match on top of the matchbox in readiness should the stove go out. "The soup will no take long. Get the tin plates and spoons ready. There's some bread in ma saddlebag. Ye can spread some butter on it."

An unexpected gust of wind flapped the tent, prompting Mal to utter, "that's wind."

"Maybe ye jist need somethin tae eat."

"No me ye eejit,.. the wind ootside...it's getting up!"

"I wish we were, and gettin away hame," Static growled, his eyes on the inviting pot of soup.

Suddenly, another gust of wind caught the door flap, and with a hiss the stove went out, plunging them into darkness. "Quick, Static, light the stove!" Mal yelled.

Fumbling for the matches, Static found the one on top of the box, lit it and plunged it into the bucket of the still hissing stove. With a bang, the stove ignited, the shock throwing him backwards in unison with the pot of soup. A hole the size of a plate miraculously appearing in the roof of the tent as flames from the stove continued to feed through their newly acquired chimney.

Flames lit the tent. Horror stricken, Mal pulled at Static's legs. "Come on, Static! Oot! Yer hurt. Yer face is bleeding!"

The tent now ablaze, coughing and spluttering, the two hauled themselves from their burning home out on to the shingle.

"Oor saddlebags and things!" Static howled, grabbing at a tent pole and heaving it aside as the flames threatened to scorch his hands, Mal following his example with the other pole.

Pulling at the ropes, they managed to drag what was left of the burning tent to the water's edge where it continued to burn itself out.

Forlorn, Static watched it die. "Well, there is wan consolation, Mal, at least yer bike will be a lot lighter on the way back."

"That's nae consolation tae me, pal, seein as it wis your turn to carry it hame."

Mal turned to peer through the rain at his pal. "How's yer face? Does it still hurt? At least, it has stopped bleeding."

Static ran a finger down his cheek. "If it's blood, it must be type Heinz 57 Positive."

Mal peered closer. "Ye mean it's tomato soup? Trust you to fill yer face wi` a' the supper." His reprimand aimed at covering his relief.

Salvaging what was left of their belongings, they hurried to the shelter of the trees.

"Whit do we dae noo?" Static wanted to know, sitting hunched under a tree.

"It'll no be long `till it`s light, then we can head for hame," Mal decided.

"I`m still starvin." Static drew his knees up to his chin.

"Efter a full can o tomato soup?" Mal mocked. He spotted the plate of bread they had laid out in readiness while waiting for the soup to heat. "There's some bread in yon plate, although it's soaked through." He nodded to where the plate lay. "If ye fancy a poultice?"

"No thanks," Static growled. "I've already come camping wi wan."

Static pulled his jerkin collar up. "Ye said it widnae rain. I dinna bring ma cape."

"Stop moaning. Nae use greetin` ower spilt milk, or in your case tomato soup."

For a moment, both boys sat glowering at one another, then as if in mutual agreement, decided that there was nothing to be gained by this silent confrontation.

"Why don't we play a gemme?" Static suggested optimistically.

"Ye mean like Hide and Seek, 'till the baith o us get lost?" Mal sneered.

Static shook his head dismissing the absurdity. "A guessing gemme!"

Mal tried to control his rising anger and his own chattering teeth. "Like I spy! There's bugger a tae see...ye eejit!" he hurled at his friend across the intervening darkness.

"Dinna be daft," the educated one replied. "Names o film stars."

"Naw!" Mal bawled, knocking over the stove lying at his feet, his temper rising. "The last time I played that wi you, the gemme wis a bogey before it got started!"

Static scratched his head, the noise loud in that eerie darkness. "Whit dae ye mean?"

"I`ll tell ye whit I mean! Half an hoor tryin` tae guess R. K....a film star...Rory Colquhoun, disnae start wi a , 'K'!"

There was silence for a time before it was broken by Static asking, "Dae ye think Claudette Cardinale is French?"

Still in no mood to humour his pal, Mal shot back. "Wi a name like Cardinale, she has tae be Polish...maybe even French Polish!"

There was silence for a long moment while Static thought through the pun. "Polish! polish! Oh that's a good wan Mal!" he laughed. Mal uttered a sound of disbelief, then finding his pal`s laughter infectious joined in.

A glimmer of light breaking out above the hills across the loch, helped to lift the campers spirits.

Mal stared at the approaching dawn. "No long noo, then we can get oor things the gither, and get away hame."

Static stretched his legs. "That doll o yours, whit does she dae?"

"She's at the college...studying foreign languages." Mal threw a stone in the direction of the loch.

Static turned up his nose. "Foreign languages? I dinnae know there were any other kind," he confessed drawing his legs back up. "Although English is a foreign language."

"To you Static," Mal agreed, wondering also, what his pal would make of him, should he tell him that the only reason for his being here, was because Liz had returned home to Inverness. A long way to go to wash ones hair, he mused.

"Dae ye mind oor teacher, Miss Sprinkle?" he heard Static ask. "She was teaching me wan day aboot the letter 'C'. Nearly the hale day it seemed tae me, until I got 'C' sick," Static reflected soberly. "Anyhow, she says tae me, sometimes 'C' can be pronounced as a K."

"So that's how ye got mixed up wi Rory Colquhoun?" Mal accepted.

"Naw. Never mind that!" Static waved his hand impatiently. "She points tae ma reading book, and says," he proceeded to mimic the unfortunate teacher. "'Drew, pronounce that word. So I says 'kankled'. "She hit me the awfu`ist dunt on the side o` the heid!" Static rubbed his head as if it still smarted from the blow. 'It's not 'kankled', you stupid boy! It is pronounced 'cancelled'! You sound the first 'C' like a 'k' and the second `C` like an 'S'! Well if that's no cheating and a foreign language? Whit is?" Static declared resolutely, while Mal sat in silent mirth.

As the dawn broke, the rain stopped.

"I think we should try a wash before we head for the ferry," Mal suggested.

"Okay." Static pulled his shirt over his head.

Mal stood back surveying his friend. "See you Static, wi yer peely-wally skin, and yer face and hair covered in tomato soup, ye look like an advert fur Swan Vestas, matches."

"And whit aboot you, Al Jolson, wi yer face aw covered in soot?" Static countered.

"Fair enough," Mal chuckled.

"Let's get goin." Their toilet over, Mal gathered up his saddlebag, clipping the Primus to the handlebars by its attachment, Static busy with his own bag. In no time, they were on the road and riding down the loch side to the ferry and civilisation.

"No long noo tae the ferry," Mal panted standing up on his pedals.

"I'll race ye there!" Static challenged.

"Dinna be daft, ye don't stand a chance."

"Want a bet?"

"How much?" Further panting.

"The ferry fare."

"Yer on."

"Hi! That's cheating!" Static burst out as Mal took off down the brae.

Mal knew, despite Static's brief cycle training on the grocers bike, that he was the faster. This, and the fact that he had the better bike. He reached the top of the next brae first, and was about to sit down on his saddle to recover from the long climb when he was almost knocked off his bike my a panting Static rushing passed, legs pumping. Uttering a swear word, he had heard from an old lady who had slipped coming out of church one Sunday, he took off after his flying friend, unable to believe he had been overtaken, this, and the fact that Static appeared to be hell bent on boarding the ferry at full speed, despite there being a four feet gap between it and the pier.

With a yell of triumph, Static launched himself at the vessel, clearing the gap in one airborne bound, to land with a thud on the deck, where an astonished ferryman arrested his speed by grabbing his saddle as he hurled passed.

"Made it! I thought I'd missed it!" Static cried ecstatically, staggering off his bike. "I'll wait fur ma pal on the other side and he can pay me ma bet!" Static panted at the astonished ferryman.

"Whit dae ye mean, made it?" The man furrowed his brows. "We're just coming in!"

"Whit?" Static cried in dismay, as the ferry landed with a thump and rattle of chains, and stood staring with dubiety at Mal coming aboard affecting an exaggerated nonchalant air.

"Nice tae see ye again pal," Mal greeted him, as he pushed his cycle passed. "Eejit!"

Crestfallen, Static gave him a withering look. "Well, noo yer here, ye can pay my fare, seein as I won." And, with that, he swung for the lower deck.

Chapter 11

Static leaned against the iron bath in Oor Bit. "I'm knackered. No as young as I used to be," he confessed with a sigh.

Mal hoisted his hip onto a corner of the bath. "Ye wid think ye were a hunner. Wan wee gemme at fitba and yer ready for the knackers yard."

The disdain in his pal's voice did not go unnoticed by Static. "Whit aboot you? You had it easy in goal!"

"There were some hard shots to stop!" Mal defended his ability.

"Only against Bobby Jackson and Tam Speedie, at least, they were oor age. But against eight and nine year aulds?"

Mal rubbed his shin. "Oh, I don't know, that wee red heided yin couldnae half kick. Sometimes even the ba."

Mal ran an affectionate eye around their old playing place, searching out any changes that may have taken place since their own tenure. "Hasnae changed much. We used tae play here fur hoors on end. Noo we're lucky tae last till half time."

Static nodded, assent. "Mind how we used tae hate mammies comin up tae ca us in?"

"We're gettin auld, pal." Mal let out a sigh. "Jist like oor mammies."

"Here's somebody who's trying hard no tae be." Static nodded in the direction of the trees where a track-suited figure had emerged, the sound of his rasping breath preceding him by a good twenty yards.

"Wid ye credit who it is?" Mal exclaimed. "If it's no ma eejit o a cousin, Calum."

"Hi, lads!" Calum rasped out a greeting, collapsing on to the grass before them.

"Whit in the name o the wee man are ye doin Calum? There is easier ways o committing suicide," Static smirked.

"Aye, like jumping oot o tenement windies!" Mal chuckled, as his cousin eased himself up into a sitting position. "And whit are ye doin by the way aw dressed up? Are ye trainin for the Olympics?" Calum shook his head. As Mal went on to ask. "Maybe jist the Empire Games tae start wi?"

"Mair like the Empire biscuit, seein he's such a crummy runner!"

Static let out a loud laugh at his own joke. "Or maybe jist plain crackers."

Calum turned a jaundiced eye on his friend. "Listen O galloping tortoise, at least I'm still trying tae keep fit."

"Mair like take wan," Static shot back, plucking a blade of grass and sticking it between his teeth.

Mal put up his hands for an end to the banter. "Come on Calum, I asked ye afore. Whit are ye doin?"

Calum turned his hot stare way from his antagonist. "I'm training for a race three weeks come Saturday. It's ower five miles, Mal."

Mal's eyes bore into his cousin, digesting the enormity of his statement, also the hidden reason behind such an undertaking. There could only be two reasons. One, for a bet. Two for love...or in his cousin's case...lust. He plumped for the second. "Whit's her name?"

"How did ye know that?" Calum asked through glazed eyes that were rapidly narrowing with suspicion.

"'Sno that hard. Whit other reason wid ye put yersel through such torture, if it wasnae fur a lassie?"

"Any wan we know?" Static's curiosity now aroused.

"Widnae think so. She's in the athletic club."

"See that's the only club she's in," Mal warned him. "Or take whit ye'll get frae yer Mammy."

Static could not resist the temptation of having another dig at his pal. "Och, Mal! Calum's no like that, ye can hardly say they're exactly runnin the gither. How far is she in front o ye Calum?"

"Very funny, Mister Creepy Crawly!"

"Ye still havnae telt us her name. Are ye ashamed of us peasants meeting her, snobbish cousin of mine?"

"Dinna be daft. I only met her aboot three weeks ago."

"And already she's got ye in a track suit and gutties? Sad...sad." Static shook his head. "Nae hope, nae hope." He heaved a long, sympathetic sigh.

Mal gave him a discreet sideways kick on the ankle. "Come on Calum, we're

waiting."

"Oh, aye," Calum said, as if suddenly remembering the question. "Isabel Brooks."

"Wid that be wan o the running brooks?" Static burst out, unable to resist the pun.

Mal himself was scarcely able to ask the next question for laughing. "Which prompts the next question, Isabel for ringing?"

Calum shot to his feet, all tiredness gone in a surge of adrenaline, arms flapping in a gesture of surrender, and frustration. "I should have known better than tae tell you two!"

"Only joking, Calum," Mal apologised. "So whit's so important aboot this race?"

Calming down, Calum faced his friends. "I really fancy her, pals. You should see the figure she's got."

"Aye, I'm looking at it," Static ventured.

"Haud on Static," Mal admonished. "This could be serious. Go on, pal."

"As I wis tryin tae say." Calum glowered at Static. "She has some figure."

Static spat out the grass he had been chewing. "We've seen the figures you've gone oot wi. Eights, nine, and even wans,"

"Do you want to hear aboot Isabel or no!" Calum barked, close to losing his temper with this moron of a pal.

"Aye, shut up Static, can ye no see the puir sods full of longing?"

"Mair like wind," Calum muttered, studying the grass at his feet.

"So, this Isabel," Mal said, encouraging his cousin to resume their rudely interrupted conversation. "She's a wee stoater?"

"No so wee, but, as they say, a right stoater. I think I'm in wi a chance if I dae well in this race. Ye see she has other admirers in the club, like the club captain, and a couple of the real fast men."

"So there are others in the running," Static mused deadpan.

Calum ignored the pun. "This race will be real hard, and I've got aboot as much chance o being near the front as a First War General, but if I can jist keep up, or finish no too far behind, it might jist do the trick."

"Is it roon a track?"

"Naw, through the woods and things." Calum shook his head at the sudden gleam in his cousin's eye. "Nae chance, Mal, it's too well marshalled tae take a short cut."

Mal was about to explain where there was a will there was a way, when the dog appeared out of nowhere.

"Where did ye come frae, fella?" Static bent down to fondle the panting dog's ear.

"That's a greyhound," Mal observed. "It must have run away. Dis it hiv a collar?"Static shook his head, tickling the dog's ears.

The animal, now having somewhat recovered, and knowing one to be judged by the company one keeps, took off at speed across Oor Bit in the opposite direction from which it had appeared.

"For a minute, I thought that wis Isabel," Static sniffed.

"Listen you!" Calum exploded.

"Lads! Lads!"

Three heads turned to where a small bow legged man, dressed in a suit and tie, cloth cap slightly askew, trotted awkwardly towards them.

"Have ye seen a wee dug? A greyhound," the wee man puffed, stretching out a hand to steady himself at the opposite side of the bath.

"There was wan here a wee while ago," Static told him, slightly worried by the wee man's condition.

"Did ye no think tae haud it?" the wheezing man exclaimed.

Static shrugged. "Naw, I jist gave its belly a wee tickle and it run away ower there."

"Then, ye better tickle mine, cause I've got tae catch the bloody thing," the wee man rasped, following Static's pointing finger.

"I think ye better have a wee rest mister." Mal sounded worried. "Maybe we can help catch yer dug."

The elderly greyhound owner took in a deep breath. "That wid be nice." He gave the boys an appreciative nod. "It doesnae usually run away, maist times it will come back when I call it – must have seen a rabbit or something."

"Have ye any idea where it might go?" Static drew closer to the speaker.

"No. I bide doon yonder." He turned to nod in the opposite direction to where the boys lived. "I'm no often up this way, too many weans playin fitba here to let the dug aff its leash."

The pals smiled at one another.

Having advised the wee man to return home, the three pals decided to spread out and search for the runaway, and if he told them where he lived, should they find his dog they would bring it to him. So, with their stratagem decided, they set off.

Static nudged Mal as Calum disappeared into the woods. "He's nae chance in that race, pal, jist look at they splay feet. He'll knock doon every tree in the place."

"That's love for ye," Mal grunted.

"Well, when I start winchin, it will be wi somebody that plays tiddlywinks fur a hobby." Static declared explicitly.

An hour later, Calum having found their quarry, trotted back to the old man's house.

"Where did ye find him?" The old man patted the excited fugitive as he jumped up on him.

"The other side o' Oor Bit."

"Where's Oor Bit?" The wee man furrowed his brows.

"Oh, sorry. It's where we met ye the night. It's whit we cried the place where we used tae play when we were weans."

The wee man nodded his understanding. "Where's yer pals?"

"I suppose they'll be away hame by this time. I'll ca' in and tell them I've found the wee dug."

"Wid ye like tae come in and have a cup of tea – meet the wife?"

Calum hesitated. "I'd like that Mister?"

"Sorry. I should have said before, my name's, Bob...Bob Mitchell."

"Mine's Calum Muir. Pleased tae meet ye Mister Mitchell."

"Same here son."

Bob lead Calum round to a hut in the back garden of a row of terraced houses, where he kept his dog.

"Nice wee hut ye've got there, Mister Mitchell. The dug will be warm enough in there."

"Thanks son. And ye can ca' me Bob." The man closed the hut door on the dog. "So, have ye time for that cuppa? Come on. I'll no keep ye long," he coaxed.

"I didnae no there was that much tae greyhound racing as that." Calum confessed after his second cup of tea and a third chocolate biscuit."

"Ye havnae heard the half o it," Mrs Mitchell attested, pouring out another cup of tea for her guest. "That wee dog gets better fed than the baith o us." She gave her husband a scathing look.

"It has tae get fed on the best if it has tae run at its best."

Sighing, his wife shook her head, having heard it all before.

"Ye see," Bob explained, lighting up his pipe. "the wee dug needs a yard or two more to be up wi the winners. I can only take it fur walks, and let it aff the leash noo and again to let it run by itsel."

"Lose it," his wife added.

Bob threw her a look of annoyance, and turned back to his guest. "It needs someone wi younger legs than mine."

Calum liked this old couple and was willing to help them in some way. Perhaps, if he was to co-ordinate his training by taking the dog a walk...or run? "I'd be happy to take it for a run noo and again. I dae ma training aroon Oor Bit."

Bob shook his old grey head. "I widnae want tae burden you wi havin tae come away doon here at night."

"Nae bother. I couldnae make it every night. But would Wednesday and Thursdays be any good?"

"Great!" Bob exclaimed. "Save ma rheumatism."

"No tae mention yer corns," his wife added from the safety of the fireside.

Wednesday night having duly arrived, Calum dressed in a new blue tracksuit, called and received possession of Tam the greyhound, both trainer and canine prodigy heading off in the direction of Oor Bit at a trot.

Mal trapped the ball under his foot to point his finger in the direction of dog and master trotting in their direction. "Here comes Little Boy Blue, Static!"

"Mair like Donald Duck, wi feet like yon," Static countered.

"Hello lads!" Calum halted to draw breath, while his companion greeted Mal by jumping up and drawing a muddy paw down his trousers.

"Having tae stop for a wee breather, are ye Calum?" Static sniggered.

Calum rubbed his leg. "Jist for a wee while. Ma right foot's in cramp."

"And yer left wan's nearly up the dog's arse, the way ye run wi they splay feet," Static commented drily.

"Who's training who?" Mal interjected, before the conversation turned into something more serious than a verbal battle between two half-wits.

"I'm giving it a run for wee Mr Mitchell. I telt ye the other day aboot it." Calum drew on the leash, pulling the impatient to be gone dog, away from Mal.

"Is yer race still on, Calum?" his cousin inquired.

"Aye. This is helping me tae get fit."

"Maybe ye should let the dug run," Static suggested.

"I've better things tae do, than stand here and get insulted!" Calum retorted angrily.

"Name wan?"

"I think ye better get on wi yer running, Calum." Mal made a face. "Static is in wan o his moods."

"Good idea. Come on boy." Calum pulled on the leash and, as the dog went to jump up on Static, added, "doon boy, that's no yer dinner. Ye know yer master will no let ye eat rubbish!"

Calum set off at a brisk pace, the greyhound gambolling by his side. Soon Oor Bit was hidden by the trees as they ran towards the outskirts of the 'scheme' (the name given to all Council Estates) where they picked up speed to round piles of garden rubble stacked against the broken fence which separated the scheme from what was left of the woods at that point, eventually coming across the odd abandoned pram; thankfully minus the wean, as well as giving discarded mattresses a wide berth, as they gave a whole new meaning to the expression 'take up thy bed and walk`.

Calum gave the leash a tug and swung away to cross the field that would take him in a long semicircle back to where the dog's owner lived, his thoughts on how pleased Bob would be at the good work out he was giving his dog, and also pleased by his own progress he increased his pace, encouraging his pupil to do likewise.

Ten minutes later, still running, Calum headed for the gap in the hedgerow, from where he would cross the field, which in turn would take him on to Bob's street.

Calum was two strides away from the gap in the hedge, the dog a little behind, when the leash was almost wrenched from his grasp, throwing him backwards. Regaining his balance, he swung round. The dog having come to an abrupt halt sat panting, tongue lolling, letting out little doggy sounds of unhappiness.

"Whit`s the matter? Ye'll no get fit sitting there." Calum's question and advice answered by the dog lying down, its sides heaving. "Come on, ye cannae be that knackered, Tam, ye're supposed tae be a greyhound...a racing dug!" In response the wee dog stretched out its paw as if inviting this long distance Ian Liddle to take his pulse.

Now, a little concerned by the sight of the dog's sides heaving like a bellows, Calum decided to give the animal a rest before completing the remainder of their journey.

It was close on dark when wee Bob Mitchell opened the door to the sight of an almost exhausted Calum carrying an equally exhausted greyhound in his arms.

"Whit in the name!" Bob stammered.

"Sorry, Bob...Mister Mitchell. The wee dug just sat doon," he stammered. "It just decided no tae go any further."

"Where was this?" the astounded man asked, helping to lay the still panting animal on the floor.

"Clunies Burn." He gave the dog a loving stroke. Not that there was much love between them since he had to carry the lazy wee bugger the last two miles home.

"Clunies Burn!" Greyhound owner exploded, "that's miles away. Ma wee dug is a greyhound, no a camel. It doesna dae long distances!"

"Sorry Mister Mitchell. I didnae know ye couldnae take it as far."

"Greyhounds can run for miles, but this wan is built fur speed, no marathons. It widnae be so bad, but its racing the morra night!" The despondent owner looked down at the dog trying vainly to haul itself to its feet. "But somehow, I don't think it will be."

"Did it have a chance o winning?" Calum asked, feeling awkward, and wishing he had never met this one man and his dog.

"Nae chance noo, unless aw the rest have bunions, and the hare short circuits...Ah, well!" Bob heaved a sigh. "it cannae be helped. I'll jist have tae stuff him, and try again next week."

The ball went out of play giving the 'captain' of Mal's team the opportunity of chastising his centre forward. Looking Mal straight in the knees, the nine year old began. "See you. If the goals were across the pitch instead of at each end, we wid be winnin five nothing." The captain's eyes travelled the long distance up to Mal's face. "Any mair o that bad play, and yer aff!" A small thumb jerked in the direction of the sideline

A little distance away, Mal's former classmates, Static, Tam Speedie and Bobby Jackson stood chuckling and winking at one another, amused by the sight of their pal being berated by a nine year old.

"Away or I'll gie ye the back o ma hand!" Mal countered.

"Dae as yer telt, Mal, he's the captain." Bobby's laughter echoed across the intervening turf.

"I'll gie him captain!" Mal exploded turning angrily on his captain again. "I suppose ye think yer that good ye'll play for Scotland some day?"

The small boy shook his head. "Canny. I'm no Scots, I can only play for Caesurae."

"Where the hell's that?" Mal screwed up his eyes.

"Don't know," the small footballer solemnly confessed, "but ma Mammy said I wis Caesarean born."

"Away ye go ye wee scunner!" Mal fumed.

"Talking aboot scunners? Here comes another wan, the noo." Static pointed to behind Mal where Calum was slowly approaching.

"Whit nae tracksuit and gutties the day, Calum?" Static feigned surprise. "Don't tell me she has gave ye up already?"

Mal turned as his cousin drew near, acutely aware of his hang dog expression.

"Whit's up Calum? Somebody stole yer scone?"

Mal's captain intervened, arms akimbo. "Are ye playin or no?"

"Naw, ye wee scunner, I've better things to dae!" Mal growled.

"Like learning tae play fitba?" the diminutive player suggested, running off to join the rest of his equally diminutive team.

"Me and Tam are aff tae the pictures," Bobby announced, lifting his jacket off the iron bath. "Fancy coming?" Static and the cousins shook their heads. "Ah, well, see yis again."

"Aye, see yis," the others replied.

When the two picture goers were as far away as the old gatepost, Mal once again expressed concern at his cousin's crestfallen demeanour. Calum obliged by briefly relating what he had done to Bob Mitchell's dog. Static for his part refrained from commenting by the affect it had had on his pal.

"And what has made matters worse is that Mr Mitchell has been paid aff." Calum went on. " Noo he tells me, he will no be able tae feed Tam the way he should. He says he will have tae sell the wee dog."

Mal folded his arms and leaned against the bath. "Maybe we should try and help?" he demurred.

"How?" Calum inquired of his cousin.

"Maybe there is a way. Jist maybe."

Calum knocked on the door and stood back, his two pals behind him. Mr Mitchell opened the door, clearly surprised by who stood there. "Hello, Mr Mitchell," Calum greeted the wee man's knees, unable to lift his eyes any higher.

"Calum," the wee man answered curtly.

Mal took a step forward, half blocking his cousin's view. "We heard ye might have tae get rid o yer wee dug, Mr Mitchell, so we thought…well me actually...we might be in a position tae help."

The dog owner opened the door a fraction wider. "Oh, aye, and how dae ye figure that wan oot?"

"Where's yer manners Bob Mitchell?" A female voice asked from somewhere inside the house.

Bob stood slightly aside. "Ye's better come away in then, and let me hear this great plan o yours."

"So we are in the greyhound business." Static thrust his hands deep in his pockets. "My Mammy always said I'd finish up goin tae the dogs."

It was now two hours since they had knocked on Bob Mitchell's door. Now on their way home, Static mulled over the plan suggested by Mal, that the old man keep his dog while they contributed to its upkeep. A decision refused at first by Bob until, seeing that he had no alternative, he agreed.

Hunched against the evening's chill, Static swung on the plan's initiator. "Ye know I cannae afford tae gie very much."

"I know that pal, yer a silent partner."

"That'll make a change," Calum quipped.

Mal hit out at a stone in the yard, hitting a fence. "The wee man knows his stuff. I'm tae go tae wan o the tracks wi him and learn the business. You two have tae keep oot o the way until the time is right fur Tam tae try and win."

"How come?" Static zipped up his jerkin, puzzled by the complexity of the statement.

"Were ye no listening tae whit wis said back there, dozy?" Mal rebuked.

"Too busy scoffing the auld woman's biscuits." Calum supported his statement with a nod of his head.

They rounded the corner of the row of buildings onto the main street. Mal put his arm around Static's shoulder, intent on explaining and drawing him into his confidence. "Bob telt us, when ye are at the track, punters watch the dug owners and their pals tae see if they are goin tae bet on their dug. If they are no, then they know their dug is no tryin` tae win. But if they see the owner or their cronies heading fur the bookies, then they know there's a chance o the dug winning and they start betting it too and the prices go doon, maybe even before the owner gets aw his ain money on it."

"That`s aw right if ye have money," Static said seriously, studying the pavement.

"If we intend making money aff Tam, we better start saving some." Mal squeezed Static's shoulder.

"Aw right fur ye, Mal, I'm hard pressed tae make ends meet as it is, I'm still on an apprentice wage." Static stopped at the kerb. Taking in a deep breath, he looked up at the buildings across the street, relishing the fresh air, if not the prospect of being more hard up, should this venture fail.

"No tae worry, Static," Mal assured him. "We'll see ye aw right. I've tae go wi Bob tae wan o the tracks next week. I'll let yis know after that if I think we should go through wi it, or no. How's that? Okay? In the meantime, Calum, you keep training the dug, ower…short distances," he warned his pal. Calum gave a sign of understanding.

"It will be a feather in yer cap, Calum, when Tam wins , and ye can tell that doll yer goin wi, that ye are a successful dog owner," Static suggested, now a little happier.

"Only a part dog owner," Calum corrected, waiting for a car to go passed.

"Which part has he got, Mal?" Static asked.

"Well Static, Bob and me, have the front half, you and Calum the back half," Mal winked at his cousin.

Static let out a long sigh. "It's aye the same wi me, always at the tail end."

Laughing out loud, the cousins grabbed their pessimistic friend by the shoulder, and ran him across the road.

A small crowd had gathered around the starting area, marked off by twin lines of white tape running from the open field towards the entrance to the woods.

Spying Isabel Brooks, Calum led his two pals to where she stood conversing with an official, a little apart from the spectators.

"Is that your doll, Calum?" Mal let out a low whistle of approval.

"Aye. Come on and meet her."

"On yis go, I'll wait here." Static drew up with the intention of mingling with the crowd until all introductions had been concluded.

Both cousins knew the reason. Having run about with Static so long, it was easy to forget his looks. Clearly, Static had not.

Mal took another look at the girl's slim figure in the neatly fitting dark blue blazer and grey pleated skirt, feeling slightly uneasy at meeting this obvious upper class bird, so he could easily imagine what was going through Static's mind.

"Oh, there you are, Calum! I thought perhaps you had already made your way to the changing tent." Isabel left the official to meet her boyfriend to run a critical eye over him. "But clearly you have not. You had better run along and get changed, it will not be too long until the start," she ordered crisply.

"I will, Isabel. But first, I'd like you tae...to meet my two...pa ...friends." Nervously, Calum stood to one side. "This is my cousin Mal. And this is Sta...Drew Little, an old school pal of mine." Buggered, he thought, if I'm going to insult Static by explaining to her how he came by that nickname.

"Pleased to meet you both." Isabel swung with a dismissive shake of her blonde curls to a group of fellow athletes already stripped for the race, her eyes only briefly having dwelled on Static , but long enough for that boy to have seen the look of revulsion that had crossed her face.

"I better get changed, lads," Calum said to cover his embarrassment.

"Aye, ye better do that," Mal agreed. "We'll see ye later. We baith know whit to dae."

Mal drew Static after him. "Stuck up cow. Who does she think she is?"

Static watched the aristocratic bovine stand chatting with her fellow peers, confessing. "I wis wrang, Mal, she's no wan o the running Brooks, she's wan o the babbling wans."

Mal nodded. "Beats me how he ever came tae get mixed up wi somethin like yon. No in oor class at a'."

Static stroked his chin. "You know, Mal, the best thing that could happen to oor pal, wid be if he wis tae come in last...an awfy bad last, then he might come tae his senses."

"I wid agree wi ye pal, except a widnae want tae gie Miss Bool in the mooth, the satisfaction of humiliating ma cousin, so we'll stick tae oor original plan. Come on, let's get oot o here."

The boys made their way into the woods, coming across the occasional solitary spectator sitting on the grass by the side of the path, patiently waiting for the competitors to pass.

"This is it." Mal nodded to where a clump of bushes half hid an overgrown path. "I better get masel ready."

Static followed Mal up the path until they came to a particular tree. "Good! The bike's still where we left it last night." Mal opened up the saddlebag of his bike. "You better get yersel back doon tae the path. If I'm no ready by the time the first runners appear, gie me a whistle. Okay?"

Static was scarcely back by the bush before a leading pack of around twenty runners appeared around the bend, followed a few seconds later by a second pack of about half that size. Static put his fingers to his lips and gave the prearranged signal.

"Jesus! Ye nearly blew ma heid aff, Static!" Mal stepped out from behind the bush, wearing a long brown overcoat that almost reached to his ankles.

Static gave a start. "Sorry pal, I didnae know you were there."

"Ony sign o flash yet?" Mal stepped back behind the bush.

Static craned his neck. "They are some comin noo, Mal. Maybe Calum's amongst them."

"If he is, then he will have tae drop back, 'till he's on his own,'" came the voice from behind the bush.

Three minutes later, another two groups had passed, followed intermittently by a solitary panting runner.

"Ye don't think he's packed in already?" Mal whispered from his hiding place and wondering if their highly technical plan had all been for nothing.

"Cannae have. No wi' a' the training wee Tam's given him," was the others dry comment.

Static stepped out on to the path. "Here he comes noo, Mal!"

The long coat discarded, Mal came out from his hiding place wearing a pair of black shorts and a white running vest, also with the number sixteen on the back, which they had made the previous night.

"Don't forget yer cap." Calum thrust it at his cousin, as he was about to move off. "Mind and draw it well doon, jist in case the marshals get a bit nosey when they're checking your number."

"We'll see ye at the ither side!" Static called out to the departing figure. He turned to Calum. "Come on, better get this coat on." He held up the long brown coat Mal had worn while waiting for him. "Get yer leg ower the bike and we're away."

The bike with Calum on the back, his legs sticking out on either side like some mobile scarecrow, wobbled as Static fought to establish equilibrium.

"Dae ye think we will make it?" Calum asked anxiously, as he held on to his pal's shoulders.

"We did when we practised it the other night," Static panted. "Noo shut up and haud on!"

They descended into a dip, forcing Static to pedal even harder than he was already doing in order to make it up the other side, which also gave his passenger his first taste of the local vegetation, from the bushes in their way.

Calum spat out a leaf. "Steady pal, I'm no really a vegetarian, ye know."

"Listen Casanova" the pedaller panted. "I'm no` doin` this for the good o` ma health, ye know."

"Sorry pal, it's jist that Isabel has high hopes on me winning the Novices Cup."

"Ye win a cup! Ye'll be lucky tae win a saucer the way you run!"

Catching sight of a group of runners through the trees to his right, Calum gave Static a nudge. "I think that's the leading pack jist passing," he encouraged the pedlar.

A little later, in order to miss a jagged thorn bush, Static jammed on his brakes, causing the bike to skid, while Calum wobbled on the back, before involuntarily vacating his seat.

"Come on Calum, nae time tae be lying doon fur a rest, ye've a race tae run," Static hurled at the prone figure.

Shakily, Calum struggled to his feet. "Whit a driver!" he criticised through glazed eyes. "I should have known better!"

Slowly emerging from his temporary coma, Calum tugged at his shorts where white skin showed through. "Ye eejit! Jist look at man guid new shorts, ye can see half ma arse through them!"

"That's only half o whit I'm looking at the noo!" Static hurled back. "So, stop yer moaning and get back on, we havnae much time."

Five minutes after remounting, the two arrived at the prearranged spot by the side of the path where the athletes had to pass.

"Right, Calum, there's naebody in sight, get goin ye'll be pretty well up in the field noo," Static quickly helped his pal to discard his coat.

"I'm glad tae be oot o that thing, I felt like a flasher," Calum moaned.

Static gave him a shove. "Good. Then get flashing. Me and Mal will see ye on the other side."

Grateful for the rest after all his hard pedalling, Static sat down on the grass to await his second pal. Two minutes later, a pack of a dozen or so runners came into view before quickly disappearing out of sight. No Mal.

Five minutes later, after another dozen or so runners had panted and puffed their way past, Static was sure there could not be many more to come. What had become of the mighty 'Wilson' his comic book hero?

Suddenly – or in this case, gradually – a hedgehog appeared, laboriously passing Static silently sitting by the path. Taking a piece of grass he had been chewing out of his mouth, Static pointed it at the insectivorous animal. "Hey you! Your number's fell aff." Adding good humouredly, "Ye didnae pass ma pal Mal by ony chance?"

From above the snout, two beady eyes peered up at him, as if to say, and if I were to answer you in better English than in which you have just spoken, would you have recovered sufficiently from the shock by the time he did arrive?"

Running a good two minutes behind the hedgehog, Mal arrived, knees glued together, held up by a slim bespectacled figure, coaxing him along.

"Not far to go now." Four eyes encouraged him.

Mal looked appealingly at Static. According to their plan this was as far as he had to go, from here on in it was up to his speedy lovesick cousin to complete the rest of the course. "Naw, I think I'll hiv a wee rest here," Mal spluttered from his state of near apoplexy, and made to flop down where Static stood.

"No! You cannot do that," his bespectacled friend commanded. "Once you sit down, you'll never get up."

That's the idea, pal, Mal thought to himself, rubbing a hamstring and now aware of having muscles in places he never knew he had.

His support drew him away from the haven of green banking

where he would lovingly have lain down to die. "Come on, you can make it, you've done very well."

Mal stared at Static through rapidly glazing eyes, hoping for some sort of support, and not necessarily of the verbal variety. To his horror and dismay, Static gave a shrug of capitulation.

"Go on, you can make it Calum!" Static called out to him, as his supporter dragged him passed.

Mal's glazed eyes lingered on his pal for a moment, before his torturer dragged him further up the path, his boiling brain inventing a hundred different ways of putting this so called pal of his to death.

Static watched the two zig-zag up the path, Mal falling to his knees, to be hauled up and encouraged by his indomitable new found friend. Why, he thought was I ever talked into this? Cycling over those overgrown paths had been hard enough without the added weight of a moron on his back. Therefore, he was due a little compensation, such as seeing the look on Mal's face when forced to run to the finish, or for that matter Calum's, when his cousin appeared, not to mention the expression of the marshals and judges when they discovered there were two number sixteen's. Nor did it bear thinking about, he chuckled, when Miss Snooty Drawers found out all about it. The best thing that could happen to a nice wee bloke like Calum, who would be much better off without the likes o yon. Aye, some day they will both thank me for this. He sat down.

Further up the path, Calum began to slow down, the curtailing of his speed a necessity due to his quadriceps now bearing a distinct similarity to the weight of his Mammy's fairy cakes; poor Mammy never could bake. He slowed down to a walk.

Although he had given up the notion of having won the Novice Cup, he thought he could not be too far back in the field, thanks to Static getting him through the short cut so quickly, despite their unfortunate fall. He put his hand down to cover the hole in his shorts. At least if his lungs lacked oxygen, his backside muscles did not. Now it was up to him to keep on going these last few miles if he was to receive the plaudits of the one he loved. Also, he took comfort in the thought that for his cousin, the agony was already over.

A few hundred yards later, he converted his remaining energy from walk, to slow run, judging he had no more than a couple of miles left to do, when, behind him he heard the sound of running feet. He looked round. A small group was rapidly gaining on him. Good company for at least part of the way before they left him behind.

Calum increased his pace expecting to be caught at any moment. He turned a bend. White tape, and spectators leaped into sight. "Gees!" he swore aloud. "I'm nearly there!"

With no other option than to keep going, Calum ran towards the finishing line amid thunderous applause from an appreciative crowd. He had made it!

Isabel was the first to congratulate him. Scarcely able to contain herself, she rushed to give him a hug in the most discreet way possible amongst the back slapping and cheering for one who had finished only slightly behind the Nation's best.

"I knew you could do it Calum! You've won the Novice Cup!" Isabel cried with delight, already visualising him standing on the winner's podium at the next Olympic Games, while she applauded from the grandstand...Official Enclosure, of course. "But I never thought you'd finish sixth overall." Her affectionate hug, squeezing out what little oxygen was left in his dazed and stupefied brain and body. "Now away and change, a champion like you must look after one's self."

Calum staggered towards the changing tent, exhilaration replaced by despondency, not to mention outright terror, as the ramifications seeped through to his fuddled brain like 'watter' through a shitty cloot` "Static, ye eejit ye've started me far too quick on that last leg! Sixth! He explained with what little energy he had left. "Noo, they will expect me tae join the club. Go oot training wi them. Maybe compete in the next event."

He reached the tent amid continued congratulations. Had it been really worth it? Isabel's delectable body floated hazily on the wall of the tent. Not if it meant going training with the best in the club, and all he had left to offer that 'delectable body' was 'skint' knees.

Mal had never seen such a red sunset, especially at three in the afternoon, from end to end, nothing but red, just like his bank book. "Come on, man!" Mal faintly heard his four eyed friend whisper from the depths of the Amazon Rain Forest...or despair...even Coatbridge. "It's not far now."

It was imperative he did not cross the finishing line. He leaned a little more heavily on his friend for support. A tree swam by. He slackened his hold on his running mate, concertinaing his legs towards the nearest tree before it too swam passed, intent on falling down and rapping his arms around its trunk and holding on. So, that in the event of his masochistic friend wanting him to cross the line, he`d either have to hold on to his feet and stretch him all the way there, or take the damned tree with him.

"Ye`ve done it, mate!" We are here!"

Mal found himself propelled around and pushed towards rows of red faced people. He blinked his eyes shut for a moment, reopening them to a crowd that had gone unbelievably pale against a background of light blue sky. A few turned from where they had been heading towards the park exits or refreshment tents to give these two nocturnal octogenarians a polite round of applause.

"Sixteen and forty two," an official called out as four eyes pulled Mal across the finishing line.

"I knew you could do it!" Number forty-two puffed out triumphantly. "You'll do better next time."

Mal gave his rescuer a wave of ambiguity, leaving it up to him to decide whether it was a victory sign or not, while at the same time attempting to dissolve amongst the remaining spectators before an inquisitive official started to ask too many awkward questions.

"Come on Mal, ower here!" he heard a familiar voice call out, and looked up to see Static waving urgently.

Without argument, Mal followed his pal through small knots of people to the rear of a refreshment tent, where Static had parked his bike against a guy rope.

"Quick, get yer claes on and let's get oot o here," Static urged, opening up his saddlebag.

Mal put out a tired and shaking hand to take his trousers out of the bag.

"Come on!" Static`s voice rose anxiously, " before ye grow oot o yer claes!"

It took the announcer on the public address system requesting, number sixteen to report to the judges tent, to spur Mal on after a cyclist already fleeing towards the exit.

Static knew he should have listened to his Granny when she told him to take his coat. Granny's rheumatism never failed when it came to predicting the weather. "Rain with wet intervals," she had forecast with a wry smile, leaving him to work out her wee joke for himself.

"And where are ye playing the night?" Mal asked wee Ian Shaw, as they sat in the dimly lit cafe, hands clasped around their coffee cups to keep them warm, although it was only mid August.

"Cambuslang," Ian replied, giving the black box on the floor a sideways kick with his one good foot.

Mal bit into his chocolate biscuit. "Dae ye get many bookings wi yer squeeze box?"

Ian puffed at his cigarette. "Aye, no bad. It's a good wee band we've got, though we're aye on the lookout for anyone interested in playing with us. We do dances and the occasional weddings."

"Still work in the Co. Office?"

"Still works is right. It's that still, nothin ever happens. It's a guid job I've got the band, it helps with the money. If ye hear o anyone needing a band...."

"We'll let ye know, Ian," Mal nodded, including the for once silent Static in his assurance.

Ian stood up. "Well, I better away then and catch the bus. See yis baith again."

"Aye, see ye again, pal."

"Aye, see ye, Ian." Static gave a wee wave of his hand. Although it was now several years since the accident at Oor Bit, he still felt uneasy in the unfortunate boy's presence.

Ian limped off, weighed down by his heavy black box, meeting Calum at the door, where he halted to exchange a few words before disappearing into the night.

"Wee Ian's fairly put on the weight," Static commented drily. "They tell me he likes the booze as well."

Mal nodded. He could well imagine what his former school pal was going through. "It cannae be easy goin through life wi only wan good leg."

Static grimaced. "Oh I don't know, some fitba players dae it every Saturday."

"I wis tryin tae be serious," Mal said, disgusted by his pal's lack of sensitivity, not knowing that Static had only said it to hide his discomfort. "It's sad tae think he's turnin in tae an alky and him only turned eighteen." Mal's eyes drifted to a young female making her way to a table at the far end of the cafe. "Dae ye think it's his leg that's done it?"

"Whit, made him turn eighteen?" Static's eyes alighted on Calum crossing the floor, and timed his next comment to coincide with his pal's arrival at their table. Also glad of the opportunity to forget wee Ian. "Here comes Scotland's athletic find o the century. They tell me yer club has picked ye fur the next Olympic Games, but no' for runnin, for they tell me yer fur the high jump!"

Sliding into the seat opposite, Calum turned a hostile eye on his pal, who's comment was as welcome as a pair of bicycle clips to a man with no legs. "Don't mention her!" He made a dismissive gesture with his hand. "All ower me like a rash when I finished yon race she wis. And the rest o the team thinking they had found a star, and wantin' me fur next week's event!" Calum's voice rose an octave or two. "Can ye imagine me a' lined up wi the best in the country?"

"Nae bother Calum," Static feigned seriousness. "All ye hiv tae do is get near the front, and wi they splay feet o yours, jist trip up anybody that tries tae pass ye."

Calum made a noise indicating his patience was quickly coming to an end. Though Static, indifferent to his pal's tender feelings continued. "So ye mean tae tell us, it's all aff? Efter whit we a' went through! Yer cousin's knees had tae be separated by a blacksmith...fair riveted the gither they were. No tae mention complications." Static registered his deep disappointment with a shake of his head.

"Complications, aw right! It wis your plan that had complications!" Calum retorted savagely.

"How come?" Static wanted to know, appalled by the very thought that his plan should be considered in any way deficient.

"Fur wan thing, ye sent me aff on that last leg, far too quick," the complainant proceeded to inform him, tapping the table with the point of his finger. "So there I wis, up amongst the best runners in the country. Me! That couldnae run oot o sight in a dark night! Wis that no suspicious fur a start?"

Mal drew his eyes away from the young lady who had eventually found herself a table. "Whit has happened tae ye then, Calum?" he asked casually, returning to look at the girl and wishing he was over there sharing her orange juice with only the one straw, instead of having to listen to this aberrant verbal battle of wits...or should it be half-wits between so called pals.

"I got banned! That's whit happened."

"You got banned!" Mal echoed, now giving his cousin his full attention.

"Then ye better see wee Ian, he's lookin fur somebody tae join his band," Static chortled, lifting up his cup to hide his smile.

"Oh very funny, Master Planner, General Disaster." Calum sneered, for he had long since given up any hope of expecting any sympathy from this pal of his.

Absently, Mal stirred his coffee. "So no Olympics fur you then cousin?"

"Don't you start, Mal!" Would this patter never cease, he thought, becoming increasingly exasperated by the minute.

"Are yous goin tae sit there aw night ower wan wee cup o coffee. This is no a bed and breakfast, you know." A young waitress hung over their table, chewing gum poised daintily at the corner of her mouth.

"Jings yer no half a wee smasher when yer angry, Sonya. I could fairly go fur ye." Mal winked up at her.

"And I could fairly go fur ye tae, Mal Moffat, wi a hammer and chisel. So noo that the flattery is ower, whit do yis want, another coffee?"

"Another coffee? At these prices?" Static cried in mock horror. "If the Highlanders had charged like that at Culloden they wid have won the bloody battle!"

Sonya turned to Mal, to jerk a thumb in Static's direction. "A right wee comedian ye've got here. Now that the jesting is over," she began in a polished accent, "whit do yis want?"

"Oh, very ladylike indeed," Static mimicked. "Call for the manager."

"Caul fur me too, Static. It's freezing in here." Mal joined in the banter.

Then as Sonya's chewing gum, started to match the speed of a football manager's jaws while watching his team getting a right doin, relented. "I will hiv a coffee, Sonya...And you Static, same again?" And, at his pal's nod, asked of Calum, "Same fur you?"

"Just an Irn Bru for me," Calum answered dolefully.

"On the hard stuff, are ye Calum?"

Static lifted his eyes to meet those of the rapidly impatient waitress. "A bad case o love Sonya. A bad case."

Sonya shifted her gum. "Looks mair like constipation tae me, wi a face like that," she replied brusquely, stooping to inspect the subject, before departing.

"Where were we before we were rudely interrupted?" Mal presumed to take up where they had left off, before Sonya's engaging appearance.

"We wis asking oor nibs here, whit Miss Snooty Drawers had tae say aboot him being chucked oot the club," Static ventured to appraise.

"Well?" Mal coaxed, when his cousin had made no attempt to answer.

Calum knew it was useless to remain silent, he would have to tell them eventually. Better now than later, as it would save him being the brunt of Laurel and Hardy's, patter. "She said," he began, "that she did not want to be associated with anyone who cheated. Also, I had disgraced and humiliated her in front of all her fellow club mates."

Static furrowed his brows. "How does she know ye cheated?"

"It's no that hard Static, when two number sixteens cross the line," Calum condescended to explain to his moron of a pal, and having no wish to further elaborate, on what had passed between Isabel and himself.

Thankfully, Sonya's reappearance gave Calum time to calm his mounting irritation aimed at his pal, while she slid the glass of Irn Bru across the table, and distributed two cups of coffee none too gently in front of her other two patrons, declaring in a voice that held about as much warmth as the tepid coffee, "That will be one and nine."

"There ye go again, Sonya!" Static stormed in mock disgust. "Wi charges like that, you should rename this place the Electric Chair! Shocking! Shocking!"

"If ye don't stump up, it will be you that's on a charge!" Sonya countered, and stood back to await payment.

"Nice wan hen," Calum chuckled admiringly, and happy at last that someone had got the better of his tormentor.

They paid up. The delectable waitress departing with a few chosen words that suggested they hastily absorb their beverages and depart. Such as "get that doon ye, and beat it."

Mal gazed dolefully at his coffee cup as if blaming it for all that had befallen them the day of the race. "I thought Static and me had got away wi it, seein as I took aff as soon as a' finished."

"As fast as ye could?" Static mocked. "Ye were aboot as fast as a pregnant duck wi piles!"

Mal rounded on him angrily. "How fast wid you hiv been, if you had tae run a that way? It wisnae in the plan."

"I had tae pedal! It wisnae easy wi two great lumps o lard on the back!" Static defended.

"Nae use complaining noo," Calum sighed. "It's all over."

"She wisnae fur you," Static consoled.

Calum looked at his pal across the table, awaiting the inevitable punch line, surprised though grateful when none was forthcoming. "Aye, maybe ye are right, but she wis a wee smasher."

Mal drew the sugar bowl towards him. "An upper crust smasher, Calum. Best ye stick tae yer ain kind in future. A lot less painful...in mair ways than wan. Never mind though, yer athletic days are no yet ower." And at his cousin's quizzical look, reminded him, "ye've still wee Tam tae train."

Chapter 12

Bob Mitchell had decided that this would be his last race meeting before handing over to Mal. He had also suggested to him that he bring his cousin Calum along, while leaving Static behind, who would therefore remain unknown to the racing fraternity until the time was right.

His edification complete, Mal proudly guided his cousin through the various stages of preparation prior to wee Tam's race. "You have tae see the tapes on the hap are on right, Calum." Mal pulled the tapes down under the dog's belly, with the number six blazoned on its sides. "Tam's in the next race. I'll gie him a wee grooming before I let the kennel boy have him."

Bob came and stood beside the boys. "They're offering three tae wan on Sammy," he said patting the dog.

"Who's Sammy? Is he a rival?" Calum asked.

"You're holding him, son." Bob fondled the dog's ears.

"How come?" Calum asked, puzzled.

Eager to show off his newly acquired knowledge, Mal explained. "Tam runs under a different name at each track, jist tae try and confuse the handicappers and the punters, no tae mention the bookies." When his cousin continued to appear puzzled, he went on the assure him. "It's aw right Calum, they aw do it."

Calum was not so sure he understood all this doggy...or should that be dodgy intrigue, but decided not to pursue the matter. "Does Tam...I mean Sammy have a chance of winning?" he asked.

"Half a chance." Bob fumbled in his pocket for his pipe. "I'll jist pit a few bob on him tae keep the punters and the bookies happy. It'll help confuse them for the next time he's trying."

The race started. Tam, alias Sammy, running second until the last bend where he was overtaken by another two dogs, to eventually finish fourth.

Sitting on the front seat of the upper deck of the bus on their way home, with Tam stretched out at their feet, Bob drew contentedly on his pipe. "The wee dug needs a yard or two more."

Squeezed between the older man and his cousin, his appetite whetted by his first experience of greyhound racing, Calum asked eagerly, "How dae we dae that, Mister Mitchell?"

Bob took the pipe out of his mouth. "He has tae trap faster. And he slows ower the last few yards. Hasnae much stamina, the wee dug. Have ye Tam?"

At the mention of his name, Tam turned his long snout towards the cousins as if thinking, "Ye can say that again, Bob, that eejit in his fancy blue tracksuit nearly knackered me yon first night. Then, jist when I thought I was safe lying there dozing in ma ain hut, I opened ma eyes and there were two o them. It's a true saying, it's a dog's life, right enough." He gave a doggy sigh.

"Then we'll jist hiv tae improve his start." Calum bent down to stroke the sleek grey body. "Won't we wee man."

They had made a trap out of old pieces of wood and wire netting. Bob gently guided Tam in to it, while Calum stood at the back, rope in hand, awaiting the older man's instructions.

Bob stepped back from the trap and signalled to Static straddled over Mal's bike, that all was ready. Contemplating a disaster, mainly his own, Static, slowly and reluctantly, pedalled the bike a few yards away from the trap across the open field, while Bob made his way between the trap and the bicycle as quickly as his rheumatism would allow.

"Get ready!" Bob shouted raising his hand in the air. Then with a sharp downward movement of his hand, "Go!"

The trap flew up to Calum's pull of the rope. Static thrust down on the pedals, the makeshift hare attached to the end of the rope bobbing as he accelerated across the uneven ground as fast as his legs would take him, and was amazed by the fact that after a few minutes of vigorous pedalling the only sound of panting was his own, while the object of the exercise poked a cautious nose out of the trap wondering what these eejits of humans were up to, before taking a hesitant step out into the fresh evening air.

A few disappointing minutes later, Mal stood tickling the dog's ear. "I knew it widnae work. We'll hae tae pit something on the hare tae make Tam chase it."

"Hare? Ye mean Teddy Bear," Calum said drily.

"It's the best we could come up wi," Mal pouted.

"I suppose I shouldnae criticise somebody who is willing tae sacrifice their night's sleep." Calum commented, tongue in cheek.

"Whit dae ye mean?" Mal eased himself on to the top of the trap.

"Well, ye'll no be able tae get tae sleep withoot yer Teddy Bear,"

Calum explained.

Mal gave an indifferent shrug of his shoulders. "I can get tae sleep o right, seein as it's your Teddy Bear!"

A few minutes later, they tried again, Tam having been severely reprimanded for his lack of co-operation.

"Go!" Bob shouted. This time, Tam flew out of the trap after a furiously pedalling Static, catching the artificial 'hare' and pulling at it with all his strength, and capsizing bicycle and its yelling rider in the process.

"I knew it! I knew it!" a disconsolate Static shouted, scraping chunks of wet grass and mud off his trousers.

"Did he do well, Bob?" Mal asked, ignoring his pal's outburst.

Bob consulted his stopwatch. "Aye, but he will have to dae better. We'll try again."

Static pushed the bike at Mal. "It's your turn, I need ma trousers for ma work the morn."

Several starts, falls, broken ropes and bruised bums later, Bob called a halt.

"We'll work on the dug's stamina on Thursday night lads, if yous can make it?"

Static rubbed his backside. "Only if it doesnae interfere wi ma doctor's appointment. I hope aw this practise is goin tae work, and that wee mongrel doesnae sit in the trap in its next race waiting fur somebody tae pedal passed dragging a Teddy Bear ahint it before it comes oot!"

"Wid yer take a look at that! Here comes Gunga Din!" Sonya stopped on her way to the counter as Mal pushed the cafe door open, a broad white bandage wrapped around his head.

"Very funny, O menial one," Mal growled, holding the door open for an arm bound Calum.

Sonya turned an amused eye on the latter. "A new war started, has it, and yous no tellin me." She followed the two walking wounded to a table, affecting an upper class accent when asking. "What will it be, gentlemen, a cup of coffee with a morphine chaser, perhaps?"

Calum turned a jaundiced eye on his waitress. "We'll wait fur Static."

Sonya made a face. "Sorry, is he arriving by ambulance or wheelchair?"

"Bugger aff, Sonya," Mal snarled, in no mood for joviality.

"Nice, very much the gentleman the day. That heidgear suits you," Sonya retaliated. "It reminds me o ma Mammy's cloutie dumpling."

After Sonya's indignant departure, Mal asked of his cousin, "How's the arm?"

"Nips a bit. The same feeling as ye get when looking at whit they take oot yer pay for tax."

"That bad," Mal commiserated, "might mean amputation."

Calum's heart sank at the sight of Static coming into the cafe, unable to relish the thought of again being the brunt of his pal's humour.

Static slid down beside them, running an eye over their injuries. "Two nothing tae the dug, then?"

Mal studied the salt shaker forlornly. "I had the feeling it widnae work."

Calum was surprised when Static merely asked, "Whit happened exactly?"

Mal took it upon himself to explain. "Auld Bob couldnae make it....some union meeting he had tae go to ower his being paid aff, or something. So we went tae yon new road they're putting in where they intend building thae prefabs."

Sonya's reappearance momentarily interrupted his explanation. A hand on hip, gum balanced precariously on her lip she asked of her clientele, "So Chelsea pensioners, whit will it be then?" The gum disappearing with a smack and inward suck of breath.

Mal answered for his pals. "Three Irn Brus will dae."

"Nothing for me, Mal." Static smiled up at Sonya. "I don't want tae spoil ma tea."

"Whit dae ye think this is then, visiting hour?" she asked of Static, flicking her pencil in the 'patients' direction.

"Maybe later, hen," Static apologised.

"Later! Don't tell me you expect tae wait here until their better? It's no a hospital, ye know."

"The Irn Bru will help them recuperate, Sonya," Static assured her. "Different if it wis wan o yon rock cakes ye sell, then maybe they wid be confined tae bed."

"Whit's wrang wi oor rock cakes?" Sonya defended indignantly.

"Nothin, Sonya beloved. Personally, I like them. I only need another five and I'll have finished ma garden path."

"You were saying, Mal ?" Static prompted. The insult to the establishments sweetmeats having hastened Sonya's departure.

Mal started again. "We were up on that new road. Nothing there yet, except a few bricks for the foonds for yon prefabs."

"A fair length that new road," Calum vouched, with a nod.

"Anyway," Mal continued. "I got on the bike, Tam on the end o the rope, and I took aff doon that road like Reg Harris himsel, the dug at ma heels."

Static sucked in breath. "Don't tell me. Tam saw a cat, and pulled ye aff the bike?"

Mal shook his head impatiently. "Tam saw a rabbit. Past me like the clappers. I wis all prepared for jist such an emergency." Mal briefly closed his eyes, to emphasis the wisdom of his foresight, the inflection in his voice changing to one of despondency. "Somehow the rope managed tae fankle itsel in ma front wheel, next thing I knew I wis base over apex, cleaning the street wi ma bum!"

"And yer heid."

"Naw, Static, I reserved ma heid for polishing kerbs."

"Same thing happen tae you, Calum?" Static drew back to let a strange new waitress set their drinks down on the table. "Where's Sonya? Is it her night fur teaching elocution at the college?" he asked her.

Ignoring the remarks, the new girl set down the last drink, informing them, "Sonya telt me no tae take ony o yer lip, or I.O.U.s. O. K?"

"Dae ye know any mair letters in the alphabet, hen?" Mal politely inquired.

Not in the least amused, the waitress held out her hand. "A shilling."

Mal smiled up at her. "Are ye willing fur a shilling?" to quickly receive a bash on his bandaged head with her tin tray for his poetry.

Calum lifted his drink, as his eyes followed the waitress's progress back to the counter, comparing her figure with that of the delectable Sonya.

Static tapped his glass to draw Calum's attention back to their conversation. "So whit happened tae you, Speedy?" he asked.

"Me?...Oh aye." Calum swung back to the table. "We thought the bike might no be a success, so we went prepared."

Static's eyes bulged, red veins stood out at his temples. "Ye mean ye took they bandages along wi ye?"

Mal shook his head vigorously to show his contempt for his pal's deduction. "Tell him, Calum," he urged his cousin.

"Roller skates," Calum announced proudly.

"Roller skates!" Static exclaimed so loudly that customers ceased 'sooking' their drinks at nearby tables to find out what it was all about.

"Wheest!" Mal warned him, "everybody is looking."

"It's a good job they were no looking at this eejit on the roller skates. Roller skates! I jist cannae believe you two." Static sat back in his seat consulting the ceiling or beyond, for some sort of rational explanation.

"At least we were there." Calum condemned his pal with a growl.

"You knew I had night school." Static defended his absence with a glare across the table. "But never mind that, whit happened tae ye and yer roller skates?"

It was better to get it over and done with, Calum decided. The sooner Static had his little fun, the quicker he could get away home and get his Mammy to have a look at his elbow, then have the bandages washed and returned to Mrs Mitchell, who had put them on for him and Mal when she saw the state they were in when they brought back Tam.

"I had everything under control, straight doon the street I went." Calum made a slicing movement with the edge of his hand. "Goin like a Rangers supporter left ahint at Parkheid, I wis. Everything right, until the daft dug saw the rabbit."

"Same rabbit as before, Calum?" Static asked, tongue in cheek.

"How wid I know that?" Calum growled, incensed by the absurdity of the question. "Tam past me heading doon the street, and me haudin on tae the rope fur dear life - like that Nanook of the North, I wis. All I had to do was shout mush!"

"No sae loud," Static warned his pal. "Or they'll be up here wi dish o the day."

"Then he hit the kerb at the far end," Mal explained. "Ye actually passed Tam before hitting that bush, did ye no, Calum?"

"I landed on something. Don't know whit I actually hit first, it could have been ma backside, before I hit ma elbow.

Static sighed. "Ye've never changed, Calum, "ye still don't know yer arse frae yer elbow."

"And I suppose you could dae better?" Calum challenged him angrily.

Static gave a slight shrug. "Maybe. I will hiv tae see whit I can dae."

"So this is whit ye have come up wi, O little genius one!" Mal stood back to admire the truck.

It had been a week now since their conversation in the café, and time for their injuries to heal, and Static to have come up with this new idea to improve Tam's speed and stamina. Now they were once again on the same stretch of new road that had previously proved a disaster.

Bobby Jackson stepped down from the cabin. "Mind, I only have this wee truck fur an hoor, then it goes back tae big Jake, the tattie man, afore he finds oot it's missing ." Bobby warned them.

"That's aw right, Bobby, half an hoor will dae it." Static waved an assuring hand. "You get yersel back ahint the wheel, we'll get intae the back. When I gie the cabin roof a thump, start driving away. Each time I gie ye a thump, jist go that wee bit faster. Mind and gie yersel and the wee dug time tae stop before the end o the road, though."

Instructions now finalised, Static, plus two cousins clambered on to the back of the small truck, Mal seating himself by the lowered tailgate where Tam looked up at him with baleful canine eyes, which seemed to say, "Here I go again, with the Life Members of the Eejits Club. Why, of all the greyhounds in the West, have I got lumbered with this lot?"

Mal patted Tam and made sure the rope attached to his collar was not too tight.

"Everything is aw right, ye can start noo. No too fast tae start wi," he threw over his shoulder settling back down by the tailgate.

At the front of the truck, Static gave the prearranged signal by thumping on the cabin roof and, in answer Bobby, revved the engine and drew slowly away, Tam following the tightening rope with a gentle trot.

"A wee bit faster!" Mal shouted to Static, who completed the instruction by giving the roof another thump. Again, Bobby increased the speed, with Tam responding.

"Up a wee bit!" Mal shouted and immediately had his instruction carried out.

When almost half way down the empty new road, the speed having gradually increased, Calum gave Static the thumbs up that all was going according to plan.

"A wee bit mair, Tam's really belting it noo!" Mal shouted with delight. He was already envisaging Tam first over the winning line at the next race.

Suddenly, out of nowhere, an Alsatian came at Tam, the larger dog snapping at the racing hound, who in turn snapped back to defend itself, which in turn tightened the rope.

"Stop! Stop!" Mal cried out. "The dug's choking!"

Static jerked round and thumped the cabin roof, and instantly the truck speeded up. "Stop the truck Bobby!" Static yelled, continuing to thump the roof.

"Stop doin that Static, Bobby thinks ye want him tae go faster!" Calum yelled out, panic-stricken now that the truck was going at the rate of knots and increasing with every thump on the roof.

Unfortunately, the driver preoccupied with trying to gain sight of the dog in his wing mirror and not realising he was almost at the end of the road until he was almost on it, stamped on the brakes, swivelling the truck round before it hit the kerb, toppling Mal backwards, who collided with Calum flying in the opposite direction, with Static landing on top off them both.

"Get aff me Static!" Calum yelled from under Static's legs"

"Gie me a chance pal, I've only jist arrived," Static snapped back angrily, while Tam, realising the back of the truck was rapidly coming closer, took a flying leap on board, landing amongst a tangle of human arms and legs.

He had just joined the Eejits club.

Two weeks had passed since the 'truck incident', Mal and Calum, with Tam between them, walked towards the exit of the greyhound stadium. Sammy Shaw, better known as Tattie, caught up with them. "Havnae seen Bob for awhile. How's he keeping these days?" The words tumbled out in time to his heavy breathing.

Tattie, in contrast to whose health he was inquiring after, was a frisky little sixty year old, who, it appeared lived on the edge of his nerves, always glancing around him as if on the lookout for predators.

Mal slowed to let the little man and his dog catch up. "Bob's been paid aff."

"Then he'll be finding it harder than ever tae feed the dug."

Mal did not reply, believing it would be wrong to discuss Bob's business with Tattie.

Unperturbed, Tattie went on. "He was tryin tae sell the wee dog afore this happened. Did not have the readies, ye see. Didn't happen." Tattie darted furtive glances around him as if expecting a dinosaur to suddenly appear from behind the 'gents' and pluck him oot o' his simmit. "Neither would his ticker stand the excitement. Maybe jist as well. Though, he's been at this game for a while. Started as a hobby, ye see." He pulled his dog away from Tam, while the cousins gave understanding nods.

"We had an agreement...See yis later..." Suddenly, Tattie was gone, heading for the nearest exit, an arm swinging like a sergeant major on parade, his dog trotting by his side.

"Some wee man!" Calum voiced. "I thought for a minute he was goin tae tell us something."

"Maybe he got caught short. Jist like me and ma bank balance," Mal winced.

They reached the gate and out into the dark ill lit street. A few punters hurried passed, heading for the bus stop. The cousins followed, both aware of someone behind them.

"Daes yis know, Big Harry Rattray?" The boys turned, surprised that it was Tattie who had asked the question. "That's why I got off ma mark back there." He jerked his head in the direction of the stadium. "I didn't want him tae see me talking wi ye two."

"Who's this Harry Rattray?" Calum asked in all innocence.

"Someone your better aff not knowing," Tattie assured him, tightening his leash on his dog. "He's the local Mafia ye might say. Doesnae bother me much, noo that ma dog`s no a threat tae his. But I've seen him eyeing up your wee dog noo that he's improving and has beat his once or twice."

Suddenly, two white faces shone in the dark street, both related to one another.

"Ye don't think he'll approach us aboot fixin races dae ye Tattie?" This time it was not just Tattie who stole quick furtive glances around.

"Maybe, maybe no. All I can say is, be on the lookout for him and his cronies."

This was getting worse by the minute the heroes thought. First, Big Harry, then Big Harry and his cronies!

Mal swallowed hard. "Does he go tae all the tracks?"

"As far as Wishaw and Coatbridge, even ower tae Dunfermline."

"International Mafia," Mal said, without humour.

Tattie drew up at the street corner. "Anyhow, as I was saying afore, me and Bob had an agreement, we would tell each other when oor dogs were trying. It worked wance or twice. We can still dae the same, although mine's no doing too well. Doesnae like the bends ye see."

"Have ye ever tried Larkhall? It's got longer straights." Mal turned up his jacket collar. "It might suit yer dug."

"I thought aboot it wance or twice, but it would mean me takin two buses. Thanks aw the same." Tattie poked his head around the corner. "Here's my bus. Mind whit I telt ye. Watch oot for Big Harry and his mob." And then he was gone.

"Malcolm!" Mal's mother's voice curled around the light bowl, out of the kitchen, down the lobby and into Mal's room, where he was pulling on a clean shirt.

When his Mammy called him by his full Christian name, Mal knew he was in trouble. The 'command' came again, this time thundering down the lobby and bouncing off his chest as he made for the door.

One hand on hip, a foot tapping in time to her angry impatience, Mrs Moffat eyed her son entering the kitchen. "And whit dae ye call this?" She pointed a rigid finger at her small fridge, a newly acquired acquisition - her pride and joy.

"It's a fridge." Mal tucked his shirt into his trousers, careful to keep the table between himself and his interrogator.

Mammy's eyes narrowed, and Mal knew he had made his first mistake. "Do not get smart with me boy!" Agnes swung the fridge door open. "I had a pun o sausages, and a half pun o mince in there." She changed swiftly to her best English, which she always did in order to emphasise her displeasure, to inquire of her son, "Can you explain their absence? And as I know you cannot have cooked them, seeing as you do not know the location of the cooker, am I to believe...!" Agnes changed to a more comfortable and colourful accent, "that damned greyhound has had them? Ye wee naiff!"

Slowly and minuscule, Mal edged closer to the door. "Ye have tae feed him on the best if ye expect him tae run fast and win."

The arm on Mammy's hip swung a little. "Is that so? Well it didnae dae you much good at the school sports when I fed you them, so whit's the difference?"

Mal dearly would have liked to have said, "An extra two legs and a tail," but, not wishing to curtail his life span, he refrained from doing so.

Accepting her son's silence as an admission of guilt, Agnes pressed on. "So it's dripping and fried breed fur you this week, ma lad."

Mal calculated the distance between angry parent and door, judging he had a foot or so advantage, which he would need to counteract Mammy's favourite weapon lying within her reach on the table, a rolled up newspaper, and reflecting, should his brains have absorbed the daily headlines as much as the back o his heid, he'd be a genius. "Ye'll get yer money back when Tam wins," he tried to console the irate woman. "We're goin tae try him on Friday."

"Good. And I hope yis find the wee mongrel guilty." Agnes drew closer to her son, as her son drew closer to the door.

"You'll no be sayin that when Tam wins, and I put a couple o pounds in yer hand," Mal propounded loftily.

Agnes eyed her son and heir caustically. "The only couple o pounds I want you to put in ma hand is mince and sausages!" She jerked a thumb in the direction of the door. "Noo git, afore I lose ma temper." He was free!

"Whit dae ye think we should do then?"

The three boys sat round the table in Calum's house, each hugging a mug of tea.

"I don't fancy getting mixed up with these hard men," Calum replied to Mal's question.

Mal toyed with his cup. "Mammy bought a wee fridge, she saved up for it hersel. Waste of money, there's never anything in it, it's all in the dug."

Calum nodded his understanding. "Bob Mitchell can hardly look after it. The wee dug can hardly get oot twice a day. It's his lumbago."

Static turned a shocked eye on the speaker. "Ye didnae tell me wee Tam had lumbago?"

"Don't start!" Calum warned his guest. "You no whit I mean. You're no that thick."

Static frowned at Mal. "Whit does thick mean Mal?"

Despite his resolution to remain serious, Mal's face broke into a smile. "See you, Static!"

Calum passed the biscuit tin around. "This is serious. First, we havnae the where with all to keep the wee dog. Second, if we do keep him, we will maist likely get involved wi these Lanarkshire hard men. I say we sell the dog as quick as we can."

Mal took a biscuit from the tin. "We'll have tae let Mr Mitchell know whit we intend to do. It's only right."

"I don't think he'll mind. Though, I think he wid be bound tae miss Tam after aw this time." Calum chewed morosely on his biscuit.

"Can we no at least get a win oot o it afore we sell it?" Static ventured.

"We are goin tae try him at Larkhall. Then we'll sell him, unless auld Bob has ither plans."

"It's settled then. First we see Bob, let him know Tam's aw set for Friday, then tell him aboot oor intentions of trying tae sell him. Efter all, he's still a partner." Two heads nodded in agreement to Calum's suggestion. "Who is going tae tell him, then?"

Two heads, that had stopped nodding, winked at Calum.

This was the big night Static contemplated, he was going to the dogs for the first time, perhaps also for the last, should they sell Tam. Bob Mitchell had seen the sense of having to give up the dog. The man's Lumbago had prevented him from taking it for nothing more than a short walk during the day, and when he had, he had been as slow as a hospital clock. Also, it had not always been practical for one of the pals to take Tam for its much needed training walks at night. The miracle was that the wee dog had improved at all.

There was also the question of finance. True, Calum and Mal had shouldered most of the burden, when he himself could not. It was not that he counted every penny, rather that he made every penny count.

It was all right for Mal, now that he was getting on fairly well in the grocers, and his Mammy working part time in Woolworth's, otherwise they could not have bought that new fridge Mal had talked about. Then there was Calum, who was doing well in his new job in the Council office. He remembered how he'd sat in his kitchen, legs tucked under his chair for fear of scuffing the Muirs' new linoleum. There was also talk of their getting one of those television sets as well. Static sighed. What chance had he of possessing any of these things, with him still on an apprentice wage? Though some day, he vowed, when his time was out…However, he had one consolation he told himself, he was in a better trade than either of his pals, and carpentry was something he was good at. Then, he reflected, maybe someday he could buy his Mammy a T.V.

Static watched his mother poke through her purse. She was showing her years. Suddenly the thought occurred to him of how much his mother might miss his father- a father whom he had never really known. He had only the haziest of memories of him, such as his father in uniform bouncing him on his knee until the 'chip poke' hat fell over his eyes…a day at the swings…crying when he went away. That was about it.

Occasionally, his mother would mention something he and his father had done together, and she would ask him if he remembered and he, not wishing to make her unhappy, had lied by saying he had.

He dared not think of the future, hating when either of his pals had girlfriends, something which, with a face like his, he would never aspire to. This, in turn, would bring on a loneliness which now made him realise what his mother might be going through each day of her life, for, as a laddie, mammies were only there to look after you, keep away all the nasty things in life. After all that was what mammies were for.

Static clenched his fists. Should he ever come into money, his mother would be the first to benefit. A new cooker, a new carpet, and should everything go well, a telly in the corner.

"Will five shillings be enough, son?" Calum heard his mother ask, while she mentally calculated the affect of losing such a large amount from the household budget.

Static pondered over the wisdom of having told his mother about Tam's chances of winning. Perhaps, it would have been more prudent not to have said anything and just put a bit extra on the dog for her. "Aye, that will be fine, Mammy, if ye can afford it. You could make it a half croon if ye like, jist in case?" The boy's chest constricted at the thought of the wee dog losing.

His mother thrust the two coins at him in a gesture indicating, that to lose the money would not be a major catastrophe, not Armageddon, and it would not matter in a hundred years time. "How much will I get if it wins?" Mammy closed her purse with a click.

"We're expecting to get four tae wan. If we do, ye'll get a pound and yer own money back," Static told his mother authoritatively, as if gambling had been an everyday occurrence to him from birth.

"And if it loses," Mammy replaced her purse in the top drawer of the chest of drawers, "ye can expect auld claes and purrich, for the rest o the week."

Static stopped, his hand on the door handle, amused by the old Scottish expression. He smiled affectionately at her. "Och, it will no be the first time, Mammy."

And, as he turned, heard her say, "Aye, and by all accounts, no the last either."

Tam, plus three pals, got off the bus one stop away from the racetrack in order not to be seen together by inquisitive punters.

"Noo remember, Static, Tam's running in the last race, so you've got plenty of time." Mal commenced his final briefing of his friend. "You go through the gate tae yer right. We go in by another gate, so we'll no meet till the race is ower. Mind ye get it right. All right so far?"

Static grunted his understanding. Mal went on, "We want four tae wan. If ye see the bookies giving anything higher, like five or six, get in there." He emphasised the significance of such odds with a downward sweep of his hand.

"Whit if the bookies don't gie four tae wan?" Static asked perplexed.

Calum closed his eyes momentarily, wondering as to the wisdom of placing this gigantic financial burden on his pal's slender shoulders, not to mention thick heid. "Have ye separated the money in case wan bookie will no take it aw?" he asked apprehensively.

Static tapped both trouser pockets as if to reassure himself that he was well in charge of the situation.

Mal drew closer to the prospective gambler, hoping the old adage of beginners' luck would hold out...at least for tonight. "If ye cannae get fours, take whit ye can. Ye better wait till the last minute though. Never mind if ye cannae manage tae get aw the money on, we'll sort things oot after Tam wins."

"Ye hope." Calum sighed, looking skywards for a sign of

assurance, such as a huge face of a benevolent bookie beaming down at him. Instead, all he got was two crows belting it hame before it got pitch dark.

Mal drew slightly to one side. "We're goin this way. You go that way." He pointed in the direction Static should take. "All the best. We'll see you at the same bus stop as we came aff at efter the race."

Inside the track, Static looked around him, slightly overawed by this new experience. Once again, he tapped his pockets as if to assure himself that he could cope. Though he may have failed academically at school, he thought, he still retained more than a modest amount of common sense. Or so he hoped.

Hesitantly, he moved towards the epicentre of noise. The scene under the eerie floodlights reminiscent of some ghostly meeting place of a religious cult, where men stood around in small groups holding their faces up to priests on pedestals besides boards adorned with strange symbols. Some with a cry of despair lifting their baleful eyes heavenwards, beseeching the Son of God...or words to that affect, to help them. While by the side of the priests, men gave out peculiar signals to other priests further down the line. All the while men would leave groups to run to other priests and groups, as if undecided on which religion to enrol.

To the rear, men rejected by the priests stared at the ground and tore up their membership cards, and angrily declared to the Son of the Lord...or words again to that effect, that they were always destined to lose.

His fantasy over, Static drew closer to the bookies. His face had started to sting as it usually did when he was nervous. Hence his almost continuous patter when it did. A trait poor Calum hated as he was nearly always the brunt of his humour.

Wee Tam was in the next race. The bookies sang out a string of odds. He moved closer, and was jostled by men rushing here and there, and stuck his hands in his pockets before someone else did, clenching the rolled up notes in his fists.

A bell rang. He panicked, remembering Mal having told him there was not much time after it rang to place his bets. He moved forward, straining to see the chalked names on the boards, searching for Tam's name and his odds. Nothing. He pushed through to another board, unable to see their wee dog`s name. Had he got it wrong? Was this the wrong race? Yet Mal had said it was the last race. He should have made sure and bought a race card.

A man stepped on his toes. An arm came up from nowhere and cleaned his nose as it reached out to the bookie. He gripped his money tighter, ready to pull it out of his pocket when needed, and pushed a punter out of the way in his anxiety to ask the nearest bookie what the odds were on Tam. Or had he got the wrong race?

Too late. A cry went up. Static rushed to the rail in time to see Tam flash passed in third place. He clenched his fists as it went into second place, never having seen his canine friend run so fast. Now in the back straight it had gone into second place heading for the home straight a full two lengths clear. A roar went up as the other dogs drew closer to it, though Tam still led, but not now by so much. Then, Tam was almost at the line. .... A blur as the dogs hurled passed, yelping and fighting one another for the artificial rodent they had been gulled into chasing.

The kennel boy came up and held out the leash of the panting dog to Mal.

"Yis hiv a right guid wee dog there."

The cousins swung round. Two mouths opened in unison.

Now no longer taller than either of them, but broader, and still capable of inflicting fear, stood, Basher Moodie.

"Basher," Mal croaked, having a deep desire to put up his hand to protect his throat. "Whit are ye doin here?"

"Aye?" said Calum, as if feeling he had to say something in support of his cousin. "Fancy. I wis goin tae ask ye baith the same thing."

Basher's voice changed from one of mere friendliness to those whom he had been in so much close contact with...mainly his fists...to one of downright hostility. "Ra boss wid like a word," the swinging on his heel, a command to follow.

Two pairs of eyes gaped at one another. Two pairs of lips quivered simultaneously, "Big Harry Rattray!"

"So these are the owners?" Big Harry reared over them.

As neither boy had recovered from shock, and were not likely to in the near, or even distant future, it took Basher to answer for them.

When Basher had finished, the face that confronted them, though flabby was of an arrogance born out of power, a power which still held the two young men speechless.

"Yer dug did well the night. Keep it up." Harry jerked back his head in the same manner as a drill sergeant does when addressing a group of squaddies. He drew closer, his eyes alighting on Mal as if electing him as the one to do business with. "Enter yer dug here for the next three weeks. Let him keep tryin. Then, on the fourth night, have him stuffed. Okay?"

Why, thought Mal, had he the feeling it was all academic to Big Harry, should he have the courage to refuse?

"Yous don't get it do yous?" Mal heard Basher laugh, but could not bring himself to look away from Al Capone Of the Closes staring down his nose at him.

"Yer dug's doing well," Big Harry condescended to explain, as Basher's cigarette lighter came out of nowhere to light, 'ra boss's' fag'. "So when it comes tae the fourth night, yer dug's odds will be a lot less than mine. Therefore..." Here, Big Harry endeavoured to sound real educated. "You will stuff yer dug and let mine do the business." End of dialogue...End of story.

Big Harry flicked his almost untouched cigarette into the darkness the way he had seen Humphrey Bogart do, his turning away an indication that the audience was at an end. "See yous next week." Their old school bully's laughter followed them into the night.

A few shaky minutes later, the cousins turned the corner for the bus stop. "Whit a shitty night!" Mal swore. "All we needed tae finish aff the night wis a command performance frae Big Harry!"

Calum blew out his cheeks. "Fancy Basher Moodie being his yes man!" He paused for a second to digest the events of the past half hour. "Whit are we goin to do aboot running the dug for the next four weeks, Mal?"

"Don't know. Suppose we'll jist hiv tae dae as we're telt."

They were now close to the bus stop. Calum drew Mal's attention to the dejected figure of Static slouched against a wall, hands deep in his pockets, in the same way they recalled seeing him do at school whilst awaiting to be called into the headmaster's office.

Mal thought of all the money lost. Besides that of their own money, there was that of Static's Mammy and the Mitchells, none of whom could really afford the loss. He shortened his stride as if by doing so it could prolong the inevitable.

Static levered himself off the wall. The gesture he made with his hands akin to a bird about to launch itself in flight. "Sorry, pals"

"It's aw right, Static, no yer fault," Mal hastened to assure him, "all the dug had to do wis stick its tongue oot tae win."

Even in the dimly lit street, the cousins saw Static's face change colour. His eyes flicked from one to the other as he stammered the question, "Tam lost?" Two heads nodded. "Well I'll be buggered!" Static wagged his head from side to side in disbelief. "And here wis I thinking I'd cost yous money."

"It would help somewhat, Static, if you were to explain," Calum challenged. "In other words, spit it oot!"

Static obliged with a grin. Suddenly, the whole world seemed right again. "Well, ye telt me Tam was in the last race, so I run up and doon like a hen on a hot girdle looking for his name on the bookies board. Nae Tam! So I couldnae get oor money on. Jist as well...Eh?"

Several yards away, people standing at the bus queue turned at the sound of near hysterical laughter at two...to them, eejits laughing their prospective heids aff, whilst one, more sensible than his companions stood mystified by their behaviour.

"Sorry, pal," Mal apologised to Static, and grinning at Calum. "It was oor fault. We should have telt ye Tam runs under an alias here, as he does at every other track. His name here is Bertie Blue."

"Bertie Blue!" Static exploded, not knowing whether to be angry or not. "Nae wonder I couldnae see his name on the boards. Lucky for ye it didnae win."

"You can say that again pal." Calum put his arm around Static, guiding him to a bus queue unhappy at being joined by eejits...although the wee dog was welcome. "Ye can say that again."

It was the fourth night at the racetrack. Basher crossed to meet the cousins as they came out of the kennel enclosure, demanding to know to whom they had been speaking.

"I hope yis are no up tae somethin, ra boss will no be pleased."

"Don't get yer dole card aw crumpled Basher, ye've nothing tae worry aboot. Yer boss has it fixed. His dog is trying the night, while we have fed oors that many pies it will maist likely come doon wi piearrhoe."

For once, Mal felt unafraid as he confronted the enemy, his bravery encouraging Calum to continue the aggression. "We've kept tae oor side o the bargain, noo it's up tae you and Al Capone ower there."

Taken aback by this, until now unheard of courage by two boys, who had given him some of his most pleasant moments in life to demonstrate his pugilistic skills, Basher's mouth fell open, his uneven teeth showing like a row of blitz houses. "Well mind that ye do."

"Aye we'll mind Basher. If ra boss's' dug losses, it's no oor fault," Mal mimicked, as Basher moved off to be by Big Harry's side.

A little later Mal leaned on the track rail, a discreet distance away from the finishing line and Big Harry and his sidekick. "It's now or never as the song says," he sighed at his cousin. "Surely Tam cannae win wi aw they pies in him?" Calum tried to assure himself.

The race started. Tam trapped well and hit the front. The cousins shouted to him to slow down or, if he felt so inclined, to stop. Big Harry's dog, Miffin was, in third place.

Calum nudged his cousin. "Dae ye see whit I see?"

"Sure do!" Mal shouted above the roar of the crowd.

Tam had began to slow, Miffin passed him with a brindled dog on its tail. Reaching the last bend before the home straight, Tam came again. "No Tam! There's a clever dug!" two voices shouted above the crowd.

Again, Miffin spurted passed Tam, and just as Big Harry's dog was about to cross the finishing line was in turn passed by the brindle.

Mal threw his cousin a look. "Let's get oot o here."

The boys quickly left the brightly lit trackside behind. Mal drew up. "I'll wait here. You carry oot the business." He nodded to the sombre shape of the kennels.

Calum snatched a look in the direction of the track, then back at his cousin. "Are ye sure? Do ye think Big Harry will want a word?"

"Maist likely, but I can handle that aw right. Noo git!" Mal jerked a thumb.

Reluctantly, Calum took a step or two away, then as if questioning the morality of his action, swung back. "Oor man can wait. I'll bide here wi you. Maybe if he sees the two o us it will..."

"Go on!" Mal ushered him away with an impatient flick of his hand. "I've nothing tae be feart aboot."

Mal swung to face the track, where punters, heads down, hands in pockets shuffled towards the exits. While others; mainly the few successful ones were loudly extolling the wisdom of their choices, to equally noisy acquaintances. From behind such a group, two men appeared, heading in his direction. "This is it," Mal muttered to himself. "Check yer guns, pull yer Ten Gallon hat ower yer een and if things come tae the worse, droon yerself in it."

Mal walked casually to meet the men. For a moment, his eyes rested on the younger one, whose grin clearly portrayed the enjoyment of the situation; or more likely, the prospect of the situation to come, before flicking to the impassive expression of the other.

"Basher. Mr Rattray." Mal greeted them stoically.

"Ma dug lost." There was more disappointment that accusation in the big man's voice.

"Mine as well."

Basher strained like a dog on a leash, awaiting the command from his master at Mal's clipped reply.

Big Harry's lip curled in a brief smile. "The brindle beat us. I'm sure I've seen it somewhere afore."

I'm sure ye have Harry, Mal thought to himself, it's Tattie Shaw's dug. I knew the longer straights would suit it.

"We'll get it right next time, I'll let ye know when." Magically Basher's lighter appeared to light his master's cigarette.

Mal didn't wait. "Don't think so Mr. Rattray." Basher's eyes lit up at the prospect of earning his wages, "unless ye can come up wi a deal wi the dog's new owner."

Big Harry glowered down his nose at Mal. "Ye mean tae tell me ye have selt the dug? Ye must have had it in mind aw this time, and no telling me."

"Sorry Mr Rattray. As the dog wisnae winning, we couldnae afford tae keep it, but we kept oor side o the bargain, which was tae see oor dug didnae win the night."

Big Harry drew on his cigarette, for a moment his eyes rested somewhere on the darkened kennels. "Well, that's it then. Maybe we'll get the gither if ye ever buy another dug." He started to move away. "S'long then."

Mal waited for Bashers parting shot, either verbally or otherwise. None came.

"Aye, so long Mr Rattray. You too, Basher."

"It worked oot aw right then?" Calum asked his cousin as they took their seats on the bus."

"Nae bother. Whit else could he dae?"

The conductress came to take their fares.

Calum brushed an imaginary speck of dust from his trouser leg. "I got the money for wee Tam. The wee dug didnae know whit was happening to it. Tried tae break its leash tae come efter me," he added sadly.

"It's aw fur the best," Mal sighed, his eyes somewhere down the passageway, not wanting Calum to see his face, and wishing he had been there to give the dog a final pat. His thoughts on what Bob must be feeling at knowing his dog would not be coming home.

At last, it was their stop. They got off the bus and started to walk to their prearranged meeting, while laughing at some of the funny things that had happened since taking over the dog.

Outside the pub, Calum drew Mal aside. "Tam's new owner gave me an extra fiver for him. He said he was worth it." He fanned the notes out.

"That wis good o him," Mal agreed. "Give it tae Bob, efter aw it was his dug."

He drew his jacket collar up against the approaching chill of the evening. "You go in, and I'll wait for Static. It would be best tae divide the winnings aff wee Tattie's dug oot here, and no let they nosey buggers in there, see whit it's aw aboot."

"Ye'll catch yer death o cauld," Calum warned him.

Mal shook his head. "Static will no be long."

"I hope he hasnae made an arse o it this time," Calum said with some trepidation.

Mal blew out a laugh. "Naw, this time I made sure he knew the name o Tattie's dug. Besides, he had Bobby Jackson wi him jist tae make sure."

Calum turned for the pub door. "See ye inside then."

"Sure, Calum. Make mine a pint."

Calum had hardly gone before Mal felt a hand on his shoulder swinging him roughly round.

"So this is yer gemm! I knew yis were up tae something!" The voice was loud, venomous. Basher Moodie stood inches away, his face thrust into Mal's, his fists clenched.

"Whit had yous cooked up atween yis at ra bosses expense?"

Unflinching, Mal stared back. "You've got it wrong, Basher.

Nane o' us can bile an egg far less cook up somethin."

"Dinnae gie me that patter, I saw yer gawky cousin gie ye money."

"That wis money we got for selling the dug. I telt ye and yer boss aboot it back at the track. If we won money the night, it had nothing tae do wi you or Big Harry."

Though convinced by the logic, Basher still craved revenge having bet on his boss's dog to win. And, although roughing up this naiff would not give him his money back, it would as sure as hell give him some satisfaction.

Apprehensively, Mal braced himself for the blow, determined not to let this brainless moron have it all his own way. As Basher's fists came up, the bully was swung round and driven to the pub wall, his eyes wide in disbelief as another hammer blow caught him in the stomach. Basher crumpled but struggled upright, bringing up his fists to shield his face.

"No this time," the voice seethed, and hit him again. Basher folded against the wall.

"Did ye no hear my pal tell ye we did everything yer boss asked us tae do. It`s no oor fault if yer dug lost. Okay?" His fists clenched in readiness, Static glared down at his old schoolboy enemy.

"Aye. Aw right Static." Basher hauled himself up by the aid of a convenient window ledge. "I suppose ye did the right thing by ra boss. Nae hard feeling, eh?" The man stretched out a hand for Static to shake.

Ignoring the gesture, Static pointed in the direction he wished Basher to take. "On yer way, pal."

Moments later, both pals stood watching Basher's figure gradually disappear into the darkness.

"Wis I no glad tae see you, pal," Mal said, without turning his eyes away from the almost vanished figure.

"Efter aw this time." Static words were almost a whisper as his thoughts travelled back over all those years of misery inflicted on them by the man whom he had just defeated. Then, as if he had suddenly remembered where and who he was with, turned to rebuke his pal. "It's freezing oot here. Come on, ye can buy me a half."

Chapter 13

It was Saturday night. Mal was disappointed that he did not have a date. Maybe he could if he tried the Larcano, there was always the few there with other things than dancing on their minds.

"Ony mair tatties Mammy?" he asked, pushing the empty plate away, rifting and, tasting the mince and tatties again.

"Whit ye eat the day ye will no get the morro," his mother prophesied. "I'd rather keep ye a week as a fortnight. It's a wonder ye can stand up withoot yer belly getting stuck below the table."

"Maybe ye are right, Mammy," Mal agreed. His face lit up. "Ony mair o they scones ye baked yesterday?"

"No. You ate them aw. And it was this morning I made them, not yesterday, ye greedy, wee naiff." The incessant ringing of the doorbell drowned out the noise of the woman's mixed diction as she angrily swept away the dirty dishes onto the 'bunker' by the sink. "See who is at the door, son, must be the Fire Brigade by the sound of it!"

Mal stood up, tasting more of his recent meal on the way.

"It's you Static! I thought it must have been the rent man by the racket."

Impatiently, Static waved the sarcasm aside, stumbling into the hallway. "I've got the fitba coupon up, Mal!"

Mal furrowed his brows in a gesture of improbability and followed his pal into the kitchen.

"Hello, Mrs Moffat!" Static drew quickly to a halt. "I hiv jist been telling Mal, I've won the coupon!"

Agnes looked passed her unexpected visitor to Mal. "Oh, that's nice son," she said calmly while her expression suggested otherwise, such as Static getting it wrong as he had done in the past. "But if ye don't mind me no jumpin up and doon at the news Static, son, it's no because I'm no happy for ye, or dinnae want tae disturb the neighbours doonstairs, wi plaster falling on their heids, it's jist," Agnes hesitated, not wishing to destroy this moment of happiness for this loveable eejit. "But ye'll mind the last time ye had the coupon up? Ye held a party here, and had bought us a' hooses before the night wis oot..." Agnes halted to let the recollection seep through a thick skull, before continuing in the nicest possible way. "Then it turns oot ye made mair frae the empties…not including yer heid…than ye did frae the coupon!"

Static spread his hands in a gesture of abject apology. "I know. That wis a mistake. But no this time. My Mammy checked it wi me. I think I've got the second dividend!"

"How many draws are there in the coupon anyway, Static?" Mal squeezed himself back into his seat at the table.

"Ten, maybe more."

Mal ran a finger round the rim of the sugar bowl. "If that's the case," he demurred, "the Co-op will maist likely pay a better dividend that your coupon."

Not to be deterred, Static rushed on. "It'll be Wednesday before I'll know how much I've won for sure. Any road, I'll shout ye tae the dancing the night!"

"Static!" Mal warned angrily, tapping the table with the point of his finger. "If we go tae the dancing, ye'll hiv tae promise tae keep yer big gob shut aboot winning the coupon. Okay?"

"Aye anything ye say, Mal." Static gave a briefly exciting version of modern dancing with his hands and shoulders.

"Got an itch, son? Maybe it's yer simmit?" Agnes suggested as she watched Static do his finest interpretation of Rock and Roll.

"An itch tae spend money he disnae have," Mal responded.

Static slapped his pal on the shoulder. "Come on, Mal, let's live it up!"

Mal got to his feet, reconciling himself to the inevitable. "Okay then. As long as ye don't have tae live it doon, ma ba`heided friend."

Mal and Calum leaned against the bath in Oor Bit. Across the uneven field a few weans played their own version of 'rounders'. Calum raised his face to the weak sun.

"Have ye seen Static lately?"

Mal bent to throw back the stray ball. "No for nearly two weeks. No since he won yon pools money."

Calum let out an affectionate laugh. "He's some guy. He wanted tae buy us a new suite."

"Same here," Mal said. "Only wi us it was a telly. I telt him tae keep his money for a rainy day...and knowing oor weather."

"Bought his Mammy wan though."

"Whit a rainy day?" Mal said, tongue in cheek.

Calum stole a glance at Mal. "Jist when I thought I wis safe frae

Static's jokes, you had tae come oot wi something like that."

Mal applauded a 'home run' for a wee dog that had stolen the ball and was now evidently 'belting' it for hame.

"He's bought a Teddy Boy suit, ye know."

"He's whit!" Calum cried incredulously. He turned to stare his cousin in the face, afraid this was another of his weak jokes.

Mal confirmed his world shattering statement with a nod. "You should see it, ye need sunglasses frae the reflection. A nuclear flash hasnae a look in."

"How aboot the hair? He hasnae got himsel a D.A.? No wi a coupon like yon."

The statement regarding Static's complexion may have sounded cruel to an outsider, but to the two pals it was only a matter of fact.

"There's worse."

"No shoes as well?"

Mal made a moue. "Worse still. He's got himsel a wumman."

"Tell me yer joking! Static wi a doll!" Calum took a pace or two away from the bath, the image of Static with a lassie as ludicrous as that of the Queen and Prince Philip arriving at Balmoral on a tandem.

"No joke, Calum, as sure as the Pope's a Catholic."

Mal dug his heel into the wet grass. "Funny, that the poor eejit never had a doll until he won yon coupon money."

For a minute or two, the cousins mulled over the ramifications of their pal being in love, and also of the likelihood of his lady love having more interest in his pocket than his looks. Then again, they told each other, was it their right to interfere and deny Static a chance of happiness, whatever the cost, even if proved correct in their assumption, that it would all end in catastrophe for their pal?

"Whit dae ye think, Mal? Should we have a word wi the poor bugger?"

Mal looked to where the weans having found a new ball were in the act of starting a new game, watched from a distance by a wee dog intent on completing another 'home' run and adding a second ball to its collection. "Maybe we should leave it as it is for the time being. See whit happens. Let nature take its course, so tae speak," Mal suggested.

Calum nodded his agreement, knowing while this decision may not be the correct one, it was at least the easiest. He turned his attention to the iron bath half filled with green slimy water, trailing a finger in the stagnant water. "I see the weans noo a days don't use this much. You couldnae play forts, stagecoaches, or the things we used it fur."

Mal hit out at a passing fly. "Aye nothing stays the same. No even Static," he sighed

It had sounded urgent. Static wanted to meet him at seven o'clock at McDonogal's. Why, Mal thought, did his pal want to meet him in a Catholic pub on the other side of the city?

He hunched his shoulders against the impending cold and prospect of rain, and briskly side stepped a couple with their heads bent against the rising wind. Suddenly, the heavens opened, negating his intentions of waiting outside McDonogal's until Static arrived or poked his head out of the pub door. The rain came down, not the big chunks that mysteriously took a while to soak you, but the wee sleekit kind that had ye drookit in seconds. Intent only on saving his 'good brown suit', (not the Teddy Boy variety), he pushed open the pub door.

It was like a scene out of a 'cowboy picture'. Simultaneously, upon opening the door, all seven heads swung to stare at him. Dominoes ceased, instead of the favoured piano. Mal focused on the bar, or more precisely the clock above it, and shuffled across the sawdust floor in the time it would have taken to cover the length of an Arizona wasteland.

"What will it be then, friend?" The barman surprised him by his lack of an Irish accent.

Mal hastily scanned the row of bottles behind the bar, searching out a whisky to steady his nerves, and was not at all surprised that they should all include the letter 'E' in their spelling. His eyes alighted on the counter pump. He cleared his throat and asked huskily, "I'll have a Guinness." There, that was safe enough.

The barman, a small lean man with a head as bald as a badger's arse, stuck an empty glass under the pump. "The Bhoys did well on Saturday?" The question was as subtle as an Orangeman in the Vatican asking a choir of pontificates to sing a chorus of the Sash.

Badger-heid let the head on the Guinness settle. "Peacock did well tae score."

A trick question, Mal thought, searching his pocket for a half crown. Fortunately for him, he had heard two fans commiserating the absence of this same said player, on the tram on their way home last Saturday night. "I think ye've got it wrang there, pal," he challenged with conviction.

The pint was placed before him. "Aye, maybe ye are right."

Mal's host picked up his half crown. "Havnae seen you in here before."

Mal took a sip of the unfamiliar nectar and wiped foam off his lips. "That's because I havnae been in here before." As if recognising a challenge, the barman's eyes narrowed. Mal hurried to explain. "I'm just passing through."

"Oh, I see."

Mal picked up his change and recrossed the sawdust desert to a table in the corner, where he sat with his back to the wall, as would a notorious gunslinger, a little reassured by the sound of clicking dominoes. He stole a glance at his watch. "Five past seven," he whispered to himself. "Where are ye Static?" He hoped his pal would not be too long in coming, or that this was not some grotesque game on his behalf. "If it is!" Mal fumed. "I'll murder ye. That's if I don't get murdered first."

Two hours later, he stole another glance at his watch. Ten past seven! He thought of the book the Day Time Stood Still.

The door opened, Mal looked up, a suitable witticism already on his lips. Instead, a man came in wearing a long black coat and matching complexion, who scowled at him on his way to the bar. Where the hell was his moron of a pal?

Again, the door opened, this time emitting the figure of a paperboy. Mal bought one and held it up with the intention of hiding behind it, when quite suddenly and, without informing his brain, his hands began to shake, forcing him to drop his paper shield before the draft blew sawdust across the desert onto badger-heid and Dangerous Dan McGrew.

Four door openings later, Static breezed in, nodding to the barman, and 'Dan McGrew' in a way that suggested to Mal he was no stranger to the premises.

"Am I no glad tae see you pal. I thought ye might no come." Static greeted him, pulling out a chair to sit down opposite.

His witticism long forgotten, Mal faced his friend across the table. "Whit's this aw aboot?"

Static pushed back his chair. He pointed to Mal's drink. "Want anither wan?"

Having already sat in abject fear of being found out, if for no other reason than his eyes were blue, Mal was in no mood for niceties. "Ye know fine Static this is no ma tipple," he reproached his friend.

Static's smile remained glued to his lips. "Ye'll no mind if I have wan?" He rose, not awaiting an answer.

Watching Static talk animatedly at the bar, Mal felt a growing uneasiness towards his pal. This was it. Static had finally cracked. All those years of belts on the heid, falling off bikes, straining what little brains he had, had finally done the damage, Static had become a Celtic supporter. There was nae hope!

Static returned from the bar, the same wide grin on his face. "There, I got ye that." He set the glass of whisky down in front of Mal. "I think ye will need it when ye hear what I've got tae say." Apprehensively, Mal waied while Static took a sip of his drink. "Ye know I'm winchin."

Mal nodded. "It's been done afore.

"But, no by me Mal, no by me. That's why I asked ye here the night. I want ye tae meet Mary. We're goin tae get merrit."

Mal choked. Amber nectar spilled down his front, blending in with the colour of his suit, but not his white shirt. Agitatedly, Mal patted his pockets in search of a handkerchief and a suitable reply...such as "yer aff yer heid."

"Ye'll like her." Static went on unperturbed.

Mal wiped his jacket. "When did all this take place? Hiv ye asked the lassie?" He was wiping whisky, but his brain was flashing signals, messages mostly in S.O.S. such as does ye mammie know? Where are ye goin' tae live?

At last, Static's smile slackened. The corrugated face darkened. "That's why I wanted a word wi you first. Ye hiv been good tae me Mal...always trying tae make sure I didnae make a fool o masel...well no too often," he grinned. "I really am in love, pal."

Embarrassed by his friend's sincerity, Mal toyed with his glass. "So whit's the problem? Besides the usual wans," he asked trying to sound cheerful.

Static looked his lifelong friend straight in the face. "Mary's a Catholic, Mal."

Mal could not have been more surprised if he had been told Rangers had signed an English Pygmy from Siberia as their new goalie. His surprise must have shown, considering that his shaking hand still fought to keep the contents of an empty whisky glass from spilling. Or that his mouth had fallen wide open, for the ever observant Static to remark. "Are ye surprised, Mal?"

"Surprised!" Mal croaked, eyeing his empty glass despairingly. "Wiped oot, mair likely." His despair all the more transparent by his friend's next remark.

"Och! Ye'll get tae like her," he reassured him.

Get! Get! The word suggested permanency.

Mal leaned forward on the table, his elbow catching the edge of the newspaper. "Hiv ye thought this thing through? Discussed it wi` yer Mammy, for instance. You know mixed marriages never work!"

"It will this time…and it's nae use ye trying tae talk me oot o it, my mind is made up," Static said defiantly, standing up. "I'll get us anither drink afore Mary turns up."

Mal's mind fought to shake off its state of shock while his friend returned with the drinks.

Static sat the glass down in front of Mal with a happy thump before sitting down. "So…will ye be ma Best Man?"

"Have ye set the date?" Mal's question sounded more like a hanging than a wedding.

"Four weeks come Friday. We couldnae get the Co. Hall for the Saturday. It'll mean ye havin tae take the day aff work."

"Who says I'll take the job?" Mal asked his friend angrily, and Static's complexion went an even deeper red than usual.

Inwardly, Mal cursed himself, not having wished to hurt his pal, but hoping the points he had raised might have brought the poor eejit to his senses. He lifted his glass. "I suppose ye've worked oot where yer goin tae live?"

Static's face brightened a little on the assumption that his pal`s change of subject was his way of accepting his invitation. He nodded over his raised glass. "With ma Mammy. Ye see, there is nae room in Mary's hoose, for besides her Ma and Da…."

"God!" Mal thought, he's already began tae learn their language. Now there is nae hope for the daft soul!

"There's her two brothers, Patrick and Joseph."

"Whit aboot weans?" Mal asked.

Static shook his head. "Nae weans. Jist Patrick and Joseph."

Mal bunched his fists in frustration. "I didnae mean that, ye daft eejit. I mean whit happens when you have weans? Besides it being a national disaster, how are yis goin` tae manage in wan wee room?"

"Nae worries pal. I'll put ma name doon for a council hoose. Then by the time the weans arrive, we'll hiv a place o oor ain."

"Yer telling me ye hivnae discussed this wi yer Mammy? Whit if she says no?"

Static ran his drink around his mouth, savouring the flavour if not the question. "It'll be a'right, Mary's a nice lassie."

"Yer Mammy might not want her in her hoose."

"Because she's a Catholic?" Static cried in disbelief.

Mal waved away the protest. "Naw, ye daft gowk, 'cause she's a wumman. Women don't like other women in their kitchen!"

Static stared at the clock. "She's late." He swung back to Mal, implying in a tone that wanted to convince himself as much as his pal. "Mammy's no like that, she'll like Mary. They'll get on like a hoose on fire."

"Not a good metaphor, Static. Fire suggests smoke...possibly blue smoke."

However, there was one subject Mal wanted to broach but did not quite know how, as he was unsure how Static would react, being well aware of his friend`s temper. He drew a finger across a pool of whisky he'd spilled on the table, and asked cautiously, "You havnae thought it even a wee bit funny that this...Mary and her folks should take ye into the bosom of their family, just like that?" He snapped his fingers, to emphasis his point. "Winning the coupon widnae hiv anything to dae with it?" Now he had said it. Watch Static's fists and await his reaction.

"I knew it wid come right doon tae that," Static chuckled. "There never has been the slightest reference tae money by either Mary or her family."

"But they know aboot the money?" Mal asked, now relieved he was not going to be beaten up by a fellow Prodie in a Catholic pub.

"Of course. I couldnae ask tae marry Mary and hiv them thinking I wis a nae user. A Protestant wan at that! Although, I agreed tae pay for the wedding, seeing as they are no that well aff. The men being on the Bru."

"I don't suppose ye mean Irn Bru by any chance, Static?"

"Naw, Static grinned. "Maybe I should see Social Services aboot the big day and see if they will no gee us a State wedding?"

State is right, Mal thought. "Talking aboot weddings, Static, is this wan in the chapel by per chance? If it is, expect tae be ostracised."

"I thought only the Jews went in fur that!" Static exclaimed.

Mal fell for his pal's deadpan expression. "I said ostracised, no circumcised! Honestly, Static!"

"I know fine what it means," Static said, in disgust. "So folk will either have tae accept me and Mary fur whit we are, or jist leave us alane. Okay?"

Mal's eyes had rested admiringly on a young woman who had entered the bar as he spoke. She was a beauty. Probably, a Catholic though. Nae chance there, Mal, thought. Raven black hair, flashing eyes, peaches and cream complexion as they sang about in songs.

He turned back to his friend. "So it all hinges on yer Mammy…and the poor soul disnae even know aboot you and this…"

"Hello Andrew. Sorry I'm late. I was held up at the shop."

At the sound of the voice, Mal stared up into the face of the raven-haired beauty.

"Mal, I would like ye to meet Mary." Static rose to put an arm around the girl, who in turn flashed a smile in Mal's direction.

"So this is Mal, the one you keep telling me about. Pleased to meet you, Mal. I think I know you quite well already," she said, with perfect diction.

"Same here...eh...Mary," Mal stammered rising.

Two hours, and several whiskies later, Mal staggered onto the last tram. He had done his damnedest to lay before his pal all the pitfalls associated with such a marriage and had failed. So be it. But what had confounded him most was the lassie. Even before he had laid eyes on her, he had decided not to like her, and had made himself believe, considering his pals looks, that all she could ever be after was his money. And, although he had sat there listening to the 'patter', and watching for the slightest hint of false affection on her behalf, he had to admit there had been none. What was worse she seemed to genuinely love the big eejit. Worse still, and it hurt his Protestant pride and upbringing to admit it, he liked her too.

This prompted him to think of how many times he had heard the old adage, "A awfy nice lassie, and a Catholic too!" As if there were only two good things in the world. A Protestant, and a Protestant referee at Parkhead.

Maybe he would see thing different...if not clearer in the morning. He'd better, for now that he was assistant manager in his grocery shop, he had a responsibility to himself and his staff. And, with that thought, promptly fell asleep until 'chucked aff' by an endearing clippie for having passed his stop.

The weather had held, which was more than he could say for his nerves. Determined to offend no one, Mal offered his sweetest smile to the guests entering the Co-op hall, giving himself an invisible pat on the back on how well the ceremony had gone. And at how he'd managed not to have bobbed up, when the rest were bobbing doon.

However, he had been right in thinking that the loving couple would not be the only hitch that day. For, when it had come to present, the ring he had found that it had managed to slip through the lining of his rented claw hammer suit pocket.

Giving the priest and the betrothed couple an apologetic smile, and doing his best to ignore a few disparaging remarks from the assembled congregation, he had, at last, after much rummaging and impersonation of a demented Penguin with a hernia, produced the ring, and had hurriedly laid it down on the open Bible, only to find to his horror it was not the ring at all but a partially chewed Polo Mint. His second rummaging had taken even longer before the correct article had been produced, prompting someone in the front pew to mutter 'daft Prodie' or some other such similar comment.

Mal put out a hand to help a lady up the front steps, wearing a flower basket on her head.

Carmen Miranda glared up at him. "Git lost, oor Mal, I'm no that haunless yet."

"Sorry Aunt Jenny, I didnae recognise ye wi that..."

"Jist you try and say it oor Mal!" his aunt challenged.

"Good fur you son!" his Uncle Jimmy, chuckled, giving him a congratulatory pat on the back. "I'll meet ye inside wi the watering can."

The bridal party were already seated at the top table, which stood at right angles to two other tables running lengthways of the hall. Static gave Mal an encouraging wink; he reciprocated by patting his top pocket to indicate all was well in hand.

"You all right, Mrs Little?" Mal asked, and had his hand squeezed in appreciation as he sat down beside his pal's mum.

She seemed right out of it here at the top table as he himself did, which is why, foregoing protocol he had elected to sit beside her.

"Andrew did well, dae ye no think so, son?" Mrs Little whispered, her eyes fixed somewhere on the far wall.

Mal put a reassuring hand on top of hers. "It'll work oot all right." Athough whether he meant the marriage or the rest of the evening, or both he was not quite sure.

"Did it go a right in the chapel?" Calum came up behind them, squatted down and poked his head between their two chairs. He, as had the rest of the 'Prodies', having refrained from attending the wedding itself, with the exception of Mal and Static's mother. "Frae where I was sitting, ye a look like the Nuremberg Trial ower here!" Calum gave a strangely stilted laugh.

"Mair like the Last Supper," Mal countered.

Calum drew closer to his pal. He gave a little nod to the barely half full table from where he had been sitting, comparing it to the other full one. "If it comes doon tae another Battle o the Boyne, we're in trouble."

"Wheest, Calum. Let's no start anything." Mal threw his neighbour an embarrassing smile, and hoped he had not overhead.

"Sorry. I better get back tae ma seat. Here come the Penguins."

Their heels tapping on the bare wooden floor, a row of black clad, white lace-aproned waitresses appeared, marching down between the tables, each carrying trays of steaming food.

"Steak pie! Whose for steak pie?" the leading waitress chanted, and was answered by a forest of arms raised by the 'short table' and moans of despair from the 'long one'.

"Oh no!" Mal squeezed Mrs Little's hand in dejection. "Steak pie, and it's Friday!" He was glad however when a second Penguin announced that there was a choice of fish and chips for those who did not wish steak pie.

The Penguins, their job done, had made their exit, the sound of a rattled spoon on glass, announcing that Father Flynn, would now say Grace. Heads went down. Amen. Heads came up.

A little later, Mal reached for his third glass of water. Nerves had begun to get the better of him. Now, he wished he had not remembered his duties until after he'd finally finished his meal. If he were to drink any more water, they'd all have to crowd into the toilet to hear him read the telegrams.

Static stuck his head round his new bride. "Mal?"

Mal screwed up his face. "Aye, I know. All right pal." The sound of his chair scraping on the floor as he rose, acted as a signal for complete silence in the hall, or to him, a deathly hush.

Introductions and appreciations over, Mal lifted the first telegram and began to read, ending with the same witticism as most of the others were to do. "And may all your troubles be Little ones...Uncle Pat and Aunt Maria," to the accompaniment of polite applause and inquiring nudges as to whom the senders might be.

By the time most of the telegrams had been read out, Mal was sweating, although the atmosphere in the hall was about as warm as a Polar Bear's arse. He started on the last message of congratulations and best wishes, holding the slip of paper closer to read, "Always oor wee boy, Aunt Lizzie, and Uncle Bob."

Static tilted his chair back to converse with his mother. "That wis nice o them Mammy. Pity they couldnae be here."

Suddenly, it occurred to Mal that although he had known Static since schooldays, he still knew practically nothing about his family. In fact, Mal thought if it was not for his and Calum's relatives, plus a few of Static's work mates and pals, he would have no guests here at all.

Aware of the silence Mal put down the last telegram and cleared his throat. This was it. Break the ice wi a few jokes Static had urged him at last night's stag party, where, he had to admit, the groom to be, had behaved rather well, despite the usual ragging, and other not so sophisticated tricks. Again, he cleared his throat. Again, there were the impatient coughs. All eyes from the 'fish' table dared him to make them laugh, or whatever he intended doing.

"I must say," he began.

"Oh no, you don't!" some wag shouted up from the 'fish' table, followed by the first genuine laughter of the evening.

Mal smiled back, and dearly would have loved to have strangled the interloper, for now he would have to start again. "As I was saying before I was rudely interrupted." He smiled to ensure that everyone knew it was a joke. "After hearing Mrs Rafferty giving her daughter advice, it has put me right off ever thinking about tying the knot."

A few stared at him blankly, his mother's expression clearly advising him to proceed with caution. "For I heard her say to Mary, 'There's nothing to be afraid of dear. First, you walk down the aisle, halt in front of the Alter then you sing a Hymn. And if you remember these three things throughout your married life, you will never go wrong. Remember, Aisle, alter, hymn!"

"Good for ye Mal!" someone shouted out from the pie table, and to his utter astonishment more than a little polite applause from the fish.

"So you see Mrs Rafferty," Mal turned to where the woman sat. "You're not really losing a daughter but gaining a Little...Andrew to be precise." Again applause, this time less forced. Mal took a deep breath and continued, grateful that he had read these quips in the newspaper. "When Mary went in to sign the register, she found that the pen would not work, however the good Father came to her aid, and bending over her, said. 'Put your full weight on it dear.' So Mary wrote nine stone five." This time, the laughter and applause was noticeably louder. The ice, though not broken, had at least cracked.

Later, they stood around in their own wee groups while the tables were being cleared, only the bride and groom circulated, unafraid of contamination from the unknown.

Eventually, the couple wove through congratulations to where Mal stood with his own folks and Static's mother.

"How's it goin so far, dae ye think?" Static asked the company in general, giving his mother an affectionate squeeze.

"Never mind that, Sta...Drew," Agnes hastily corrected herself in front of Mrs Little. "Where are yer manners? Ye havnae introduced me tae yer bride!"

"Sorry, Mrs Moffat...Mary, I wid like ye tae meet ma good friends, Mal's mother, Calum and his folks."

Mary smiled sweetly, amid protests that she would be unable to remember all of their names.

Calum drew Mal aside. "She's a wee smasher, Mal. How in the name o the wee man did a bloke like Static manage tae get a haud o something like that...and her a..."

"Don't say it!" Mal warned. "If I hear that again, I promise you I'll turn a Catholic masel."

Calum drew back, taken aback by Mal's unexpected rebuke. "Nae offence pal. Nae offence."

The women had commandeered the bride, while a little further away the men stood clustered around the groom, laughing and joking until an announcement that a bar had been set up in the anti-room had them drifting in that direction, headed by the groom's father-in-law and his sons, the former with an affectionate arm around his new 'son'.

Aware of a sudden draft, Mal looked towards the door, where Ian Shaw struggled across the floor under the weight of his squeeze box'.

"Good tae see ye Ian," Mal greeted him, hurrying to take the big black box from him.

"It's a right Mal, I'm used to it."

Mal helped him up the stairs to the stage. "Ye found the place aw right?" he asked, offering a nod and a smile to a tall thin man, who was heaving more from the affects of the cigarette, hanging from the corner of his mouth, than the weight of his drum kit.

"Nae bother. Been here afore." Ian dropped his box, and ran an eye over his 'customers' below.

"You sure ye can cope, Ian? We've got mixed company the night, so no breaking into the 'Sash' or any o they provocative songs. Okay?"

"Aye, nae bother pal." Ian opened up his box. "However, whit do we do aboot requests? Such as the Soldiers Song, or the Wearing of the Green? If ye take my meaning, as we are here to please."

Mal eyed his former school pal belligerently. "Jist take wan request frae me, don't play any. Okay?"

Wee Ian lifted his squealing instrument from its case. "Sure, Mal, sure. Anything ye say. As I said afore, we're here tae please."

The tables had now been cleared away and guests began to seat themselves, one long row on one side of the hall, a shorter one on the other. Already, Mal envisaged the dancing evolving into one large group at one end of the hall, and one small one at the other. The Co-op's answer to the Iron Curtain.

Laughter, strangely out of place, burst out of the anti-room. At least some were enjoying themselves. Mal descended the stage steps and nodded up to wee Ian.

There was a whine from the microphone followed by Ian inviting the guests to take their partners for the first waltz.

A few heads looked this way and that. Buxom middle-aged ladies clung to their handbags on their laps as a means of defence, or made quite unnecessary adjustments to their attire. Weans, sensing the calm before the storm, scurried off the floor for the protection of their parents.

Wee Ian and his band struck up, and the floor remained as empty as a Cranhill street when the polis came looking for someone to help them with their enquiries. Four choruses and five verses later, the floor's sole occupants were a five year old boy and his baby sister. The first weans they'd ever seen in their lives, by the look of interest from both sides of the hall, where there were also a few muffled inquiries as to whom the children may belong. Or, was this perhaps the floorshow put on by the co-op, or just weans left behind from the last wedding?

Despairingly, Mal glanced up at wee Ian and shrugged. Ian shrugged back and squeezed out a few louder notes.

Out of the corner of his eye, the Best Man caught sight of the happy couple being ushered on to the floor by the good Father, who, his duty done, returned to his seat. A small cheer of encouragement followed as the couple started to glide around the floor.

Watching them, he offered up a prayer of thanks that Static and he had been taught at school, as it was now his own duty to seek out the Chief Bridesmaid and follow his pal onto the floor.

Having found his partner, Mal swung her round gracefully in time to the music. She, unlike the bride, was of slightly different proportions, and articulation. "Ye think I had the plague, or something. Dinnae come near me at the table. Are aw Prodies like you?"

Mal looked into her upturned face, wishing to state he was one of the nicer ones, and also suggest she heel to starboard and get aff his feet before they ran out of dance floor. Instead he said, "Sorry, but Sta…Andrew's mother was a wee bit nervous, so I sat beside her."

"Nice of you." She nodded her approval, if not forgiveness.

By the time the dance had ended, a few more had joined the happy couple. The music also ended Mal's interrogation as to his connection with the groom. Now, he needed a drink.

The makeshift bar was crowded: faces lit up with booze, grinned foolishly while they listened to folk talking just as foolishly. He looked around in search of a face he knew. Calum stood in a corner surrounded by Bobby Jackson and some of Static's work mates, who were already well into their cups. Calum saw him and waved him across.

"Where's the lucky man?" Bobby asked, referring to the groom. "Under the thumb already, is he?" he tittered.

"Ask him yersel, Bobby." Mal nodded to where Static was threading his way through little groups of drinkers to join them.

"How's it goin', you lot? I thought ye'd be oot there dancing."

"Early yet, Static," one replied, hiccupping slightly. "Need a swally or two tae get started."

"Aye, there's no that many tae choose frae," another ventured to proclaim.

"There's plenty." Static stared accusingly at his guest.

"Och! Ye know whit I mean," his guest replied, finding his glass suddenly interesting.

Mal saw Static's face turn a warning red. The last thing they needed was the groom fighting with one of his Prodie guests.

Bobby Jackson saw the danger. "My, Static, that wis a good speech ye gave." He forced a laugh. "Whit dae ye think boys? On behalf of my wife and myself..." He mimicked.

Static's complexion relaxed. "Dae ye think so, Bobby?"

"Of course, I wid no be saying it if I didnae mean it. I liked how ye telt aboot taking Mary oot for the first time tae that posh restaurant. How ye tried tae impress her by lighting her fag wi a candle, the way they dae in the pictures, and burnt her nose!" The group guffawed, and the tension eased.

Static spied his new in-laws. "I better away and mingle as they say in the best of circles, as well as the back stalls, I believe," he said, now back to his jovial self, and willing to forgive any small misunderstanding that may have arisen amongst pals.

"You dae that Static," Bobby nodded in agreement, adding to help things along, "we'll be oot shortly tae help wi the jigging." He turned from the disappearing figure to add with a sigh. "Poor bugger."

"Whit dae ye mean?" Sammy asked.

"Well. Look who he is mixed in wi. Yon Rafferty looks a right waster, and his sons don't look much better."

"He didnae marry the Faither, Bobby." Mal hastened to defend his friend.

Bobby took a sip of his beer as if deciding whether or not it was worth pursuing the subject, then, obviously thinking it was not, gave a dismissive shrug of his shoulders.

"Come on, this is a wedding. Static's wedding, and I need a drink." Mal said in a way that suggested they forget what was just said.

"Yer right, Mal," another said. "Come on we could all do with a drink."

The evening had escalated into a talent competition, where both sides had put forward their most talented singers and dancers. Mal had just returned from the bar in time to hear the 'fish' side's best singer, a woman of indeterminate age 'geeing it wally' as they say, finishing to thunderous applause from the bride's relatives.

Not to be outdone, Mal's Aunt Maisie, representing the 'pies' had brought along three of her young dancers, who tripping lightly on to the middle of the hall floor, took up stances for the start of the Irish Jig, greeted by a little above average applause from the bride's side, who appreciated, if not the gesture, at least the three wee girls attired in green skirts and Shamrock bedecked aprons, anxiously watched by a perspiring teacher.

"I brought along wee Bridgette because she's wan o them," Maisie confided to her sister Agnes. "She's no that good, so let's hope she disnae fa on her arse as she did at rehearsal."

Mal, together with his cousin Calum, had decided to forego the competition, electing instead to mourn the loss of a good friend, and despite his resolution to remain in control of his senses Mal was now practically legless. "Wan doon, wan tae go!" he commiserated, an arm round Calum.

"A don't know aboot you Mal, but I think I'll wait a wee while. See how things turn oot wi Static."

Mal hiccupped, unable to fathom why there were now two barrels of Guinness on the bar top when a moment ago there had only been one; and why there should be one dead man with four arms hugging both barrels.

"Jist think, it wasnae that long since we were a playin at Oor Bit." Calum wiped his nose with the back of his hand to muffle a sob. "Who wid ever have thought that it wid come tae this?" Sobbing harder.

"Yer right there, Calum." Mal fought back an accompanying sob. "We've failed. We should have taken mair care of the daft eejit. Noo it's too late. Nae mair Oor Bit for him."

"Dae ye think his weans will ever play there? Keep the tradition going so tae speak?" Calum sobbed harder and louder at his paralytic friend.

"Don't say things like that when I've been drinking, Calum. The image o wee Statics running aboot is jist too much to bear."

Calum had not thought of that. In fact, Calum was rapidly becoming incapable of thinking anything. "It's a good job we don't know whit's in front of us." His head slowly made the acquaintance of his chest.

Mal lifted his drink. "Nae use worrying aboot Static's weans. A lot can happen before that disaster."

"Like whit, for example?" Calum mumbled, his nose in mid discovery of a missing button on his shirt-front.

Mal threw out an arm. "Like the world being hit wi a haemorrhoid frae outer space. Whit a bum way tae go."

"Yer right. Whit a bummer."

Dejected by their friend's fate, Calum made a brave attempt to rise. "Come on, cheer up, Mal. Let's get oot o here and see whit's happening. You're the Best Man, ye know. Have ye had a dance wi the bridesmaid?"

Mal rifted. "Aye, but I've got ower that noo, the circulation's back in ma feet. Talk aboot a weight aff yer mind! "

Calum lunged against the wall for support. The wall, anticipating the lunge, moved away.

"Whit are ye doin doon there Calum? There are plenty of seats."

With the aid of a chair, and the back of someone's jacket, Calum hauled himself drunkenly back on to his feet.

Yells of enjoyment, mingled with hoots of laughter, invaded the anti-room and both cousins staggered to the door, where on the hall floor a Paul Jones was in full swing, the two 'sides' for the first time 'mixing' it, however unavoidably.

Mal staggered to the foot of the stage, where wee Ian, accordion in full swing, winked down at him.

"Look at the state of you, and you supposed to be the Best Man!"

Mal shifted his cumbersome weight around to face his mother. "'Saw right Mammy. Want a dance?"

Mrs Moffat glared at her son. "Dance! I'll gie ye dance!"

Unable to control himself at his mother's angry expression, Mal sniggered.. "So ye think yer son cannae dance? I could gie exhibitions if I'd like." He put his arms out invitingly.

Agnes pushed them aside. "Ye'll make a right exhibition o yersel, aw right. Show us up ye will in front o them." She jerked her head where the 'fish' were mainly seated. "Jist when everything is starting tae go well."

Mal took a hazy look at the floor full of dancing swirling feet. "How did this happen?" he hiccuped, steadying himself against the stage.

"Mary's side liked yer auntie's wee dancers. I think seeing them wi their Irish rig oots did it, for the next thing I knew everybody was clapping and cheering."

Agnes stopped to glare at her son. "But why I'm I telling you this? Yer supposed tae be the Best Man! Heaven help us!"

The dance ended to howls of delight and uproarious applause, the dancers making their way towards their respective sides of the hall.

Giving them time to settle, Ian drew his microphone closer, announcing. "And now Mr Gerry Mulligan will favour the company with a song." Amid much clapping from his relatives, and surprising encouragement from the others, the singer ran lightly up the stage steps.

Mal slapped his swaying cousin on the back. "Come on, let's hiv another wan until this joker's finished."

By the time the inebriated duo had returned, the warbling crooner still stood on stage, wee Ian's microphone held expertly in one hand, a smoking cigarette in the other, 'geeing it wally' as they say in some circles; probably the same ones as Static had referred to earlier. After the third restart of the present rendition, and a few accusing looks at the pianist, 'Frank Sinatra' started again, this time exonerating the pianist vainly trying to follow him, by blaming his failure to comply to his usual standards, on the smoke from his cigarette.

"Gee him a pint, and tell him tae sit on his arse." A far from sober Bobby Jackson suggested, turning back to the anti-room.

"Could you do better?" A wee bald headed man asked, hooking his thumbs under a pair of green braces.

Bobby brushed past him into the anti-room where someone lay asleep over the makeshift bar top, his arms lovingly encompassing a beer barrel.

"A pint of something better than that," Bobby requested of the barman and pointed stiffly to the barrel.

"You can't get better than that," the volunteered barman responded, none too friendly.

"He's right, friend," the wee man in the braces confirmed. "Guinness is good for you."

"A lot o good it's done you," Bobby challenged. "Seeing as yer aboot the right height for toasting breed at ma Granny's grate."

The little man let go of his braces, his eyes bulging. "There is no need for cheek, young man. Where I come from, young folk respect their elders."

Sammy came into the room. "Where wid that be, grandpa? Ireland?"

"No. It's no. I am as Scottish as you are," the wee man fired back.

Tripping in behind Static's work mates, the cousins steadied themselves against the swaying wall.

"Scottish, is it?" Bobby sneered. "That widnae be Dublin Scottish, by any chance?"

The scene was rapidly turning ugly, matching the mood and complexion of those entering the bar, drawing Mal out of his drunken stupor.

The wee man, more confident now that reinforcements were arriving drew closer to Bobby. "Let me ask ye something, son?" He peered up into the taller man's face. "How many Prodies were there at the Battle of Bannockburn?" The wee man gave a short tantalising laugh.

"No as many as they were at the Battle of the Boyne!" Bobby quickly countered.

"That's it!" The wee man gasped. "You Prodies have been waiting all night to get that one in!" So saying, the wee man raised himself on to his toes, and aimed a blow at his antagonists chin, who, spurred on by a burst of passing adrenaline on its way to his head, hit out at the Leprechaun, both men missing and landing on the floor on top of one another.

Instantly, the barman let out an oath and quickly ran to protect his supply, as the fighting became general. Two of Static's work mates proceeded to hang the Leprechaun on a coat hook, where he commenced to yo-yo by the elastic of his braces, shouting and swearing, while implying that none of the cowardly attackers had birth certificates.

It happened too swiftly for Mal's fuddled brain to comprehend, although somewhere a voice at the back of his brain was telling him he must do something. "That's enough!" He stood up without the aid of the wall. "Listen! I'm the Best Man!"

"Prove it!" someone challenged, and hit him on the mouth.

Mal staggered under the blow, passing Calum on the way down, who was himself unsuccessfully trying to get back off the floor.

How it would all have ended no one was to know, for at that moment Static appeared, hurling bodies out of the way as he cut a swathe to the centre of the room. "Will yee's no stop! It's supposed tae be a wedding, Mary's and mine, ye crowd o naiffs!" He boomed out above the cries of anger and injury.

Little by little, the antagonists backed away from one another, leaving the groom centre stage. "I'm ashamed of yis a. Bigots! That's whit yis are! Mary and me invited ye here as oor guests tae celebrate oor marriage! The beginning o a new life for us baith. And look at yis!" Static's eyes slowly encompassed the room, until they found Mal. "And you Mal. I made you ma Best Man, seein' as you were ma pal."

It was the worst moment of Mal's life. Static had entrusted this duty to him and he had failed. Static, the class dunce, the one with no brains, who was the only sensible one here. He made a gesture to express his apology, but Static had turned his back on him, arguably for the first time in his life. He felt sick, and not from the drink.

A row of angry faced women blocked the anti-room door, Mary amongst them, until she disappeared behind a group of women pushing themselves to the front.

One jerked a thumb in the direction of the dance floor, another wagged an accusing finger, a third with a face like thunder stood there arms akimbo in the narrow doorway.

"Oot! Oot oor Mal" said the first.

"It's past yer bedtime Calum." The second commanded.

"So this is whit ye dae when ma back is turned!" The third accused.

Mal took a hesitant step forward. Nervously, not knowing what his friend's reaction might be, he tried. "Jist like auld times in Oor Bit, being cried in. Whit dae ye say, Static?"

To his relief, Static's face broke into a reluctant smile. "Aye. Maybe no quite the same."

"Come on you lot!" Mrs Rafferty pushed through the crowded doorway. "Is this a wedding or a wake, be Jesus?" Her eyes flew to her husband at the bar. "And as for you, Pat Rafferty, you should be ashamed of yourself. And don't think you two have got away with it, either," she demanded of her sons.

In the main hall, the Palais Glide had just ended to an empty floor. The guests in the doorway, dispersing now that the second floor show of the evening was over, allowing Mal to make an almost straight line to the foot of the stage where he suggested to wee Ian that he strike up another Paul Jones, whereby, the floor was quickly crowded, all happy to exchange partners, and only too eager to forget the recent altercation.

Also, unfortunately, all had forgotten the wee bald headed man, who still dangled from his braces from a coat hook in the anti-room.

Chapter 14

Somehow, it had seemed natural to have headed for Oor Bit after Bob Mitchell's funeral, even though they were only vaguely aware of having done so.

Mal leaned against the old bath, the focal point of all their recent meetings so it seemed.

"Sad day," Mal said quietly. "I felt that sorry for Mrs Mitchell at the funeral. Doesnae seem so long ago since we were training his wee dug."

Static examined the ground from where he stood at the head of the bath, as if seeing the images of those bygone days in every blade of grass. "Dae ye mind…" he started with a chuckle, and began to relate some of the funnier episodes when training the dog, with the cousins joining in.

Their reminiscences over, Calum tapped a heel on the side of the bath. "Two years since ye got hung, Static?" he asked casually.

"Seems longer" Static replied dolefully.

Mal cast an eye at his cousin, then back to Static. "Nae trouble I hope, pal?"

Static flicked a toe at the grass. "No really, jist two women in the same hoose." He quickly qualified his remark before his pals jumped to the wrong conclusion. "It's no that Mary and ma Mammy don't get on, its jist, they both have their ain way of doing things. That, and the fact it's no a very big hoose. Sometimes Mammy sits doon tae watch wan programme on the telly, and me and Mary would like tae watch another wan. Wee things like that."

"Why no buy two tellies?" Calum suggested. "You and Mary could watch whit yis like frae wan room and leave the kitchen tae yer Mammy."

"We thought o that. Except for the noise. We'd finish up listening tae each other's programme while watching oor ain. Besides, whit dae ye thing the neighbours wid say?"

"While knocking doon the wall?" Mal chuckled.

"Exactly, Mal," Static agreed.

"Ye'll jist have tae get yer ain hoose," Calum said stiffly.

"Oor names are doon on the list. But how long we will have tae wait is anybody's guess."

"Buy wan. Ye've got the money." It was out before Calum could check himself.

Static, much to their surprise gave a nonchalant shrug. "Ye mean the coupon money? That wis a long while ago."

Calum chanced a look at Mal, who returned a look implying, that since he was stupid enough to have raised the subject, he may as well continue, and should he get his heid kicked in fur being so nosey, not to blame him.

Calum cleared his throat in preparation to his next question, calculating how much speed he may have lost since he had stopped training all those years ago. "Ye havnae gone through all the money, surely?" There, it was said. Should he start running now?

Surprisingly, Static gave another indifferent shrug. "Mary's folk have been oot o work fur quite a long while. I try tae help oot noo and again."

So that was it, Mal thought. The Raffertys' had taken the poor bugger for a ride. It was as they had all suspected. Static had been accepted, religion and all, just so long as his money held out. Then what? Would the remonstrations begin on how they knew their Mary had married beneath herself. What had she ever seen in a pockmarked eejit, etc.

Now that the subject had been broached, and, out of concern for his friend, Mal decided to ask what Mary thought of it all.

Static, kicked the side of the bath, and gave his fingernails a close inspection. "She doesnae know. I didn't want tae worry her." He hitched himself on to the bath. "Ye see, she is no like the rest of her family. Mary's refined. Ye've heard her talking. Dead posh is she no? She's worked hard since she left school in yon dress shop. No like her brothers..."

"Wasters?" Mal suggested.

"Aye. Wasters." Static's jaw tightened. "But that's the last. They'll get no more frae me. Ye wid think I was their ain personal Social Services or something. We'll need whit's left tae furnish oor hoose when we get it."

Static levered himself off the bath, to face his friends. "I really love the lassie. She has been good tae ma Mammy as weel. Always willing tae help in the hoose as best she can. We never really quarrel. And she saves every penny."

"Then it's no right, that Mary should work her feet aff, so you can gee the money tae her no use brothers," Calum snapped, angry at what had happened to his pal.

"I wonder if oor weans will ever play here." Mal gazed across the open stretch of ground, his change of subject deliberate.

"The country's no ready for that," Static told him seriously. "Besides, there is something called marriage before that happens. Weans don't jist appear ye know."

"I did," Calum challenged. "According to my Mammy, I came doon wi a shower o rain."

"Ye must have landed on yer heid," Static replied grimly.

"Aye, weans are a miracle," Calum confirmed with all the solemnity of a high court judge. "I was jist reading in the paper the other day aboot a woman wi two wombs."

"That's nothing," Mal said, curling up his nose. "My Mammy has two wooms and a kwitchen."

Calum made a moue at Static and the old joke. "No so much a miracle as the wean born ootside the fallopian tube." His look dared his pals to repudiate his statement.

"Whit do ye make o that Static?" Mal asked. "Wonders will never cease."

Static gestured he was unimpressed. "I hope it didnae catch cold waiting on the platform."

"No that sort of tube ye eejit!" Calum stormed.

Static's eyes gleamed. "Ye tell me that, do ye?"

Calum shot a look at his cousin then back to Static. "No again! See you and your humour, Static!"

They turned for home. Despite the solemnity of the day, and, at other such times in their lives, there was still a place to which they could turn. A place immune from all sad and bad things in life. There was always Oor Bit.

Humming happily, Mrs Little closed the oven door. One week! One whole week with the house to herself! The woman glanced at the clock on the wall. Mary had been given the Saturday morning off work in order to catch the three o'clock train to Ayr, where she and Andrew were to spend their week's holiday. She would be in soon.

Andrew would be in a little later as he was going to pick up some paint for their new house which they had just learned they had acquired: the second reason for her happiness.

Not that she did not like Mary in the house. Bless her, she was the best thing that had ever happened to her son. But, again, it was her house, and although she would miss them, it would be nice to do as she pleased for a while.

She heard the door close and Mary's footstep in the lobby.

"Hello Mary hen! The dinner's nearly ready!" She greeted her daughter-in -law with a cheery smile.

"Thanks Mrs Little, my feet are really killing me. I'll change my shoes and come and help you."

"No need, everything is ready. Jist waiting for Andrew when he comes in wi the paint. So, ye jist go and make yersel ready, and make sure ye don`t miss the train."

Slipping her shoes off, Mary headed for the bedroom door. "We should be using this week to decorate the house instead of going off on holiday, but Andrew would not hear of it."

"And quite right, too. You both need the break. Ye have the rest o yer lives tae get the hoose ready." Mrs Little waved a hand. "Noo away and get yersel packed."

It was a full twenty minutes before a red-faced Static appeared, pots of paint under his arms.

His mother threw a sharp look at the clock, the way mothers do when they are about to scold their offspring for not being as organised as they themselves would have been. But then who would be? "If ye don't want tae miss yer train, ye better get a jildy on." The woman of the house emphasised her displeasure with a flick of her cloth.

"Plenty of time. No tae worry." Static stacked the paint in the lobby cupboard, beside the rolls of wallpaper.

Mary came out of the bedroom at the same time as her husband entered the kitchen.

"Hello, Mary!" Static gave his wife a smile. His intention of further conversation with his wife terminated by his mother urging them both to the table. "Wis ye busy the day, Mary?" Static lifted his fork to a steaming plate of mince and tatties.

"I should say I was. Run clean off my feet."

"Less o the gabbin, you two, and get on with yer dinner," Mrs Little rebuked, adding in the same breath, "Are you both packed?"

The older woman decided it had been an eventful week. What, with these two going on holiday, and getting a new house, and her best friend Sarah McKinlay leaving to join her son and his wife in

Australia! She gave a little flick of her head. Sarah was giving up her house too...and at her age! Which reminded her she must return Sarah's rent book and spare key to the Council, as she said she would. She would miss Sarah, they had been friends since first meeting at the Women's Guild all those years ago.

"Mammy!" Static had finished his dinner and was emerging from the bedroom carrying two suitcases, interrupting her reflections. "If ye see Calum or Mal, ask them if they will take the paper and paint roon tae the new hoose."

The woman eyed her son sharply. "I thought ye telt me, yer pals didnae know ye had a hoose yet? And here ye are asking me tae do yer dirty work for ye."

Static set down the cases. "They'll no mind. They can see the hoose at the same time. The address is on the label on the key."

Although she did not relish the idea, but badly wanted to see the back of her lodgers, the woman held her tongue and ushered them to the door, as if denying two diarrhoea sufferers the use of her newly cleaned toilet. Then with a flurry of goodbyes, they were gone.

It was Monday night when the two cousins entered the close, where they caught Mrs Little returning from the 'midde' where she had been busy emptying her pail.

"Hello Mrs Little. We heard Drew has got a hoose," Mal greeted the woman enthusiastically.

"That's right, son. But him and Mary are away doon tae Ayr fur the week."

"I didnae know that." The boys made to turn. "We'll see ye again when they get back."

"No, come away up." The woman stepped onto the bottom step of the stairs. Now, she thought was her opportunity to casually mention the paint. As the boys hesitated, she suggested, "I've got the key, if ye wid like tae go ower and see the hoose?"

"That wid be fine," Mal agreed, with a nod to his cousin.

The woman led them up the stairs. "In fact, Andrew has left some paper and paint," she puffed. "It would be awfy good o yis baith if yis could see yer way tae maybe taking a can or two wi` ye."

"Nae bother, Mrs Little," Calum assured her.

They reached the appropriate landing and the woman hurried into her house, pointing to the lobby cupboard as she passed on her way to the kitchen. "The stuff is in there. Wid ye like a cup o tea? I'm fair dying for one masel."

While Calum opened the cupboard door, Mal followed the woman into the kitchen where she set down her pail. "We'll no bother wi the tea, Mrs Little, if ye don't mind."

"Aw right, son. The keys on the dresser. The label will tell ye where it is. It's no too bad a stair. Quite clean neighbours by the look o it," she threw over her shoulder, as she turned on the tap.

It had been Mal's idea that they should help out their friends by starting to strip the walls the next night, although he had decided that any alterations, especially the carpentry, should be left to Static's greater expertise.

"Where do ye think we should start, Mal?" Calum glanced around the kitchen come- living room of the two bedroomed flat.

"In here is as good as any." Mal nodded.

"Do ye think after we have stripped the walls, we should start and pit on the paper?" Bobby Jackson asked, having been volunteered to help.

Mal picked up a roll of wallpaper from the floor. "He's got two kinds here. Wan for in here, and wan for wan o the two bedrooms."

"Two bedrooms?" Calum frowned.

Mal crossed to the bedroom that ran off from the kitchen. "We'll leave the papering the noo. See how far we get wi the stripping. There's an auld wardrobe in here that will get in the way."

Calum moved in the opposite direction to where an old fashioned sideboard stood in a corner of the living room. "Ye wid think the last folk tae bide here wid have taken their rubbish wi them an no leave it for other folk tae get rid o."

"And that auld wireless standin there like a coffin for a midget," Bobby acquiesced.

"Mair junk fur Static tae get rid of," Calum said in disgust.

"I could maybe get a loan of a van on Friday efternin, and dump this junk doon at Baxter's the scrappy, and maybe get a bob or two for Static oot o it," Bobby offered.

"Aye, Okay Bobby, that wid be fine." Mal lifted a scraper from off the floor. "I could do a bit here on ma half day on Wednesday. Maybe even skive a bit time aff on Friday. But that's aboot it."

By the time the three pals had met on Friday, the living-room-come-kitchen had been papered, and thanks to Bobby's additional work throughout Thursday, so also had the smaller of the two bedrooms been painted, where they were now gathered to admire his work.

"I'm sure they meant tae paint this room, and paper the other two rooms." Bobby tried to sound convincing.

"Oh, I think yer right, there," Mal agreed, giving Bobby's handy work a closer inspection. "Though I'm surprised they picked blue. Blue aye looks cauld looking, especially fur a bedroom."

"I know whit ye mean," Calum nodded, joining in his cousin's inspection. "It's no a colour I wid have thought Mary wid have picked. Oh well, it's no for us to criticise other folks tastes."

Mal gave Bobby a mischievous wink. "I know exactly whit ye mean Calum. I've seen whit you've gone oot wi`"

Calum curled his top lip. "At least the wans I went oot wi hadnae won a prize at Crufts."

"Come on you two!" Bobby laughed, afraid of where the patter might lead. "Or we'll no get anything done." He turned back into the kitchen. "The van has tae go back the night."

Calum and Mal followed him, the latter sweeping an eye around the room. "Right, Bobby, we'll take the auld wireless doon first, then that sideboard. The wardrobe last."

"Gone dae us a favour, Calum?" Mal asked diffidently.

"Like whit?" Calum asked suspiciously.

"Like maybe gettin` Bobby and me a pie? We're fair starvin...and wan for yersel, of course," he added hastily.

"Oh, I suppose so." Calum stopped at the door. "Ye no wanting a hand tae carry that wireless? It looks gie heavy."

Mal shook his head. "No, we'll put it on the Light Programme."

"Very funny. See you, Mal, if ye were as shitty as ye are witty, you'd be in a hell of a mess," Calum retorted in exasperation.

"Away and get the pies, afore I fa through ma trousers and hing maself on ma braces!" Bobby ordered his disconcerted pal.

"Aye, aw right." Then, as if he had suddenly remembered, "I'll no be able tae stay too long the day, I've a got a heavy date the night."

"Is that the wan wi danger wide load printed on her arse?" Mal asked.

Calum threw his cousin an icy stare as he took a step outside. "That's you had yer pie, son."

Calum cursed as he climbed back up the stairs. He should have known the bakers would have been closed for lunch.

The big wardrobe stood in the middle of the bedroom, blocking out the light from the window, he'd have to move it if he wanted to see to paint the skirting boards.

Taking hold of the sides, Calum attempted to push it corner by corner. If he had to move the damned thing, he could at least help by guiding it towards the door.

Three successful moves, and four unsuccessful ones, later, Calum was almost on the brink of giving up and awaiting his pals return from the van, when he decided to give it another try.

Opening one of the wardrobe doors in order to gain more leverage he pushed, and felt it stick on the floorboards. Then, with one hand on top of the wardrobe, the other grasping the inside of the door, he tilted it away from him, intending if he could of rocking it. Suddenly, the weight of the wardrobe was too much and it began to fall, pulling him with it. To make matters worse, the sleeve of his pullover caught on the inside of the door lock as it crashed to the floor.

All Calum knew, as he passed out, was that he was falling on top of the wardrobe, or rather inside it, as his forehead hit the hat rack, before the door slammed shut behind him, then utter darkness.

Returning from loading the wireless and other small articles on to the van, Mal poked his head inside the bedroom door, expecting to find his cousin hard at work on the skirting boards. "I knew it! The wee buggers skived aff! No even the decency tae leave the pies afore he did. Wait till I get ma hauns on him!" Mal cried out angrily.

"Nae use worrying noo, Mal." Bobby stood by his side. "We might as well take that wardrobe doon tae the van. Calum must have laid it on its back before he left so he could see whit he was doing."

Accepting this logic, Mal took hold of the top of the wardrobe. "Coup it on its side, Bobby, and we'll carry it through the door long ways."

This done, they then proceeded to lift it upright, angling it through the front door to the stair head.

"You know we've lifted it upside doon?" Bobby puffed at his pal.

While inside, a newly conscious Calum could have told him just that, had he not at that precise moment landed on his head, which prevented him from using his arms to attract the attention of his two ba heided pals. Instead, he tried to yell, but found standing on ones hands and using ones ankles as earmuffs, the sound was liable to come out of every orifice except the correct one. This was swiftly followed by a falling sensation which informed him his removers were now carrying the wardrobe long ways. Also the fact he was now lying face down. A slight sideways jolt had him guessing by the sound of traffic that they were now out of the close and into the street.

Once again, Calum felt his 'coffin' come upright, before his optimism, and his wardrobe came crashing down, and that damned hat rack hit him on the head once more.

"There ye are Mal, nae bother!" Bobby cried out triumphantly at having lifted the wardrobe on to the back of the van.

Mal wiped his hands on his overalls. "Aye, jist when we could have been doin wi Calum, he's nae where tae be seen. Aye the same, never aroon when he`s needed. Noo fur that auld sideboard."

Mal and Bobby returned to the house and had managed to carry the old sideboard as far as the middle landing before they were forced to lay it down for a rest.

"We'll slide it doon long ways on its casters, Bobby. There's plenty of room on the stairs."

Bobby squeezed passed the wardrobe. "I'll get doon the stairs first, and haud it frae the bottom. You haud the top end."

"Right when you are." Mal nodded down to his friend. "Lift noo!"

Slowly, the long sideboard was carried and manoeuvred round the middle landing, Bobby stepping backwards down the stairs, until unexpectedly his foot slipped and, he lost his hold, falling backwards. The long sideboard rattling down the steps on top of him, while Mal did his best to hold on and not lose his own footing.

"Are ye aw right, Bobby?" Mal shouted down to his friend as the runaway makeshift sledge came to an abrupt halt.

"The bloody thing's stuck," came the muffled reply. "The doors have swung open and jammed themselves on the stair wa!"

Mal peered down between the sideboard and the stair wall. He gave the sideboard an optimistic shove. "Yer right, pal."

"Whit are we goin tae dae?" Bobby stared up at Mal across the furniture. "We cannae get a screwdriver tae the doors. No even a wee saw, and we'll waste it if we force the sideboard and break the doors, then we will only be able tae sell it fur a rabbit hutch."

"Excuse me young man, but I wish to get passed."

Mal swung round at the sound of the voice, to be confronted by the image of an elderly lady, dressed in a neat two piece suit, a fur stole at her throat. "Sorry missus, it's stuck," he apologised.

"Then, you had better get it unstuck young man for I have a doctor's appointment at two o'clock." The tall feather in the woman's hat waved in time to her diction.

Mal eyed the lady, who could have passed for a pantomime dame he had seen as a laddie, wondering if she could get STV on that feather.

"Nae chance hen," Bobby peered up over the sideboard, making a moue at the 'dame'. "Though, on second thoughts, maybe if yer were tae put your weight ahaint it, it might jist budge."

The woman could not have been more astounded if she had been physically assaulted with a wet kipper, or had been accused of not voting Conservative, by this wee scunner's suggestion.

"I will do no such thing!" she exclaimed, gathering her stole more closely around her neck.

"Aw right then," Bobby gave in. He nodded at the stole. "Maybe ye could get yer ferret tae gie it a pull?"

Mal's eyes shot to the stair ceiling. That was all they needed.

The irate woman thrust out a handbag-clad arm at Bobby. "I hope you are not inferring to what I think you are inferring," she demanded to know.

Mal drew his pal an angry look. He turned to pacify the woman. "Not at all missus. He widnae know the meaning of the word."

"Very well." The woman smoothed her skirt as well as her temper. "But I must get passed, I'm under the doctor you know."

"Does yer man know aboot this?" Bobby commented in a stage whisper. Mal threw him a look.

Oblivious to the sarcasm, the woman plunged on. "I've had to wait three weeks for him. This is the only day he can do me."

Mal stabbed a finger over the sideboard at Bobby. "Don't say another word, we're in a big enough mess as it is!" he warned.

Unperturbed, the woman went on. "And, if that was not bad enough, I've been waiting for the chimney sweep as well as having a doctor's appointment all on the same day. He left me with a rod sticking up my flue," she declared indignantly.

"You should see the medical board aboot that missus," Bobby suggested deadpan. And, in return, received a stare that could have frozen the Panama Canal.

"Maybe ye could climb ower it, missus?" Mal tried to divert her attention away from his pal's devious remarks.

"Climb over it! I should say not!"

"She could never manage it, Mal," Bobby sympathised, ducking down behind the sideboard, "No wi a rod sticking…"

"Shut up!" Mal hurled blindly at him.

Using all of his restraint to remain calm, Mal turned his attention back to the woman. "Perhaps if yer were to get a chair ye could ston...stand on it..."

The senior stair inhabitant swung her stole round her neck. "I'll get the chair, but I will not subject myself to such an indignity as sliding ower…over that on my..." Leaving the rest unsaid, she turned for the stair.

Five minutes later, she was back. Mal helped her to climb on to her chair. "If ye bend ower the top of the sideboard, missus, howf a leg up, maybe ye could get onto yer stomach. Then, all ye have tae do is let yerself slide. Bobby widnae let ye fa, he would catch ye."

Only the thought of losing her appointment persuaded the lady to attempt Mal's suggestion. Standing on the chair, she carefully eased herself forward over the obstacle, then gingerly swung her left leg on top of the sideboard, showing a gap of bare leg between the top of her elasticised stockings and a long pair of pink drawers, convincing Mal more than ever that she was a pantomime dame.

"Yer doin fine, missus," Bobby encouraged. "Jist swing yer leg roon a bit mair, then get the ither wan tae follow frae the ither side." He suggested and in turn received a withering look, beneath a hat all askew.

"Hi Mammy! Come and see the gemme missus Gemmell is playing!"

Mal took a sharp look round at the little boy, who stood there, eyes aglow at this strange unexpected treat of the 'tyrant' of the close in such a precarious position, who, with one look at the lady in question's posterior shouted up the stair . "Can I get ma catapult, Mammy?"

"Bugger aff!" Mal shouted at one of the youngest delinquent's in the business, as the mortified woman gave a final heave of her left leg.

The additional weight did the trick. Without warning, the sideboard shot forward and downwards, with it's unfortunate passenger hanging on, (and over it) like grim death, and knocking Bobby out of the way as it clattered passed on its way to the close mouth, where it shot across the pavement, narrowly missing a woman pushing a pram and on to the street, and causing an ice cream van to collide with a truck travelling in the opposite direction, which in turn spun round spewing turnips, cabbage and a various assortments of other greens across the street, the sideboard at last hitting the opposite pavement, and hurtling its occupant heid first half way up the close mouth, prompting a friend to comment "we don't often see you up here, Mrs Gemmell. Especially legless!"

Mal reached Bobby's side. "Come on Bobby, let's get oot o here!"

Watching the large backside disappear up the opposite close, Bobby ventured to ask, "Whit aboot the sideboard, Mal? Are we no for getting a few bob for it?"

Mal's answer was to run down the last step on to the street, throwing over his shoulder as he did so, that they had done more damage to this street than Hitler had ever done during the entire course of the war, leaving Bobby to catch him up, if he could.

Mal and Bobby returned to the scene of the crime on Sunday morning. The sideboard-come-spaceship, which was now the focal attention of the local weans, lay on its side a few feet away from the close mouth where the 'dame' had disappeared in a flurry of flying fox fur, and a broken feather.

Bobby eyed the remains of the wardrobe. "I hope yon wumman is no waiting for us up the close, Mal."

Mal shuddered. "We'll jist hive tae chance it, and creep up as quiet as we can."

They reached the appropriate landing, both boys surprised that they should find the door wide open. Puzzled they went inside.

"In the name o the wee man! Whit's happened here?" Mal exclaimed, closely followed by Bobby's not so clean superlatives.

Crumpled bits of wallpaper lay strewn on the floor, the walls stripped bare, all of their hard work destroyed. Without speaking, Mal crossed quickly to the newly painted bedroom, unable to believe his eyes.

"That's her brothers did this!" Bobby seethed, pushing past his pal. "They didnae like blue so they changed it tae cream! But they could at least have left the paper on in the kitchen."

"This must be them, Hugh! Ask them what they are doing here!" A tearful woman in her early thirties cried, pointing an accusing finger at the erstwhile decorators as she appeared out of the small bedroom, followed by her husband.

At a loss, and about to ask what it was all about, Mal caught sight of Mrs Little, Static and Mary coming in the front door, their appearance a welcome sight.

"Static! Maybe ye can explain aw this. All we did was tae use the paper and paint ye left. I hope we used the right paper and aw?" Mal cried to his pal.

Static nodded a greeting. "Oh, ye got the right paper aw right. The only thing is, ye got the wrang hoose!"

"Whit! Efter aw oor hard work tae hiv the place nice fur ye coming back!" Bobby threw his hands in the air in exasperation.

"Maybe it was my fault" Mrs Little confessed, colouring. "Ye see, Mal, ye lifted the wrang key. Yon was Sarah Mckinlay's spare key ye lifted the other night. I didn't notice it until yesterday. I meant tae take it back tae the Council afore this. Then I decided it could wait 'till the morn." She screwed up her face at Mal in apology. "I think this hoose belongs tae these two folk." Her voice slowly trailing off, as if hoping the floor would open up and swallow her whole.

"Yes, you are quite correct," the husband of the distraught woman started indignantly, his face looking like a busted tomato. "This is our house! He rocked back and forth on his heels. "We've painted the small bedroom and have started to strip the paper." He gestured with disdain at the littered floor. "Some people have some queer tastes you know."

"Cheeky bugger," Bobby whispered.

"Also, I thought my brother had not dropped off the furniture as he said he would do, until I spoke to him this morning, when he informed me that he had done so at the beginning of the week."

The woman choked back a sob, her hankie at the ready. "So, where is my furniture now?" she asked tearfully and fearfully. "Has it been stolen, or what? I had a wireless, and a sideboard. But most importantly..." The hankie rose a few inches. "A wardrobe my grandmother left me." The woman cast an almost hopeless eye around the embarrassed group.

Static glared at his pals fearing the worse. "It was a real solid wardrobe" she went on. "pre-war. They do not make them like that anymore."

"Ye can say that again!" A familiar voice broke in, as its owner walked up the hallway from the open door.

"No again," Mal moaned at the sight of his bandaged headed cousin.

"Where have ye been? Some heavy date you've had!" Bobby inquired, still remindful of missing out on his much looked for pie.

"Heavy date! Heavy date! I'll gee ye heavy date!" Calum exploded. "See this!" He pointed to his bandaged cranium. "The only heavy date I had was with the Royal, fur concussion!"

"But we only sent ye fur pies!" Mal hunched his shoulders in perplexity. "Where were you when we were moving the wardrobe?"

"Inside the bloody thing!" Calum roared, adding in exasperation at the flicker of a smile on Static's face. "And don't you say a word!"

The devastated furniture-less woman had heard enough. "But where is my furniture?" she howled, having rapidly lost patience with these plebeians, while her husband rocked back and forward on his heels in time to his own mounting anger.

It was now time to edge closer to the door, the furniture removers decided.

"Ye see, it was like this missus...," Bobby started. Suddenly, he gave his pal a push. "Now, Mal go fur it!" he shouted, and gave a good impersonation of wee Tam, those years back as he ran up the lobby. Mal close on his heels, neither pal halting until they had reached the close mouth.

"Well we managed tae get oot o that wan Bobby, but I don't fancy the others chances up there, especially Statis's Mammy wi her lumbago." Mal wiped sweat from his brow.

Bobby let out a long breath. "Dear knows whit that wifie will say when she learns where her precious furniture has got tae."

"No tae mention her sideboard ower there." Mal nodded to where the piece of furniture in question had been transformed into a double decker bus.

Bobby followed his pal's gaze. "I don't think we should hang aroon here too long."

"Ye can say that again pal!" Mal jabbed a thumb over his shoulder, where an irate female doctor's patient was limping down the stairs, intent on having a few well chosen words with two catastrophic young men.

Chapter 15

March 1964

Mal stopped at the bus queue. He leaned the carrier bag against his leg, scarcely able to believe he had done it. Tomorrow, he would be leaving all this behind for Australia.

Originally, it had all began with the letter his Mammy had received from Mrs McKinlay in Australia, saying what a wonderful country it was, and how well her son and family were doing. This, in turn, had led him into thinking of his own future.

Self Service shops were the thing to come, small groceries would soon have had their day. But to be part of this, one needed capital, a commodity he was not likely to acquire on his present salary, or in this country. Nor did he wish to become just a manager making money for some anonymous face.

It started to smir, something else he would be glad to miss

The bus came and he climbed on board. Again, Mal went over all he would need to take with him. What an opportunity! A sea voyage, and all it entailed. Places to see...all for the princely sum of Ten Pounds, the only proviso being that he had to remain there for two years.

Of course, he would miss his pals, but there again they all had to make their own way in life. Mammy? Well, that was another matter. He would send her money, just as soon as he got a job and settled down. Maybe even send for her. Who was to know what lay ahead. Perhaps, he would eventually open a Self Service out there.

His stop came. He got off the bus and walked up his street, acutely aware of its noise and smell, as if savouring its atmosphere for the last time. He had spent all of his life here. Happy and sad times. For some reason his father came into his thoughts, and he wondered where he was now. Of how hard it had been for his Mammy without him. Harder still with him.

It would soon be dark on this cold March evening. He turned the key in the lock and went inside, groping for the light switch in the darkened hallway.

"Surprise!" someone shouted. And, all at once, there were folk everywhere, relieving him of his parcels. A drink was thrust into his hand, and he was pushed affectionately into the kitchen, where his Mammy stood beaming. Relatives and pals laughing and shouting at what he did not know, all crammed into that tiny space.

By ten o'clock on that Friday night, with the exception of Mal and Static's Mammy, all were drunk. But, then again, it may have been a wee drink that had Mal's Mammy sitting in the corner sobbing. His Aunt Maisie's arm was around her, consoling her by reminding her that Mal was only away for two years, and Static replying that was the reason for her crying.

Bobby Jackson answered the doorbell, returning to lead wee Ian carrying his box into the room, more drinks while Ian set up his accordion and the singing began.

More laughter at childhood memories: Static's flitting, and other incidents since then.

Mal knew he was drunk, and was grateful that it was only the train to London tomorrow, and not the boat, or he'd be seasick as well. He saw Static leave Mary sitting in a corner and went over to talk to her. "How's it goin then, Mary, hen?" he asked, swaying slightly.

She smiled sweetly up at him, as if not quite sure whether or not she should be here- fitted in. "So you are off tomorrow. Quite an adventure, would you not say?"

"Aye. I suppose so…I'll send you a postcard. Wish you were her."

She threw him a curious look. "Don't you mean here."

Mal leaned on the wall before it fell on top of him. "Jist a wee joke, Mary, hen."

He took a fuzzy look around the room at all his family, pals, neighbours, and Static's Mammy, then back to the girl. "You're the best thing that ever happened tae Stat...I beg your pardon, Drew." Mary gave him a look that suggested he was drunk and she did not know where this conversation was leading. "I mean it, Mary...even..."

"Even though I'm a Catholic?" she ventured.

"I wis goin tae say." He rifted. "Sorry aboot that," he apologised, "even though you are too good fur the daft eejit. I mean ye are edi..."

"You mean educated?" she suggested, helping him with the word.

"Aye, that's the word. If ye could see yer way o lending it to me, I'd post it back tae ye."

Mary smiled forgiveness at him.

The drink was making him sentimental, Mal thought. Static was his pal and he wanted to let Mary know how much he would miss him. Also, how much he thought of her. "Look after him, Mary, and yersel too. I wish I had met someone..."

"Whit's this, Moffat? Chatting up ma doll?" Static put his arm protectively around his wife. "I think it's a good job yer leaving, a man's wife is no safe wi you around." Static scolded his pal in mock seriousness.

"Yer right there, Static," Bobby agreed coming to stand by Mal. "If only we had seen her first. Eh Mal?" He gave Mal a nudge.

Mal took a sip of his drink, and pointed his glass at the woman. "Ye'll no know this, Mary, but see when Static telt us he wis winchin...though he didnae tell us tae who, mind ye."

Static's eyes dropped to the floor, sensing the sensitivity of his pal's sentence. Oblivious, Mal pushed on. "He says tae me, Mal, whit shaving lotion dae ye think I should pit on tae impress her? She's a wee smasher. So I says, try lavender water. Next night he comes in to the pub wi a bandage roon his heid. I says, Static whit happened tae you? He says, don't talk tae me aboot that water! There I was, kneeling doon splashing it on ma face, when the seat come doon and hit me on the heid!" His tale bringing a burst of laughter from those gathered around. "Static, I says, I said lavender water, no lavatory..."

"Aw right Mal, we get the joke," Static broke in, giving in graciously. For, after all, it was his pal's farewell party. He squeezed his wife, flattered by the attention and the obvious compliment.

"But whit aboot you, Muir?" Mal surveyed his cousin through slit eyes.

"Whit aboot me? Whit aboot me?" Calum asked hurriedly.

"Don't gee me that, as if ye don't know." Mal waved his glass. "Yon time you decided to impress yon doll you were winchin. You know, when you took yon mail body building course to improve your muscles?"

"I knew I widnae get away wi it," Calum moaned, staring at the floor.

Mal turned to face the company. "Ten weeks body building he did. Got the instructions sent tae him through the post every week. That wis three years ago, and he's still waiting for them tae post on his muscles!" Mal guffawed. Behind him, someone spilled their drink while leading the ensuing laughter.

All too soon, the party was over, pals had said their farewells, and now only the family remained behind.

Agnes put the kettle under the tap. "Ony wan for tea?" she hiccupped. Each replied solemnly in the affirmative in their own way, for it had reached that time in everyone's party when faced with the harsh reality of sobriety.

"I wonder whit yer Granny wid have said if she knew ye were goin tae Austrailya, Mal?" his Aunt Jenny inquired of him.

"Probably help pack his bags," Mal's Uncle Jimmy chuckled, the company seated around the table responding in a suitable manner while studying their respective cups.

Suddenly, the room and the atmosphere had gone cold. "Best wake I've been at in a long while," Maisie opinionated harshly. "Come on, let's hiv another drink while the kettle's biling!"

Several drinks, and as many kettles off the boil later, the family were back into their cups.

"Dae ye mind the day Granny had the sair hip?" Maisie slurred, already tittering at what she was about to remind them of. "I asked her what had happened to her, she said." Again, Maisie's tittering infected the company who waited good humouredly for the ending to the story. "She said…" Tears rolled down Maisie's cheek, sending her sister Agnes into raptures.

His patience at an end, Jimmy asked his sister-in-law what she was laughing at, who in turn shook her head, and said she didn't know, but it was funny anyway.

Hughie slapped the table with his drink, demanding that his wife get on with it before Mal missed his boat.

Clearing her throat of the mirth still sticking there, Maisie started again. "I said tae yer Granny, Mal. How did ye come tae hurt yer hip? And she said, well it wis like this, I was reading the instructions on a packet of biscuits where it said, `pierce here and tear back`. So I tore back and ran into the cooker!"

Everyone lapsed into laughter, perhaps not so much at Granny's wee joke but to her memory, prompting Agnes to go on. "Dae ye mind the day the doctor came to examine her? He was sounding her back. He says tae her, say ninety nine Mrs Findlay. So yer Granny says ninety nine, and the doctor says, one more please, and she says one hundred.!" Again, peals of laughter.

"And..." said Jenny, anxious to keep the party going. "When I said tae her, mother ye are beginning tae forget things, she says tae me, aye, Jenny, I think I'm suffering frae auld timers disease!"

No one remembered the party breaking up.

Next morning, Mal heard the alarm go off. Turning up his nose at the taste in his mouth he stared up at his bedroom ceiling. Hazy recollections of last night floated passed. Bobby Jackson singing. Wee Ian belting oot We're no Awa Tae Bide Awa. Lassies greeting, laddies not so very far behind. Mary giving him a kiss before politely saying goodbye; Static, informing him he'd see him in the morning and help him to the train. The room emptying as well as his own emotions.

Now, he realised how many good friends he was leaving behind, but how good would they be if he was to suddenly tell them he had changed his mind, they'd probably kick his heid in and take back their presents.

He sat up. It was time for him to rise, wash and shave. Across the tiny room his best shirt hung on its hanger, washed and ironed, Mammy`s work.

For a time it became a symbol of what mammies were all about. He`d never thought of mammies having ambitions. Never thought of asking what would make them happy. Washing and ironing, making dinners, giving advice you knew was sound but would not take, was what mammies were there for.

When he entered the kitchen, Mammy was frying ham, eggs, black pudding, fried bread, enough to get him to his destination without the ship ever having to stop.

"Did ye get yer clean shirt?" Mammy asked, without taking her eyes off the frying pan.

"Aye" he said simply, and sat down at the table. 'The last breakfast'.

His Mammy talked incessantly throughout the meal, advice after advice. Remember he changed his pants often, just in case the ship sank. Always have a clean hankie. A lot of good that would do in a lifeboat, Mal thought, as Mammy went on to remind him to mind his manners, etc. etc.

He'd finished packing. This was it. The worst part. He came out of his bedroom.

Mammy sat with her back to him at the table, hands around her tea cup. His eyes settled on the nape of her neck. He was leaving. How would she cope? Oh, he knew his aunties would always be around, and most likely Static and Mary, now and again, until, like a death, his mother got over his not being there and their visits became less frequent.

Two years was not long, he'd be back. With all the optimism of youth, it had never occurred to him what life may have in store for him during that time.

"It's time I was away then, Mammy." The lump in his throat almost choked him.

His mother nodded, without turning round. "I'll say cheerio here then son, I hate railways."

He crossed to stand behind her, and bent to hug her cheek against his own. "Ye've been a good Mammy tae me. I'll miss ye." It was the closest he could bring himself to say that he loved her, to thank her for all the sacrifices she had made for him, all her struggles to make ends meet, which, young as he may have been, he had taken for granted.

Agnes put up her hand to hold his. Unlike her son, she was not so optimistic. Though time flew with each passing year, two years could be a long time when you missed someone, even someone like Erchie her man. Bugger though he was. "God bless ye, son." She let go of his hand. Then more in keeping with her usual self, added, "Away and no miss yer train. Static and Calum will be waitin fur ye."

"Aye. I suppose so."

Mal thought he heard his mother crying as he closed the door. He looked round as Mrs MacWhirter, still sprightly for her age, climbed the stairs to meet him.

"So you're away then, Malcolm? Well good luck, son. Drop me a wee card and let me know how you're getting on."

"I will Mrs MacWhirter," he promised her.

The old lady halted on the landing to draw breath. "I've just came away up to keep your mother company for a wee while. I suppose your aunties will be around sometime."

Mal nodded. "That's nice o ye. Well I better away. No miss my boat. Cannae swim a' the way, even if it is a' doonhill." He gave her a smile, and a final farewell.

Static and Calum stood on the railway platform, Bobby Jackson, having said his farewells as he sat at the wheel of a borrowed car. The whistle went, and Static looked up at Mal leaning out of the carriage window. "Ye better pull yer heid in Mal, or ye'll hiv folk thinking this is a cattle truck." His quip meant to conceal his real feelings.

"Aye, aw right, Static. Ye never change, do you?"

Calum put up his hand. "Cheerio pal. And this is something frae the gang tae remind ye o us." He held out a small box with his other hand.

Mal took the box, studying it for a second.

"No tae worry!" Static shouted, as the train began to pull away. "We've paid the first instalment, you've jist another fifty nine tae keep up!" And, then, all too quickly, the train had gone.

Mal sat staring out of the window for a time, the compulsion to jump off at the next halt almost overpowering at the thought of what he had done. He had left his pals behind! Maybe never see them again!

Suddenly, as he realised he was still holding the unopened box, he slowly began, almost lovingly to tear open the paper. The small cardboard box was about three inches square and in the inside of the lid was a folded piece of paper with another covering its contents. Mal unfolded the paper not knowing whether to laugh or cry at the crude attempt at poetry, as he read.

Take this bit grass where ever ye go.
Ye never know, it may grow.
Then again, maybe no`
And when yer lonely and miss yer ain.
This bit of Oor Bit, will aye be hame.

It's just the beginning.

Printed in Great Britain
by Amazon

21334213R00130